TRANSFUSION

Also by Nick Oldham from Severn House

The Henry Christie thriller series

CRITICAL THREAT
SCREEN OF DECEIT
CRUNCH TIME
THE NOTHING JOB
SEIZURE
HIDDEN WITNESS
FACING JUSTICE
INSTINCT
FIGHTING FOR THE DEAD
BAD TIDINGS
JUDGEMENT CALL
LOW PROFILE
EDGE
UNFORGIVING
BAD BLOOD
BAD COPS
WILDFIRE
BAD TIMING
SCARRED

The Steve Flynn thriller series

ONSLAUGHT
AMBUSH
HEADHUNTER

TRANSFUSION

Nick Oldham

SEVERN
HOUSE

First world edition published in Great Britain in 2021 and the USA in 2022
by Severn House, an imprint of Canongate Books Ltd,
14 High Street, Edinburgh EH1 1TE.

Trade paperback edition first published in Great Britain and the USA in 2022
by Severn House, an imprint of Canongate Books Ltd.

severnhouse.com

British Library Cataloguing-in-Publication Data
A CIP catalogue record for this title is available from the British Library.

ISBN-13: 978-0-7278-5015-7 (cased)
ISBN-13: 978-1-4483-0737-1 (trade paper)
ISBN-13: 978-1-4483-0736-4 (e-book)

Typeset by Palimpsest Book Production Ltd.,
Falkirk, Stirlingshire, Scotland.
Printed and bound in Great Britain by
TJ Books, Padstow, Cornwall.

For Belinda

ONE

He was an old man. His health was failing on several fronts. He had an enlarged prostate and often needed to insert a tube just to be able to pee. He had a heart condition, narrowing of the arteries, and the stents that had been inserted to keep his blood flowing through those clogged-up vessels had all but collapsed themselves, like broken umbrellas. There was also a good chance that his wafer-thin aorta, that most crucial of blood vessels, the main and largest artery in the human body, would one day burst spectacularly within him at any moment, without warning, and finish him off in a flash of agony.

His eyesight was failing and the lenses of his spectacles had become, by necessity, much thicker over the years. His weak eyes constantly streamed and were always squelchy and bloodshot.

His leg muscles were weak, his knees arthritic; he needed a cane to help him walk any distance. Occasionally he had to be pushed along in a wheelchair by his one remaining son, but because the old man despised any obvious display of vulnerability, the wheelchair was a last resort and rarely used in public.

However, despite all this physical decline, he was still a man whose brain was as knife-sharp as it had been at the age of seventeen, some sixty-three years ago, when he had lured his main business rival into a dark alley one night and brutally stabbed him to death before ripping that young man's thick gold chain from around his neck and claiming it as his own.

That had been a real turning point in his life.

That glorious moment when he stood astride the twitching, bleeding-out corpse like a mighty Colossus and raised the heavy chain up to the night sky like an offering to the gods. Then, as a cop car crawled slowly, unexpectedly, into the alley, he and his beautiful girlfriend – who would later become his wife and life-long partner – had fled the scene, giggling as if they'd just stolen apples from an orchard, into the black night of Tirana, Albania.

He had then merged two previously warring criminal organizations into a single mighty one which over the years had expanded with ruthless ferocity and untold wealth.

The old man was now almost eighty-one years old.

But inside his fragile frame he was, intrinsically, the same youth who had murdered in cold blood, without conscience, remorse or guilt.

He had expected by this time in his life to have handed over the running of his empire to his elder son, but that was not to be.

Death and circumstance saw to that.

As a consequence, the old man had been obliged to take back full control of the enterprise and steer it by himself.

As much as he loved his younger son, he wasn't inclined to allow him to take charge. Although he was loyal enough, he didn't really have the nous or acumen required to take on such a tough role, even if the son believed he had those qualities.

The old man was now seriously on the verge of handing things over to his one and only daughter, who had blossomed and come to surprise him with her strategic foresight, edge and, of course, the necessary mindset to be able to stick a knife into a man's heart and twist it or fire two bullets into the back of his head and walk away feeling nothing.

She had done both those things in the last three years.

Unlike his one remaining son who was much more interested in enjoying the pleasures of the flesh that came with the wealth of the family business – which was easily approaching the twenty billion euros mark. Despite this, the old man was very grateful to him for being capable of running a finely balanced double-cross against a tenacious and dangerous FBI agent which had enabled the old man to squirm out of the clutches of the authorities and go into hiding in Cyprus, from where he continued to rule his empire.

Since his first son's death – at the hands of that FBI agent and others – the last four years had been a very testing time for the old man and his family.

Other rivals – sensing weakness coupled with opportunity – had tried to muscle in, believing the old man was past his best, too frail to wield any real power, supported by an equally weak son and, some believed, daughter. Such moves had resulted in clear messages being sent out by the old man in the form of throat cuttings and mass family executions; others had been dealt with by way of unambiguous warnings that had served their purpose.

Some rivals had tried a more subtle approach and had been successful in pitching the idea of partnership working, which the old man found more appealing only because he retained full control of each new initiative.

The old man sighed, feeling and hearing his lungs rasp as he inhaled and exhaled. They were in good working order and were ragged with age rather than disease.

He thought about the last three years as his finger and thumb played with the gold chain around his neck, the one he'd taken from the dead boy a long time ago.

Four years ago, he had actually taken a step back and handed over the running of the business to his elder son, who'd done well, forging ahead with expansion across Europe. That was until he had made the fatal error of judgement by underestimating someone.

Until his own dying day, the old man would never forget the fate of his beloved son and would always seek out ways to bring about the downfall and deaths of the two men he held responsible for his son's violent demise – the FBI agent and one other. He would always be on the lookout to take these men down, take any opportunity to have them brought before him, make them kneel in penitence, beg for their lives . . . and then behead them and raise their severed heads high. And if he did not succeed in this endeavour in his own lifetime, he would make his daughter promise on her life to take on and complete the task.

He closed his tired eyes and imagined rolling the two heads like bowling balls, their eyes still open, tongues lolling out, both having died in the knowledge that to cross this old man, to harm his family in any way, ended with the ultimate retribution.

The old man grinned at that image in his mind's eye, then opened his actual eyes and said to himself, 'One day, my friends, your time will come.'

True, he was an old man, but he was still a stone-cold killer.

His name was Viktor Bashkim.

'Father!'

Viktor Bashkim jerked out of his revenge-tinted reverie with a snort and turned his head to look with a smile on his thin, withered lips, because the voice from behind was that of his daughter, Sofia.

She was thirty-five years old. Bashkim had had her relatively late in life – the youngest of his three children and the spitting image of her mother after whom she was named. When Viktor slid his spectacles back into place, he could almost have been looking at his wife, the woman who had been such a key figure in young Viktor's rise to power in Tirana. It was she who had enticed the unsuspecting young man – one of his early business rivals – down that dark, dank alley in 1958, making him believe he was going to fuck her up against the wall and get one over on Viktor.

Bashkim had been eating his simple breakfast – figs, cheese and a mug of lemon and ginger tea – on the balcony of his huge bedroom in the immense villa in which he now lived on the edge of the Akamas National Park in western Cyprus. From the balcony, which was protected by a screen of greyed-out bulletproof glass, he could see out across the rugged, barren beauty of the park, but no one could see in. He was screened from the eyes of anyone who might be interested in getting him in the sights of a sniper rifle.

'Father, we need to be setting off,' Sofia said. 'The cars are ready.' She smiled warmly at him, walked up and touched his shoulder lovingly.

'I know,' he said wearily.

In the huge courtyard below the balcony, this also protected from peering eyes by a high stone wall, three black Toyota Land Cruisers, all with smoked-out rear windows, had assembled in a mini-convoy. The trio of armed drivers, all young men, dressed in T-shirts and cargo shorts, each with a handgun shoved into the waistband at the small of their back, stood together chatting and smoking while four bodyguards clustered around the bonnet of the lead vehicle, dressed similarly to the drivers but busy checking their weapons and fitting their personal body armour. Each of these men had an automatic pistol and a machine pistol; two pump-action sawn-off shotguns were laid out on the bonnet, having been loaded and checked.

Also among these men, mingling with them as though he was the party host, was Nico, Viktor's younger son. He was laughing heartily, making jokes, chewing the stub of a fat cigar – unlit – and with his jet-black hair and luxuriant moustache, and two huge dogs following his every move, he looked every inch an Albanian gangster.

Sofia helped the old man to his feet. He teetered unsteadily as she gently threaded his arms through his ultra-lightweight ballistic vest, fastened it for him with the Velcro straps and handed him back his walking stick, the head intricately carved from poached ivory into a three-dimensional representation of the double-headed eagle of the Albanian flag.

'Do you need to pee?' she asked him.

'I'm fine at the moment, thank you . . . If I need help later, you'll be able to assist me, won't you, darling?'

'Of course, Father.' Sofia's smile faltered slightly. She had somehow assumed the role of full-time carer and had become a reluctant expert at inserting the firm yet flexible tube down his urethra to help him pass water more easily on the occasions when his iffy prostate was playing up, which it did more and more these days. Once more, the thought of manipulating his aged genitalia made her feel slightly queasy, daughter or not. He refused to wear an indwelling catheter because it was another sign of weakness.

'You're a good girl . . . but yet . . .' His fingertips touched the gold chain around his neck, then reached out to touch her neck. 'You refuse to wear it.'

'I know,' she said. He was pointing out her reluctance to inherit the gold chain he wanted to pass on to her. Initially he had gifted it to Aleksander, his elder son, but on his death it had been returned to the old man; Viktor had then kept hold of it in his grief and then while he assessed Sofia's competence to take control of the '*fis*' – the family clan. To Viktor, the gold chain was a symbol of leadership. Whoever wore the chain headed the organization.

Nico had been deeply offended it wasn't him who was to inherit the chain, and Viktor had tried to control him with money, property and women.

'Father, you know it is too heavy for my slim neck,' Sofia said. 'It's men's jewellery.'

And it was. Clunky, unwieldy and certainly not fashionable. She would have suggested that it be melted down and refashioned into something more modern and ladylike, but she knew he would not approve of that.

'You should at least wear it for these meetings,' he urged her.

'I will, Father, if you so wish,' she consented.

Viktor unhooked the chain from around his neck. Sofia leaned forward to make it easier for him to loop it around hers.

'There,' he said.

She adjusted it to make it as comfortable as possible.

'It's symbolic of our proud history and will ensure that everyone knows who is in charge.' He nodded approvingly, then took one last look from the balcony and frowned as he saw the gates of the courtyard open automatically – they were controlled by one of the security guards who patrolled the estate in which the villa nestled – and allowed access to an old man whom, as he adjusted his glasses to focus better, he recognized as a local goat farmer who supplied the household with cheese and milk.

Viktor watched as the farmer rushed across to Nico and began to talk hurriedly to him, turning and gesticulating towards the hills of the Akamas beyond the walls. Nico listened and nodded, patting the man on the shoulder and finally pushing him gently towards a bench in the shade by the wall. Nico then turned and strode towards the villa.

Sofia had also been watching the exchange in the courtyard, recognizing the farmer who was paid a generous monthly allowance to keep his eyes peeled and report back any unusual or suspicious activity in the area, including any cop movements.

'What was that about, do you think?' Viktor asked Sofia.

She shrugged.

Moments later, Nico entered the bedroom.

Viktor said, 'I saw Giorgos. What did he want?'

Nico glanced at Sofia, his dislike for her apparent in his look, even greater when his eyes caught sight of the gold chain, something that physically jarred him for a moment and made his throat tighten, before he gathered himself together and said to Viktor, 'Giorgos's son says a man has been in the hills for two days now.' Viktor knew the son was a goatherd and grazed his hardy flock over the rough, rocky terrain surrounding the villa. 'And he is now watching us with binoculars from behind a natural wall of rocks. He has some sort of gun, too. His son does not recognize the man, but says he looks like a tourist. He arrives in a wreck of a car which he parks on one of the tracks in the banana plantation.'

'Has the man seen Giorgos's son?' Viktor asked.

'He has, but his son has pretended not to see him.'

'Could it be one of the Toskuses?' Viktor asked, naming an organized gang operating out of Tirana with whom the Bashkims had had several territorial confrontations recently and who, like some others, were flexing their muscles against Viktor's family with a view, it was believed, to taking over some of the lucrative routes across middle Europe, carrying people, drugs and money. This was one of the few rivals that Viktor had yet to put down properly, although they were on his to-do list.

Nico shook his head. 'I don't think so. Toskus himself is in Tirana, according to our people. He's involved in some shipping fraud and is too busy for trouble.'

Viktor scratched his head through his wispy grey hair. 'Who, then? The FBI or some other law enforcement agency? As far as they are concerned, I'm a dead man.'

Nico shrugged.

'An assassin, then? What sort of weapon does he have?'

'I don't know. Giorgos's son is a goatherd, not a ballistic expert.'

'Father,' Sofia interjected. 'Perhaps we should cancel the meeting and keep you safe within the villa walls for the moment while Nico leads some men to flush out this interloper?' She glanced slyly at her brother who she knew would be horrified at the prospect of doing anything that might endanger himself or his hairstyle. From the brief look of terror that flashed through Nico's eyes, she knew she was correct. Inwardly, she smirked with satisfaction.

'Neither,' said Viktor decisively. 'Nico, get Dima to take men out to see if they can bring this individual in alive if possible. I want him here, kept in the basement, for when I return . . . but if he has to be killed, then so be it.'

TWO

Flynn had sailed into Cyprus a few days earlier and moored his boat – his beloved forty-five-foot sportfisher called *Faye* – in Kato Paphos harbour. He'd spent a couple of idyllic days in the town with his travelling companion, a recently resigned British cop called Molly Cartwright, exploring on foot, eating and drinking well and living on the boat. Then they had hired a four-wheel-drive Suzuki and driven along the coast to Coral Bay and beyond into the Akamas, the national park that formed the western tip of the island. As many tourists did, Flynn and Molly enjoyed throwing the vehicle along the rough, unmade roads in that part of the country-side. On the second day of exploring the Akamas, they looped back out of the park on one of the less-used roads in order to drive past the long, winding track which was essentially the driveway up through a banana plantation to the mega-villa in which Viktor Bashkim was allegedly holed up.

Flynn had slowed right down and been tempted to turn into the track, but he held back and headed for Paphos instead.

Next day, he hired an off-road buggy, which sounded like being on board a hovercraft, popular in that part of Cyprus to further explore the Akamas. And this time it seemed a much more innocent thing to do to turn up the track to the villa and, if necessary, claim they were exploring in the buggy just as hundreds of other tourists were doing that day and that they hadn't seen the sign at the bottom of the track which read *PRIVATE – Trespassers will be prosecuted* in both English and Greek. There was also a picture of a pair of ferocious-looking hounds from hell and the caption *Beware of the dogs*.

Flynn stopped the buggy at the beginning of the track and ensured his bandana was wrapped securely around his face, his Police sunglasses fitted correctly and the peak of his baseball cap pulled low; Molly did the same. This, too, was not particularly suspicious as most of the buggy drivers and passengers were similarly attired because of the voluminous clouds of dust thrown up from the bone-dry roads, but it did help to keep their identities under wraps just on the off-chance that the old man was in residence. If he saw and recognized Flynn, things might not go well and those hounds might be unleashed.

So prepared, Flynn engaged the gears and set off in the excess-ively noisy vehicle up the track through the banana trees, bouncing along on the very springy suspension towards the gates of the villa. His approach could not have been more visible and audible as there was nothing subtle about the buggy, and as the walls surrounding the villa came into view, an access door set into the wall by the front gate opened and two tough looking, muscle-bound young men stepped through, their threatening body language enhanced by the machine pistol each had slung across their chest.

Both men held up their hands in a 'stop' gesture.

Flynn drove up to them, waving nicely. 'Hi, guys, we're just exploring off the beaten track . . . hope it's not a problem.'

One stepped up to him, resting his hand on the roof frame of the buggy, and leaned in, glanced at Molly, then stared at Flynn and said in heavily accented English, 'You fuck off. Private land.'

'Really? I didn't know that!'

'Yeah, well, now you do's, so fuck off, yeah?'

By this time, the guy behind him had swung his firearm into his hands and was holding it meaningfully with an accompanying glare and chewing gum.

'Hey, guys, sorry,' Flynn said. 'You guarding royalty or something?'

The man at the car leaned in a tad closer, giving Flynn a whiff of his cologne and body odour. 'Jus' go.'

'Getting the message loud 'n' clear,' Flynn said, giving him a peace sign. Then he pretended to look around. 'Thing is space is a bit tight round here. These bastards have the turning circle of an oil tanker. Any chance you can open the gates and let me swing round in there?'

The man stepped back and took a menacing grip on his machine pistol; he didn't say anything because the message was abundantly clear: it was a 'no' from him.

'Gotcha,' Flynn acknowledged with a wave.

He selected reverse, twisted in his seat to look backwards and also so he could speak to Molly. He began to negotiate the vehicle back down the track, a journey of about two hundred metres.

'Armed and dangerous,' he said to her.

'Surely that's against the law, even here in Cyprus?'

'Probably.'

'We phone the cops, then?'

'I doubt the effectiveness of that.'

'How . . . why? Oh, yeah,' Molly said, realizing the meaning of Flynn's response.

'What did you make of the guy's accent?'

'Russian, maybe?' Molly guessed.

'Which kinda fits the rumour,' Flynn said as they reached the end of the track and he slewed the buggy into the road before gunning it back towards Paphos. He dropped it off at the hire company's lot and they strolled hand in hand down through the town to the harbour and back to *Faye*. They both showered on board and then, as evening drew in, they drove back towards the Akamas and settled in for an evening meal at the Sunset Tavern on the edge of the park, ordering kleftiko which had been slow cooking most of the day.

It tasted amazing.

Up to that point, Flynn had said very little – not that he often had much to say anyway – but Molly watched him nervously, wondering what was coming next. Finally, Flynn's terrible habit of keeping everything in his head made her boil over a little.

'Time to talk,' she said. 'What's the plan?'

Enigmatically, he sipped his ferociously chilled pint of Keo, one of the island's home-produced lagers, while he mulled things over and had deep thoughts. Finally, he explained what he wanted to do. It wasn't complicated and he promised it would be time-bound; Molly knew that whatever she said, she would be unable to talk him out of it. Not that she really wanted to; she understood his motivation, but she wanted him to stay safe, not take unnecessary risks, and she told him so.

'It's just me watching the place for a couple of days.' He shrugged. 'I'm not going to storm it or anything, and if nothing comes of it, nothing comes of it,' he said philosophically.

Molly stared at him with undisguised disbelief. 'How is that statement even remotely true? Just because you might not see him doesn't make it certain he isn't actually there or still alive . . . I know you, Steve. You'll want to confirm it one way or another . . . which begs another question: what happens if you do spot him?'

Flynn put another mouthful of the tender lamb into his mouth, rolled his eyes with delight, chewed, swallowed, drank more lager, wiped his lips with a napkin, looked at Molly in a deep, significant way – and said nothing.

'Just as I thought,' she said. She knew exactly what the answer was and he didn't have to say a word because his expression on its own struck a chord of terror in her heart.

*   *   *

Next morning, Flynn was up early. He walked up the hill into Paphos town to a used-car lot he'd spotted a couple of days earlier, which sold a range of very ropy vehicles from a small forecourt out front. Around the back was a huge, high-fenced enclosure jam-packed with a further array of even more battered vehicles, from which he chose a very dilapidated Renault 4. He haggled with the owner who gratefully accepted cash, no paperwork and, more importantly, no questions.

He drove the exhaust-popping vehicle back down to the harbour where he explained his plan to Molly and, pointing to the wreck on wheels, said in conclusion, 'This is just in case I need a quick getaway that can't be traced.'

'A getaway?'

He nodded.

'*In that?* That's a getaway car?'

She looked at him and shook her head. He held out the ignition key between his finger and thumb – no more than a worn, thin, slightly twisted length of metal.

They were standing on the quayside.

'I'll see you in about an hour,' he told her and kissed her on the cheek, then walked along the jetty, stepping aboard *Faye*. Molly watched him throw off the mooring ropes and slowly ease the sleek boat out of her space, then sail out of the harbour.

She exhaled a long sigh, then smirked as she suddenly remembered the first time she had ever met Flynn, not so long ago in a pharmacy in Blackpool that he had tried to rob to get painkilling drugs for a gunshot wound to his leg. Molly, then a firearms cop, had been obliged to Taser him to the ground. Yes, it wasn't such a long time ago, but much had happened since.

She clambered into the wreck, already refusing to call it a car – it was just a chunk of metal on wheels – and gingerly sat at an unusual angle on the driver's seat to avoid being jabbed by the broken spring protruding up dangerously through the fabric so it didn't stick into her bottom. She put the key into the ignition – it went in with a lot of wriggle room – and started the engine which popped a lot.

In the boat, Flynn turned west out of the harbour and kept fairly close to the shoreline, passing the *Edro* shipwreck wedged on rocks at Peyia, where it had met its end one very stormy night without loss of life; it had never been re-floated and had since become a tourist attraction. From there, he passed the outcrop that was Yeronisos Island, executed a sharp right turn into the tiny fishing harbour at St George's and, as he had previously arranged via an exchange of euros, moored *Faye* alongside a row of colourfully painted fishing boats which operated from there.

Molly had already arrived in the car, leaving the wreck in the car park behind the beach café, and was there to watch Flynn manoeuvre *Faye* into her berth. As ever, she marvelled at his boating skills, realizing he was most at home on board.

She stepped on as he tied up and kissed him.

'That was nice,' he said.

'Well, I'm beginning to think I love you,' she admitted hesitantly.

Flynn instantly clammed up and Molly noticed the sudden tension in his being. Among many other things she had learned about this man was that he was very poor at masking his feelings as well as admitting them.

'Maybe I shouldn't have said that,' she said quickly.

'No,' he said, his eyes playing over her. 'No . . .' His rigidity dissolved. 'What I meant is that, no, you should have . . . it's fine . . . great, in fact,' he said, beginning to blabber a little, caught off-guard by her revelation. Sure, these two people definitely had feelings for each other and the past year or so of living together in the confined conditions of an albeit fairly spacious boat had demonstrated how well they managed to rub along from simple lust to basic domesticity – but the 'L' word had not reared its complex little head before. There had been moments – mainly for Flynn in post-sex moments when he was at his weakest – but he had never actually spoken the word. He said, 'More than good.'

'You didn't quite give me that impression, Flynnie,' she said, beginning to feel slightly uncomfortable, the creeping redness of embarrassment slithering up from her chest to her neck like a flame. 'Forget I said it.'

'It's not something that's easy to forget,' he said. He stooped slightly – he was six foot two, while she was five feet and ten inches – and looked into her eyes. 'Look, let's just get this job over with, shall we? Two days at most, then it's done and dusted, whatever, and we're gone. We head back to Ibiza, finish off whatever's left of the season in this godforsaken year, then sail back to Puerto Rico and go big game fishing.' He paused for dramatic effect. 'Then get on with the rest of our lives – together.'

Molly sighed heavily down her nose. 'Thing is this, Steve,' she said, reverting from the casual 'Flynnie' to the more formal use of his first name. 'I came into this with my eyes wide open, not expecting commitment or anything more than a good time. But' – she shrugged helplessly – 'I've fallen in love with you. Can't help it, just have. And now I think we've reached our Rubicon. Y'know, the point where decisions have to be made one way or the other . . .'

They held each other's gaze.

Finally, Flynn said, 'Two days, eh? I can't stay watching the villa for ever and I don't particularly want to, but if Viktor Bashkim is still breathing, I need to know, because if he is, neither of us will ever be safe.'

'OK,' Molly conceded with a twist of her lips. 'Two days, then we get on with the rest of our lives.'

'Two days,' he confirmed.

She knew he was probably lying, despite his best intentions.

After Flynn and Molly had been unequivocally told they were trespassing on private property and the two heavies at the villa had demonstrated a show of aggression, Flynn had reversed back down the track in the buggy, keeping his eyes open for any suitable position from which he might keep a watch on the villa.

When he finally said goodbye to Molly the day after their verbal dalliance about love, he knew roughly where he was going to hide, at least to start with.

He parked the old Renault on a dead-end track in the banana plantation about half a mile from the villa and went the rest of the way on foot. He was dressed in a khaki-coloured shirt and cargo pants to help him blend in with the sand-yellow coloured rock of the area and had a small rucksack on his back with a couple of bottles of water, a few high-energy bars and a couple of packs of peanuts to keep him going through the day. He was only going to be there in daylight hours because he didn't have any night-time kit with him, but his usual binoculars were adequate for what he wanted to achieve.

Although he was pretty certain the position he'd identified on that backwards journey away from the villa was a good one, he spent some time slowly circumnavigating the villa in a circle about 300 metres distant to see if there was a more suitable spot to lie up. In the end, he was reasonably content with the place he'd initially chosen and settled into it behind the rocks and under the shade of the trees.

He placed the rucksack by his side and took out one of the water bottles and also his Ruger automatic pistol, which he usually kept in a hidden compartment in *Faye*'s engine room. He had brought it along without Molly's knowledge.

There wasn't much going on at the villa.

The wrought-iron front gates, backed with green mesh netting that made seeing into the courtyard beyond difficult, were kept closed mostly, opened when an occasional vehicle came and left. There was a delivery from a local supermarket, and an open-topped Jeep left with two men on board and returned with the same two a few hours later.

What was clear was that the premises were well guarded. Flynn counted at least eight heavies, including one female, who were clearly on protection duty. The only CCTV he could see from his position was a camera covering the gate. Over the course of that first day of watching, the side gate opened a few times to let different pairs of guards out to stroll around the perimeter of the villa walls, always armed but not necessarily mentally switched on. The patrols seemed perfunctory and were usually interspersed with long cigarette breaks and a lot of time spent on mobile phones.

The heat grew in intensity throughout the day and, probably because he was out of practice, there was a point mid-afternoon where Flynn leaned back against the rock in the dappled shade provided by the trees; his eyelids began to feel heavy and droop, and although he fought it, he nodded off.

He was awakened by something cold and hard pressed into his cheek. Immediate thought: muzzle of a gun.

He jerked awake, scrabbling to find his own gun, and in so doing terrified the goat that had stumbled across him and placed its snout on his face to check out its discovery.

'Holy shit!' Flynn hissed as the goat reared away bleating and bounded off to join its flock of accomplices being herded across the barren ground by a young man.

Flynn froze, feeling the slimy mucus from the animal's nostrils on his face, hoping the young goatherd hadn't seen him or, if he had, didn't think anything about a guy catching forty winks in the shade. Whatever, the young man showed no sign of having seen him and carried on herding the goats away.

Flynn's heart rate decreased. He took a long swig of now luke-warm water and settled back to watch the villa, knowing he could not afford to doze off again.

'Obviously something's going on,' he said later to Molly as they ate fresh seafood pasta on the rear deck of *Faye* down in St George's harbour. 'It's some sort of fortress,' he said, shovelling two large prawns into his mouth. 'Somebody's being guarded, even if it isn't old man Bashkim, and I'm pretty sure that any non-corrupt law enforcement body would be interested to know who *is* holed up there.'

'Have you spoken to Karl Donaldson yet?'

Flynn shook his head.

It was Donaldson – an FBI agent – who had alerted Flynn to Viktor Bashkim still being alive, though he needed an official sighting to confirm it. Flynn suspected that Donaldson expected him to check it out on his behalf, like setting a Jack Russell after a rat – a ruse that had worked well.

Flynn recalled the phone call he'd taken from Donaldson a couple of weeks earlier when he and Molly had been out on *Faye*, having found a very secluded bay on the north of the island of Ibiza, where they were enjoying a long, lazy bout of skinny-dipping and sunbathing.

Flynn had been stretched out on the foredeck of the forty-five-foot boat with a face towel draped modestly over his private parts, one area that had never been allowed to catch the sun's rays, alongside Molly who was much less cautious and seemed happy to let everything fry. He'd heard the sat-phone ringing in the cockpit and had grudgingly gone to take the call.

'Flynn? Me, Karl Donaldson,' the conversation had begun abruptly and without preamble.

Flynn was instantly on guard and tense even though he had no idea why Donaldson should call him out of the blue. They weren't friends, although both had a connection to retired detective superintendent Henry Christie – a guy who was somehow often a catalyst for bad things happening.

More recently, though, Flynn's connection to Donaldson had been because of the Bashkim crime family from Albania.

Through no fault of his own, Flynn had become embroiled in the activities of the Bashkims in the Canary Islands when they had been attempting to expand their already extensive activities. It was the start of a torrid, violent relationship between Flynn and the Bashkims which had ended in tragedy for Flynn and a muted revenge of sorts four years ago when he believed that a vehicle Viktor was travelling in had been blown to smithereens in Malta.

That had effectively ended Flynn's connection to Donaldson, who had been investigating the Bashkims for other reasons, mainly because they had murdered an undercover FBI agent who had infiltrated their operations; Donaldson had been the guy's handler, so he felt the responsibility and loss greatly.

Viktor's death had been a win-win for both men.

'What do you want?' Flynn asked bluntly.

'Hey, how are you?' the American asked.

'Was pretty good until you called.'

'Why don't you switch on your camera and we can see each other, yeah?'

Flynn glanced down at his tanned body. 'You might not like what you see,' he said. 'Give me a minute.'

He hung up the sat-phone and ducked into the stateroom to grab a pair of shorts. He switched the camera on and went to lounge in the fighting chair on the rear deck.

'You're out at sea,' Donaldson noted. 'Still with Molly?'

'Uh-huh.' Flynn was non-committal. 'What can I do for you?'

Donaldson hesitated.

Flynn took a stab. 'This about the Bashkims?'

Donaldson nodded. 'I'm calling you with some intelligence and to ask you to take care.'

'Go on.'

'The explosion that killed Viktor Bashkim?' Donaldson prompted.

'I remember it well.'

Remembered seeing a convoy of three Range Rovers, the middle one containing Viktor, blown up in front of his eyes, each car and its occupants vaporized. There never had been any confirmation from Donaldson about who exactly had blown them up, and Flynn didn't expect there to be. Donaldson was a man who very much operated in the shadows and, Flynn guessed, did things that had to be done.

Flynn guessed, 'Viktor wasn't in the car, was he?'

On the phone screen he saw Donaldson's lips purse.

'Sometimes these things take time,' Donaldson said.

'OK.' Flynn drew out the word. 'What takes time?'

'Identifications, forensics. DNA analysis . . . that kinda stuff.'

'Four years?' Flynn said.

'That plus intelligence gathering, information analysis.'

'OK – stop prevaricating,' Flynn said, wondering where he'd managed to dredge up that word in his limited vocabulary and whether it was the right word in the circumstances.

'You're right,' Donaldson said. 'I think Viktor is still alive.'

Stunned, Flynn went silent. His punt might have been a guess, but one he didn't want to be true. He spun the fighting chair to see a now bikini-clad Molly standing behind him, able to overhear the conversation between him and Donaldson on speakerphone. There was a look of horror on her face on hearing those words: she too had been a witness to Viktor's supposed demise in the explosion.

Flynn gave her a twitch of the head.

'Tell me,' he said to Donaldson.

'Well, as you can imagine, identifying the victims in such a terrible explosion was going to be hard, not least because we didn't know who they were to start with – except Viktor, that is.

'Anyhow . . . it took a long time. Nine bodies to identify in three separate cars, all blown apart by extremely powerful bombs which left nothing much of them or the cars. It didn't help that the local law enforcement in Malta was under pressure following an attack on a journalist who'd been reporting on organized crime groups with links to cops, so they were being heavily scrutinized and were watching their step.'

'You'd think that would have motivated them to bend over backwards,' Flynn said.

'Yeah, well, they didn't,' Donaldson drawled. 'They were trying to solve their own problems . . . Anyhow, eventually eight of the nine bodies were ID'd. All were low-level hard men and enforcers from around Europe, not one of them legitimately in Malta, all having entered with false passports, which left the remaining body to be identified.'

'Viktor Bashkim?'

'Or not. The remains of that person were not in any DNA database the FBI had access to, so whoever it was had never been convicted of a crime in any country that takes DNA samples as part of the custody and conviction process.'

'Had Viktor ever been actually convicted of a crime?' Flynn asked.

'Not since he was twenty-five, over fifty-five years ago . . . which means his DNA was never taken because that was way before DNA was even a tremble in its daddy's kneecaps.'

'Shit.'

'However, we did find out that Aleksander, his son – you remember him – was arrested ten years ago in Romania for an assault on a cop, and convicted, which was something we didn't know about before.'

Flynn knew Aleksander was Viktor's beloved, now deceased, elder son; he knew that for a fact because he and Donaldson had been present at his death. In fact, Donaldson had pulled the trigger.

'Familial DNA?' Flynn guessed.

'Yep. We ran a comparison from the Romanian database, via Interpol, with the one remaining, unidentified body. Not even close.'

Coldly, incredulously, Flynn said, 'You're saying Viktor wasn't in any of those Range Rovers?'

'Nutshell,' Donaldson confirmed. 'And that last body still remains unidentified.'

'But how?'

'Pick any card,' Donaldson said. 'He either didn't get into the Range Rover or somehow managed to trick you into thinking he got in – but didn't; or somewhere on the route before the explosion he managed to get out.'

Flynn looked at Molly, who was as confused as he was.

Her brow furrowed as she tried to recall the day when she and Flynn saw Viktor get off his superyacht moored in the harbour in Valetta and get into the car to be whisked away.

In her mind, she was certain she had watched the three-car convoy set off, Viktor on board, never taking her eyes off it.

But had she? Now doubt was beginning to fester.

Flynn said to Donaldson, 'I'll call you back.'

He ended the call and stared at Molly.

'Viktor definitely got in,' Molly said.

Flynn nodded, visualizing the scenario from four years ago that was still very clear in his mind.

Viktor getting off the boat, getting into the middle one of three Range Rovers, and then all setting off.

Those moments had induced panic, when Flynn and Molly had been left stranded on the quayside without any transport to follow the crime lord to wherever he was being taken. Flynn had managed to commandeer – at a steep price – a moped belonging to a young waiter who had just arrived for his shift at a café by the water's edge, from where Flynn and Molly had been discreetly watching Viktor's boat.

In those moments of bartering with the waiter, Flynn had lost sight of the convoy, but only briefly. Seconds later, he and Molly were eyeballing the trio of Range Rovers and, in Flynn's mind, from that point on the vehicles were always in sight up to the moment they blew up.

'Or were they?' Flynn mused out loud.

Molly knew what he meant. 'I'm sure we never lost sight of them,' she said, and closed her eyes tightly, reimagining the pursuit through the streets of San Giljan. Were there a few moments as they threaded their way through that busy town when they did lose sight?

'Did we just *imagine* we had them in view the whole time?' Molly asked.

Flynn had his eyes closed too, his head nodding, reliving the images.

'We must have. There must have been time for him to get out and be whisked out of sight without us seeing him at some point. If it was slick and pre-planned, everything in place, then possibly – *possibly* – it happened, like a magic trick. It would only take seconds. Stop. Door open. He leaps into a waiting car or even into a building, the latter being more likely.'

Flynn was crestfallen.

He picked up the sat-phone and dialled Donaldson but didn't use the video link.

'It could have happened,' he confessed. 'I don't know where or how, but it could've.'

'Which also means Nico pulled a fast one on me,' Donaldson also admitted, referring to Viktor's younger son with whom he had been negotiating a secret deal to sacrifice Viktor so Nico could assume control of the Bashkim empire. At his end of the connection, Donaldson grimaced at the thought that Nico had played him like a fish on a hook, and now he knew that the feckless son, who liked cocaine and prostitutes, had double-crossed him, Donaldson felt stupid and naive.

'Family ties at the end of the day,' Flynn said. 'Blood runs thick . . . and supposedly killing Viktor got the FBI off the Bashkims' back.'

'I should've seen through him,' Donaldson spat.

'Hmm . . . the price of an education,' Flynn said philosophically. 'So is that it? Is that as far as all this goes?'

'Not entirely, Steve.'

Flynn waited.

'My problem is that the world of the FBI has moved on in the last few years and we've become a political football, certainly in the higher echelons, and in some respects I think we've lost track of what we're about. Anyhow, as you know, I was on the Bashkims' case because they'd murdered one of my undercover agents, but now no one's really interested in putting valuable resources into them. They're just another organized crime group.' He paused. 'Except for me, the poor little legal attaché based in London who still wants to grind that family into dust,' he said passionately. 'But I can't get the go-ahead to look into any of this "Viktor's still alive" stuff. It's water under the bridge.'

Flynn's mouth had gone dry. 'Meaning?'

'Well, first, as I said, more than anything this is a heads-up for you to be aware that Viktor is alive . . .'

Flynn interjected. 'It's not as though we've been lying low' – he glanced at Molly – 'so he could've come for me at any time and I'd be dead, but he hasn't.'

'I get that . . . but while Viktor might be old, he plays long games . . . you could still be on his hit list, Steve.'

'Or not.'

'Or not,' Donaldson conceded. 'But there is a flip-side to the dime.'

'Which is?'

'He murdered Maria Santiago, or at least ordered it.'

The chill that rippled through Flynn with these words was physical. 'I know,' he whispered hoarsely, hardly able to speak.

'So I'm going to leave you with this,' Donaldson said.

'Karl,' Flynn said cautiously, knowing he was going to be thrown some bait.

'Hear me out. If it means nothing, then fine . . . but you and I both have unfinished business with that family.'

Flynn ran the palm of his hand across his closely cropped hair, a nervous gesture meaning he was conflicted. He didn't want to hear another word, yet he wanted to hear everything. He knew Donaldson would be lighting a fuse and he, Flynn, would be rocketed into something he didn't need. He'd lived in peace for the last four years, other than helping Henry Christie out with a little problem, and had managed to compartmentalize Maria Santiago's horrific murder while forging on with, initially, a long-distance relationship with Molly, then a very close one with her aboard *Faye*.

Yet . . . reluctantly and irresistibly drawn into this, Flynn said, 'Go on.'

He could almost imagine Donaldson smirking at the far end of the connection or doing an air punch.

'Having learned all this,' the American said, 'I spoke to many of my contacts who are still dealing with sources across Europe and also kept my eye on all the intel coming in from that neck of the woods, and it seems, though this is unconfirmed, that the Bashkims have cosied up with the Lyubery – I'm assuming you know who they are.'

Flynn did: a prominent Russian mafia criminal organization – very violent, very wealthy.

'They've tied in with a particularly ruthless section of this lot and it seems they provide protection for Viktor, guard him, move him around, provide accommodation – and guess what for?'

'I can't even begin.'

'Viktor gifted the head of this particular clan with *Halcyon* – his superyacht.'

'That's gotta be worth thirty million euros,' Flynn exclaimed.

'Rough estimate.'

'So they are his protection detail . . . in Russia somewhere, I presume?'

'No. Cyprus at the moment. But he could move at any time.'

'And how can you be certain of this?'

'Trust me, I know these things,' Donaldson said.

Flynn was up early the next morning after his first day of watching the villa in Cyprus for any sign of Viktor. He spent twenty minutes swimming back and forth across the small harbour at St George's before showering on board and making scrambled eggs and coffee for breakfast.

As he was restocking his rucksack with water bottles and energy bars, Molly emerged from the master bedroom, stretching and yawning. She rubbed her eyes, slid her arms around him and snuggled in tight. To him, she felt amazing, warm, and her contours seemed to jigsaw into his body perfectly. He hugged her back and kissed the top of her head.

'Mmm,' she purred, then withdrew and looked inquiringly at him.

'Today it's done,' he promised.

She gave him her half-smirk look, which he loved and understood.

He threw the rucksack over his shoulder, then stepped off the boat on to the quayside, giving her a quick wave before walking to the Renault in the car park behind the café.

Five minutes later he'd parked up on the banana plantation track and was making his way carefully to the observation point he'd used the previous day, hoping not to fall asleep only to be awakened by a goat's snout. He settled down behind the rocks, took out his gun – which Molly knew nothing about – and peeked at the villa which was just waking up for the day.

THREE

The day was as stifling hot as the previous one, but the shade from the trees and lots of water made it bearable.

Having learned his lesson, Flynn made sure he didn't nod off this time. Probably an age thing, because he recalled times when he was on surveillance ops in the Special Boat Service in his early twenties when he could easily do a forty-eight-hour stretch while holed up in a target's back garden and never even begin to fall asleep.

The goats came and went and didn't even seem to notice him, which was good, though it made for a tense few minutes as they trundled past close by with the young herd. Once they'd moved on, he settled back, watched the villa.

There had been a couple of cursory foot patrols around the outer perimeter of the walls by guards who didn't really seem too concerned and could easily have been surprised and overpowered had there been a need.

The front gates opened and closed a few times. Once to allow a delivery from the local supermarket; Flynn didn't know if the vehicle was searched or not, but it reappeared and left ten minutes later. The next vehicle was a taxi which was waved through the gates as though expected. Flynn had heard the approach of the vehicle and was ready with the binoculars trained on the back-seat passenger. This time the gates didn't close and he watched the taxi drive into the courtyard and sweep to a stop at the front steps of the villa. A dark-haired woman got out of the back seat, paid the driver in cash and trotted up the steps as the taxi left the compound, the gates closing behind it.

Flynn got a reasonable but fleeting view of the woman – dark-skinned, attractive, maybe in her forties – and didn't recognize her at all.

There was a lull in villa activity then and Flynn did have to fight the nodding-dog syndrome but he became alert when he heard the sound of several vehicles with powerful engines approaching up the track. The gates were thrown open and three four-wheel drive Land Cruisers thundered dramatically into the courtyard and pulled up nose to tail in front of the villa steps.

That was all he saw as the gates closed.

He settled back again, now very alert, watching and listening.

The next arrival was an elderly man, wearing a battered old trilby and overalls, on a dusty moped. He rapped on the door by the gate and after a shouted exchange was allowed into the courtyard on foot.

He stayed about ten minutes, then left, and Flynn didn't think too much about that. What intrigued him were the three Land

Cruisers that reminded him of the three-vehicle convoy in which
Viktor Bashkim had supposedly met his death.

Now he wondered if they had come to take Viktor out for a drive
in the country, depending on whether the old fellow was actually in
the villa or not, whether there was any substance in what Karl
Donaldson had fed him. He knew Donaldson reasonably well.
Although he was based in London at the US embassy, Flynn knew
he was also an experienced field agent and that there was something
slightly mysterious about him – hidden depths that Flynn discerned,
something unspoken that told of a darker side to the American. He
also knew Donaldson would not be foolish enough to act on poor
information, so imparting what he had done about Viktor meant he
must have been pretty sure of its validity.

Flynn raised the binoculars and scanned the villa walls, seeing
the door by the side of the gates open and two men step out, separate
and take up positions on either side of the gates. They had machine
pistols slung diagonally across their chests and, for the first time,
the men looked tense and alert: no smokes, no phones.

As Flynn's lenses roved across the top of the walls, he also saw
the head of another man looking out, this time with binoculars, and
Flynn guessed there must be some kind of walkway around the
inner walls like a medieval castle might have; this was the first
time he'd seen such activity. There was a whole different vibe about
the place now – a tension – and he knew the arrival of the three
cars had triggered something unusual.

Maybe someone important had arrived, he speculated.

Or someone important was leaving.

Flynn wedged his binoculars on the rocks and took out his smartphone. He took some shots of the men standing by the gates and
the head of the guy on wall duty. Despite the distance, using the
zoom function, he got some decent mugshots which he would send
to Donaldson in due course to see if they meant anything to him.

Then he heard the unmistakeable sound of the Land Cruisers
starting up, the big throaty engines being revved.

Something was about to happen.

Along with this noise, he heard other engines starting up, too
– those of motorcycles.

And the excited barking of dogs.

Definitely all happening.

He pocketed the phone and picked up the binoculars again.

The engines continued to rev and then, quite dramatically, the gates were dragged open and the Land Cruisers surged out of the courtyard and accelerated down the track with Flynn no wiser as to whether they had dropped someone off or picked someone up, which, for a very short-lived moment, frustrated the hell out of him.

It was so short-lived and briefly puzzling because the gates did not immediately close as he might have expected. The reason for this became obvious as four pairs of young men astride four scrambler motorcycles with their engines screaming burst out of the gates, but instead of turning on to the track behind the convoy, they sped straight up the rocky slope in his direction.

And behind them, two men on foot unleashed two very large Rhodesian ridgeback dogs which followed the scramblers. Flynn suddenly realized with cold dread that his position had been compromised, probably by an inquisitive goat.

Within moments the bikes were just a hundred metres from him, powering directly and recklessly towards him, the two ferocious canines tight behind them.

The two lead riders concentrated on staying upright as they crossed the rock-strewn landscape almost side by side, while the pillion passengers leaned out, braced machine pistols against their shoulders and began to strafe the ground in front of Flynn's position behind the outcrop, sending up a spray of jagged stone chips.

Behind the bikes, the dogs ran effortlessly, silently.

Flynn grabbed his rucksack, spun and began to scramble away, keeping low but also having to reveal himself briefly as he flung himself over a small rise which he rolled over and down a gravel-like banking towards the edge of the banana plantation behind where he had been hiding. He was only fifty metres ahead of the bikes when he ducked into the plantation and zigzagged between several of the trees as the guns opened fire again. He felt the zing of bullets and heard their thud as they struck the tree trunks and the low-hanging bunches of unripe fruit, several of which burst open with a 'splat'.

As he ran, clasping his rucksack to his chest, he dipped his hand into it, fumbling for his own weapon which he hadn't removed and checked since the day before – another sign of lack of preparedness and age? He managed to get his fingers around the handle and drag it out and, while keeping running, he swung the pistol behind him and without aiming loosed a few shots backwards, hoping he would either hit or at least discourage the riders but also not hit either of the dogs, even though they were probably just as dangerous as the men.

Behind him, he realized the bikers had entered the plantation, their machines swerving and skidding as they negotiated the trees and fruit. Clearly they were being slowed down by the obstacle course, which pleased Flynn, although he was less pleased by the prospect of the dogs overtaking the bikes because there was no way the plantation would slow them down. They would revel in the chase, he guessed.

He upped his pace and discarded the rucksack, which was having a negative effect on his own speed and ability to swerve, but kept the gun and fired another flurry of unaimed shots behind him.

He could tell he was putting some distance between himself and his human pursuers but had no idea where the dogs were and fully expected to be ambushed by them in some sort of deadly pincer movement, at which point he would be ripped to shreds.

Somehow he had to get back to the Renault before the dogs or riders.

He ran, focused intently, side-stepping tree roots, dodging the fruit, powering himself until he emerged on the track where he'd left the Renault, sprinting the last fifty metres up to the vehicle, which of course did not have remote locking, but was unlocked by the worn-down key which he managed to get out of the knee pocket in his cargo shorts and insert first time.

Then he was in, trying to get the key into the ignition.

Just as he twisted it and the engine coughed to unhealthy life, the pair of dogs emerged from the banana tree line, paused and seemed to sniff the air and, as one entity, bolted towards him as he crunched the car unwillingly into reverse and started to swerve backwards along the track, one eye over his shoulder and the other on the fast-approaching hounds which loped towards him at a deceptively slow pace. Deceptive because it was very, very fast indeed.

The car, however, was less quick, especially going backwards, even though Flynn was almost standing on the accelerator.

Then he over-corrected a swerve and glanced off a tree trunk, dislodging a heavy bunch of bananas which crashed down on to the roof of the car, burst and showered him with fruit.

As he tried to get the car going backwards again, the dogs caught him.

One skidded up to his door, rose up, paws scratching, its snarling face smeared up against the window.

'Good boy,' Flynn said, rearing away, then rearing in another direction as the second dog launched itself courageously on to the bonnet and slithered right up to the windscreen, crashing against it.

Up on the track, the first two scramblers appeared out of the undergrowth and pivoted towards him.

Flynn jerked the car forwards to dislodge the dog from the bonnet, sending it sprawling; the other one was still clawing wildly at the side of the car.

To his right he saw a narrow path into another section of the plantation. Yanking the steering wheel to the right he aimed for it, jammed his right foot down and plunged the small vehicle in, leaving both dogs behind – hoping he hadn't hurt them. They were immediately replaced by the bikes.

Flynn ducked as a bullet shattered the rear window. He didn't feel where the slug went, just knew it had missed him.

He heard more being fired and felt the rounds zing off the body-work, knowing how lucky he was being at that moment, but also realizing things might change in an instant. On a tarmac surface, the bikes would have already caught up with him and riddled him and the car with bullets.

At least here in the plantation he had a sort of chance as long as the route he'd just chosen didn't suddenly narrow to nothing but actually led somewhere. If it came to a dead end, he would have to bail out and go on foot again.

More bullets slammed into the back of the car and pinged off the roof, all badly aimed as the bikes negotiated the uneven terrain.

The Renault bounced horrifically on its ancient and delicate suspension, crashed into a mound of soil, careened off, side-swiped a tree but carried on going.

A quick glance in the rear-view mirror.

Flynn grinned as he saw the pillion passenger of the bike directly behind desperately trying to reload, but even as he grinned, he then grimaced and swore as the bike pulled to one side and the rider gestured for the one behind to take the lead and continue the fusillade.

His head smacked the roof as the car crashed and bounced on the ruts in the path, but he managed to keep it pointing forwards, wondering if he had stupidly worked himself into a trap. Then, without warning, the plantation ended and he found himself emerging on to a tarmacked side road.

He swerved and tried to force some speed out of the car which screamed hoarsely at him at this punishment.

'Don't give up on me,' he breathed.

Fortunately, Flynn recognized his location: that had been another fear at the back of his mind – that he wouldn't have a clue where the hell he was – but he recognized this road as one on which he'd travelled a couple of times over the last few days. It was one of the routes into the Akamas, and a quarter of a mile in the other direction it intersected with the main road to Paphos. If he went hard right at that junction, he would be about a mile from the harbour at St George's where *Faye* was moored and Molly was waiting.

He went in that direction, making the Renault scream as if it was being throttled, but as he accelerated away, the first of the bikes skidded out on his tail.

He cursed again, gripping the wheel tightly with his left hand while lifting his right arse-cheek off the seat and contorting his body into a position where he could get his right hand into his shorts pocket and find his phone. He managed to pull it out and wedge it between his thighs, just as he reached the junction at which he needed to do a hard right on to the main road and head down the hill towards the harbour.

The leading bike was just behind him as he braked sharply, almost upending the Renault on to its nose and causing the riders to split either side of him in order to stop ramming into him.

The one on the right lost control and the bike went from under him and his passenger. The bike skidded in one direction and the riders slithered away across the road like spinning tops. Both slammed brutally into a low wall surrounding a villa and stopped moving instantly.

The other rider managed to stay on his machine but had to swerve up a gravel verge, taking off like a display rider with the pillion passenger holding on for dear life, but the landing didn't go well. The bike smashed down on to its front wheel, somersaulted and catapulted both men over the handlebars like circus acrobats. The rider hit the ground head first, which might not have been so bad had he been wearing a crash hat.

Death was almost instantaneous.

The passenger smashed into the ground at an angle that sent him doing multiple rolls, ending up in a concrete drainage channel at the side of the road, into which he disappeared.

But Flynn didn't have time to mourn.

There were still two bikes with four riders behind him and he was in a car that didn't have any chance of outpacing them as he turned at the junction in second gear.

The remaining bikers did not stop to offer assistance to their fallen colleagues.

The road ahead was quiet.

Flynn steered with his left hand, picked up his phone from between his thighs and speed-dialled Molly's number using his thumb, then wedged the device between his ear and right shoulder.

One of the bikes appeared alongside him.

Flynn twisted his neck to look and recognized the driver as one of the guards he had watched patrolling the perimeter of the villa.

Flynn smiled at him.

He responded by holding up a mobile phone and presumably taking a photograph of Flynn's face, though Flynn was more concerned by the actions of the pillion passenger whom he could just see out of the corner of his eye. He was a young lad, maybe twenty, raven-haired, and he raised a handgun towards Flynn's face.

Flynn immediately released the accelerator.

Caught by surprise at the sudden loss of speed, the bike shot past, braked and began to perform a U-turn with the rider using his left heel as a pivot, by which time Flynn had stepped on the gas again and aimed the car at the bike.

Flynn saw the fear in the faces of both of the lads on the bike as the passenger tried desperately to aim his handgun at Flynn, who in turn leaned sideways as he ran into them, a glancing blow, knocking both off the bike and continuing down the road, being followed by the remaining double crew who, Flynn hoped, might be a bit more circumspect in view of the injuries sustained by their colleagues.

Flynn heard Molly's voice on the phone which was still wedged on his shoulder.

'Flynnie?'

'Molly – start the engine and release all the mooring ropes,' he said as coolly as he could. 'Just keep hold of one until I arrive, understand?'

'Yeah . . . eh? But?'

'Just do it . . . I've encountered a big problem,' he started to say, but as he moved his head, he lost his grip on the phone, which dropped between the seat and the door as he swerved the car violently across the road as the last motorbike nosed up alongside. The bike dropped back and the passenger used the rider's shoulder to rest his hand on to steady his handgun.

Flynn saw this happening in the wing mirror – then the mirror exploded as a bullet hit it.

He swerved again.

They were approaching a sharp bend, a left-hander this time, after which the road descended steeply down to sea level; at the bottom of the hill was another tight right-hand bend with the harbour about two hundred metres further on.

Flynn prayed Molly would react instantly to his hurried instructions.

She knew what to do, having sailed with him for months now, and was fully conversant with the boat. He just hoped she wasn't standing there scratching her head wondering what the hell . . .

He knew she wouldn't be.

Flynn powered the small car down the last section of the hill, knowing he would have to take the corner at the bottom ten times faster than normal and hoped he wouldn't flip over.

A glance in the rear-view mirror: the bike was still behind, though it had dropped back slightly. He guessed the two men believed they would now have him trapped down here because he was essentially driving into a cul-de-sac as the road came to a sudden end when it met the harbour and the sea. He had to hope they would be caught off-guard by the fact he had another getaway vehicle ready and waiting in the harbour – hopefully with the engine running.

Ahead, Flynn saw the back wall of the shack-like café behind the small beach, and straight ahead the road itself merged into the quayside, allowing authorized vehicles to travel along it with the breakwater to the left and all the boats moored to the right.

Faye was moored at the very far end of the harbour.

Flynn's mind whirred as he worked out his rapidly evolving tactics.

If he sped to the end of the harbour, the bike would be right behind him and, quick as he might be, it would still take him vital seconds to get out of the car, leap on to the boat and get it moving, by which time his pursuers could have caught up and would finish him off. Bullets would fly before he and Molly could sail away.

He knew he had to make time for himself and somehow put a bit of distance between him and the bike.

As he sped down the last stretch of dusty road, he braked suddenly and veered into the wasteland that served as a car park behind the café, still unclear about what he was planning to do as he fought with the wheel and raced towards the wooden building, little more than a shack overlooking a tiny, rocky beach and the harbour.

He aimed for the right-hand corner of the café where there was a short pathway between palm trees leading through to the beach. It was to this gap that Flynn aimed the Renault.

There was still about fifty metres between him and the bike as he slammed on and virtually wedged the car between the leaning tree trunks. He flung himself out of the driver's door, not forgetting to grab his gun and phone, and twisted around, went down on to one knee and fired off a burst – six shots – at the bike just as it came into the car park.

Though hurried, his aim was deliberate, and he went for scare tactics by spraying bullets around the surface of the car park just ahead of the bike, causing panic, putting up spats of grit like little explosions. The rider swung sideways, lost control, the front wheel wobbled and the bike tipped over, sending both men rolling.

That done, Flynn was up, abandoning the car under the trees, sprinting past the café, then diagonally on to the harbour and running fast towards *Faye* where he could see Molly on the rear deck with one end of a mooring rope in her hand, keeping the boat steady.

Flynn reached the boat within seconds and leapt across.

'What the heck's—?'

Flynn gestured at the two armed men running down the quay.

'Oh, shit,' she said, releasing the rope as Flynn slammed the throttle down and the powerful engine, which had been idling as requested, came to life instantly. The sportfisher raised her nose like a thoroughbred and surged away from the mooring in a welter of seawater from the propellers.

By the time Flynn's pursuers reached the point where *Faye* had been moored, he and Molly were beyond the headland, racing out to sea.

FOUR

T he convoy of three Land Cruisers arrived at Paphos Airport less than half an hour after leaving the villa, having forced its way relentlessly in, around and through other traffic with no regard for anyone else's safety.

The cars drew up on the restricted parking area at the front of the main airport building, and Viktor and Sofia were escorted at his speed – slow – but less than discreetly by the clearly armed body-guards, through the front doors and then diagonally across the concourse to a door marked *PRIVATE – Authorized Personnel Only*. As had been prearranged, a well-reimbursed customs official was there to meet father and daughter on the other side of the door, which was as far as the bodyguards were allowed to go. The influence of the mafia on the Cypriot authorities was immense, but even they couldn't swing getting armed escorts into the departure lounge complex.

Their false passports were checked – and on the computer system no warning bells rang out anywhere because they were read as genuine – then they passed through the metal detectors and body search procedures into the departure lounge. Viktor's walking stick had to be checked manually because it set off the alarm on the metal detector due to the intricate gold and silver inlay around the head and the steel tip. They were then escorted to a private lounge where there was some time to kill before their plane was ready for take-off.

'Why can't we board immediately?' Viktor grumbled. He was

unused to waiting around for anyone or anything and at his age he hated it vehemently.

'Because the plane has only just landed and needs to be cleaned and refuelled,' Sofia explained patiently.

But at least the lounge was exclusive, comfortable and discreet, and Viktor could get a good cup of tea.

'We've got about half an hour before someone collects us,' Sofia said.

'Is this really necessary?' he asked. 'All this travel?'

'So it seems. Awkward people need the hard word,' she said, 'and you are our hard word, Father.'

'And all the standby arrangements have been made?' he asked, not for the first time. 'Just in case.'

'They have,' she assured him.

The old man nodded with satisfaction. 'That is good. You think things through.' He paused. 'Do you have the papers and the demands for me to read again, to see what we are up against?'

Sofia had an attaché case with her. She placed it on the coffee table in front of Viktor, clicked it open and extracted a thin sheaf of papers and handed them across. 'These are the projections.'

Viktor took them in his arthritic-gnarled fingers, rearranged his glasses on the bridge of his hooked nose and skimmed through the figures, which were just that – a set of numbers without context, unless, of course, the reader knew what the context was. In fact, the figures related to the projected earnings that could be achieved over the next year and a half for several new ventures across Europe and into the United Kingdom, which was a voracious consumer of all the goods and services that Viktor and his associates imported into that troubled land. There had been much work done already in terms of setting up and sourcing these 'goods' and establishing a supply chain from North Africa and the Middle East, and the returns looked spectacular for not much risk. There were many layers and buffers between Viktor and the end users and their consumption for him to have any worries. And even in a post-Brexit Britain in which the UK was no longer part of the EU, the plans were still very much on 'go'.

In the next eighteen months, the figures estimated that the income for the Bashkim crime family would easily clear a million pounds per month on top of their already existing business.

Viktor was satisfied with the projections.

He sighed as he handed the sheets back to Sofia. 'And the problem is?'

She took them, tapped them back together and walked over to the corner of the room to a paper shredder. She fed the papers into the machine one at a time.

Task done, she returned to Viktor.

The tea had arrived.

She sat down opposite him and said, 'As ever, Daddy, the problem we have is greedy, greedy people.'

It was at that moment her mobile phone vibrated to indicate an incoming text message.

The driver of the lead Land Cruiser was a Moscow-born hoodlum called Mikail Sokolov who now worked for a Russian gangster based in Nicosia, the capital of Cyprus. Sokolov had been a hard guy all his life, from a ten-year-old on the back streets of the Russian capital through military service where he excelled as an infantryman, then back in Moscow where he established a good reputation for assassinating anyone who crossed or caused problems for whoever his boss happened to be at the time.

The complication for Sokolov began when he was dispatched to assassinate an irritating Russian politician who, fleeing for his life, had been discovered living below the radar in a country other than Russia, which meant that another, generally speaking, less corrupt law enforcement agency than a Russian one had to investigate the horrific crime.

In Sokolov's case, that meant the Metropolitan Police.

Although Sokolov had done his best to avoid identification for the killing – simply a brutal murder in which he had put two very large-calibre bullets into the politician's head while he was sleeping post-intercourse in a high-class brothel in London with two sex workers – he had made one big error which was that, as many criminals had found out to their cost, the capital of England was awash with CCTV cameras. Despite the fact that Sokolov was on a Moscow-bound plane two hours after the killing, thinking he had got away with it, the Met was already on his trail and only just missed him at Heathrow.

While all this was happening, Karl Donaldson was unofficially still investigating the activities of the Bashkim family. Donaldson was based at the American embassy in London, had been for over twenty years, lived in Hampshire and commuted daily, usually, and had an excellent working relationship with the Metropolitan Police Special Branch and various intelligence units. Which was good because Donaldson's job was to analyse and disseminate intel and liaise with law enforcement agencies, including the Met and Interpol, across Europe and the globe. There was another side to his work at the embassy that occasionally involved using less savoury skills than number-crunching and data analysis and sometimes took him to far-flung places, often to hightail it out of countries in which certain individuals might have met sticky and inexplicable ends.

Since the death of Viktor Bashkim, Donaldson had been keeping one eye on the family which, supposedly, had been left in the less than capable hands of Nico, the playboy son who preferred screwing around and snorting coke to running a huge criminal enterprise.

Although other commitments at work meant Donaldson couldn't spend as much time as he would have liked on the Bashkims, mainly because his focus and expertise was on Middle Eastern terrorism, he still managed to pick up a few titbits of intel that crossed his desk at the US embassy, now located on the South Bank of the River Thames and within walking distance of the UK's Secret Intelligence Service – MI6 – building on Vauxhall Bridge.

Those titbits were that the Bashkims had got into bed with a Russian mafia clan called the Lyubery (Donaldson never called these moves 'forming an alliance' because such relationships often ended up with both sides fucking each other over, so 'getting into bed' was a much more realistic metaphor). Although the Lyubery were predominantly based in Moscow, they were known to have operations up and running in several European countries, including Cyprus. They were a particularly ruthless bunch, so they actually made good bedfellows for the Bashkims . . . but this information was really only of passing interest to Donaldson because he was dealing with more pressing issues in his daily work. It was just an eyebrow raiser, one for the backburner.

However, the piece of information that aroused his interest was spread all over the newspapers and other media: the shooting of a

Russian politician and businessman in a brothel in Soho, London. He read the reports as avidly as any member of the public would, but being an FBI agent, he wanted to know more, wanted to know what wasn't in the papers or online, just in case it was of any use to him.

That meant a speculative phone call to a certain detective chief superintendent in the Met called Melling, whom he knew very well and who gladly regaled him with all the gory details – including the fact, not reported publicly, that they had identified a suspect who had fled to Russia.

Melling was happy to forward a series of photographs of the actual crime scene, plus stills downloaded from CCTV footage which essentially trailed the suspect from the scene of the crime at a premises in Dean Street to a nearby hotel and then to Heathrow and on to a flight to Moscow.

'Not the sharpest knife in the drawer,' Melling commented, while at his end Donaldson had opened the secure email and was scanning the images. 'Bit of an amateur, really.'

Donaldson mostly agreed with that conclusion.

The suspect had been easily tracked, often unwittingly showing his face to the cameras, even though he was wearing a baseball cap; his image was captured at the airport, brazenly checking in for his flight. Donaldson was loath to dismiss him as a complete amateur because he clearly had the capacity to blow someone's brains out; maybe 'cocky' was a more appropriate word to sum him up.

'We were just a tad too far behind him at the airport,' the DCS admitted, 'and by the time we alerted the Russian authorities – for what *that* was worth – he'd cleared customs at Moscow and disappeared into the ether.'

'What's his name?' Donaldson asked.

'Mikail Sokolov. Low-level enforcer, intel tells us, working for the Russian mafia. Intel seems to suggest he actually works for a particular clan which has interests all over the place, including Nicosia and along the southern coast of Cyprus.'

At his end of the phone, Donaldson blinked; at the other end, Melling sensed a change in the American.

'Mean something to you?' the DCS probed.

Donaldson said, 'A Russian mafia clan with ops in Cyprus? Would that be the Lyubery?' His voice quivered just ever so slightly and he crossed his fingers.

'That's what's written down here,' Melling confirmed.

'Can we meet?'

Later that day, they convened on the north bank of the Thames, bought a hot sandwich and coffee each and strolled along the Embankment, past the building which now housed New Scotland Yard where Melling had his office. It was chilly and both men were wrapped up warm.

'You got a river view?' Donaldson asked him.

Melling snorted. 'My office is right at the back. If I stand on my chair and peer out through the top of my window – "window" being a very generous term for what is more like a letterbox – I can just about glimpse Whitehall. On the plus side, I can come out and stroll along the Embankment with friends.'

Donaldson took in the view of the London Eye on the opposite bank and said, 'Yes, that's a good plus side.'

Jack Melling, tall and lanky, in his early sixties with fair hair plastered back across his head, took a bite of his sandwich, sucked in a breath because the cheese filling was burning hot and said, 'What can I do for you?'

Donaldson sipped his coffee through the little hole in the plastic lid, licked his lips and said, 'I'm obviously interested in Mikail Sokolov, murderer on the run.'

'I gathered that, Karl.'

Although nothing had yet been discussed between the two men, Donaldson already knew this would be a tense conversation.

He sighed. 'I'll come straight to the point.'

'What? No dancing around?' Melling smiled, chiding him amiably. 'No foreplay?' He was used to dealing with delicate matters, though more often with the CIA than the FBI.

'Look,' Donaldson began, 'I realize you want Sokolov. After all, he has committed a brutal act on your patch . . . less than a mile from here as the crow flies.'

'Which has already got the Russians twitchy. Obviously, they immediately think we're going to blame the Russian state for sponsoring another murder in the UK and, contrary to what the media portray, the Russians don't really like bad publicity.'

'Are you?'

Melling shook his head. 'Obviously, Whitehall is going to enjoy teasing them, but the ultimate answer is no. The man was killed because of his links to organized crime, not because he dissed the Russian president.'

Donaldson nodded. 'OK, that's good . . . So, how desperately do you want Sokolov?'

'As desperately as any cop wants to nail a murderer on the run,' Melling said. 'It's what we cops are like.'

'Thought as much.' Donaldson's face was tight, then he narrowed his eyes and said, 'I want him, too.'

Melling blinked, although the declaration didn't surprise him. 'Really?'

'Yup.'

'I'm not sure the senior investigating officer on the case will be very forthcoming.'

'I want him. I want to know what he knows. I want to play him a bit.'

'Meh.' Melling did a slow shrug.

'Having the Sword of Damocles hanging over him – that is, having to face a possible murder charge – will obviously bring pressure to bear on him.'

'Still, meh! And I have to ask: what's in it for us little guys?'

Donaldson took a punt. 'How about the payoff being bringing down not one but two of the most powerful organized crime groups operating in Europe at the moment, or at least putting a fucking big dent in their bodywork?'

'Sokolov has this power?' Melling asked cynically. 'The guy's a gofer, numbskull, hardman and a killer.'

Donaldson could not quite answer this one. 'I don't know,' he admitted. 'But he may know . . . things,' he said limply.

Melling was conflicted. 'Just be honest with me, Karl.' He took another bite of his sandwich which had cooled down somewhat. 'Thing is we have a nasty killing on our patch, as you rightly say, but it is the killing of a Russian low-life, someone who won't be missed or grieved for. That doesn't make it right that we don't pursue Sokolov to the ends of the earth and bring him to justice, because as well as the murder, two sex workers were in bed with him and are still traumatized, and although they're "only" sex workers, they are our people, our community.' It was an impassioned speech from the heart of a good cop and reminded Donaldson of another good cop he knew, a guy called Henry Christie.

'Your response is entirely laudable,' Donaldson said. 'However, we have a bigger picture here. I've done some research into the Lyubery crime organization. They are huge and the suffering they cause others is untold – drug and people trafficking, money laundering, gun running – and the dosh they make is off the scale . . . billions.' Donaldson laid it on thick and creamy.

'You said two crime families, though.'

'Yes, I did, and I'm interested because the Lyuberys have recently formed an alliance with an Albanian crime organization in which I have a particular – and personal – interest. The Bashkims.'

'I've heard of them, but not so much recently.'

'They're big here in London and across the UK.'

'I know.'

'And if these two are in cahoots with each other . . .' Donaldson shrugged and took a bite of his tuna melt. 'More suffering caused, more deaths, more bad people getting rich by screwing over others.'

Melling thought about this for a moment, then said, 'Run whatever it is you want past me, I'll speak to the SIO, get her take on it and get back to you. But I'm not promising anything.'

The cocksureness of Mikail Sokolov was plainly evident to see when, shortly after his return to Russia, and after keeping a low profile only for a day, he flew to Cyprus.

The journey was discovered at the Cypriot end when Sokolov entered Paphos Airport; as his passport was scanned, his details, without him or even the customs officials knowing it, were red-flagged digitally and transmitted instantaneously to GCHQ near Cheltenham, Gloucestershire, the UK government's hi-tech listening station, and a warning came up on one of the hundreds of computers inside the secure, circular building known as the Doughnut.

As per instructions, the details of Sokolov's whereabouts had been immediately forwarded to the senior investigating officer in the murder case.

After Jack Melling spoke to her and convinced her of Donaldson's intentions, he called the American to share the information to confirm Sokolov's whereabouts, then said, 'But there may be more,' and ended the call, leaving Donaldson hanging on a thread of expectation.

As well as the alert triggered at the customs desk at Paphos Airport for Sokolov's passport, the GCHQ techies had also ensured that if Sokolov booked into any major hotel or self-catering accommodation and was required to show his passport, there would be a further alert to GCHQ. This software, incidentally, which was like eavesdropping on a phone line, had been developed by a twenty-two-year-old geek, recently graduated from Cambridge and headhunted by GCHQ, and had secretly been planted in customs and border control agencies and hotel databases across the world. It was used mainly to track terrorists as they flitted across the globe but was also very helpful in tracking murderers.

One hour after Melling's first call, Donaldson – who had been on pins in his office – took another from the Met guy.

The British cop said, 'Got him!'

Much to his boss's mouth-spluttering protestations, Donaldson left his office within ten minutes of receiving Melling's call and was on his way home to pack. After a tedious train journey, which he normally enjoyed, he disembarked at Winchfield in Hampshire and was picked up by his wife, Karen – formerly a cop with Lancashire Constabulary, but now retired and running an online business selling wine from their home in the beautiful countryside close to Bramshill. By the time he slid into the front passenger seat of his convertible Ford Mustang, his phone had bleeped to inform him that his e-tickets for his flight from Heathrow to Paphos had arrived.

He kissed Karen on the cheek as she pulled out of the station car park and she stuck her tongue out at him.

'Nine tonight, Heathrow,' he said.

'Mmm . . . sun and sea,' she said dreamily and turned to face him mock-challengingly. 'But no sex for Mr Donaldson.'

'Promise,' he said.

At three a.m. the next morning, Donaldson landed in Paphos, jumped into the waiting car rental and was driving to a five-star hotel on the beach in the resort where he threw his hand luggage on to the spare bed in his allocated room, stripped off, showered and slid between the sheets. After texting Karen, he fell asleep.

Breakfast was self-service and socially distanced, and with a plate full of freshly prepared omelette, a large juice and coffee, Donaldson found himself a table on the outdoor terrace where he aimed to have a leisurely meal with a nice view of the Mediterranean and read the thriller he'd brought along to pass the time.

All he had to do was wait.

Donaldson hadn't expected Sokolov to be alone, and when he eventually appeared, just minutes before the end of the breakfast service, he was accompanied by two other young men and three giggling women who, it didn't take a genius to work out, were paid escorts.

The group scooped up copious amounts of food from the self-service display, bullied the female chef into making numerous fried eggs and then decamped to the terrace, drawing furious looks from the maître d' whose handlebar moustache quivered indignantly.

From behind his shades, his paperback thriller and coffee, Donaldson watched the group guzzling their food and Bucks Fizz, annoying all the other guests, who had been contentedly finishing their breakfasts, with their raucous behaviour.

The problem was how to get Sokolov alone.

It helped when the girls left – a taxi arrived for them to pile into – and the group thinned down to the male trio, all of whom looked bronzed, fit and very brutal.

Heavies, Donaldson pegged them.

Donaldson concentrated on Sokolov who was chillaxed almost to horizontal, laughing dirtily with his compatriots. Donaldson half wondered what kind of man could put two bullets into another man's head and a few days later be out for a laugh with his chums.

But that train of thought didn't last very long as he caught sight of his own reflection in the coffee pot in front of him.

Finally, the threesome rose and left. Sokolov stuffed a wodge of euros into the maître d's mitt as he passed as recompense for their bad behaviour and patted his cheek patronizingly.

Donaldson tipped the last of his coffee down his throat and closed his book as a waiter began to clear his table.

'A little bit noisy, those guys,' Donaldson remarked.

The waiter snorted. He was a small, middle-aged man. 'Russians and prostitutes.' He snorted again.

'Really? Russians?'

'Cyprus is overrun by the communist bastards,' the waiter responded vehemently. Donaldson got the impression he would have spat if he hadn't been waiting on tables. 'Property, smuggling, whores, drugs and people smuggling . . . all goes on here. Mafia,' he concluded bleakly.

'I take it you don't approve?'

'On the other hand, they pay good tips,' he said philosophically.

'Ah, well, that's good.' Donaldson rose, took the hint and left five euros on the table. He took his cup of coffee and went to the outer terrace to another table, where he took his time and considered his options, knowing that the one he chose would have to be the one that gave him the quickest result, which would probably mean a short, sharp shock for Sokolov, not least because Donaldson's own time on Cyprus was limited.

He sighed, ordered more coffee which came quickly, and as it did, Donaldson perked up as Sokolov sauntered alone on to the terrace dressed in running gear. He trotted down the steps to the coastal path which curved along the seafront into Kato Paphos one way and towards Coral Bay the other, several miles long and ideal for an easy, level jog. Sokolov adjusted the Fitbit on his wrist, did a few stretches and set off in a westerly direction away from Paphos. Donaldson thought he looked tough and fit and obviously remained hyper-confident he had managed to evade the clutches of the British police.

He returned forty-five minutes later, sweating heavily but not really out of breath; he did a few warm-down stretches and trotted back into the hotel. Half an hour later he was out by the pool with his friends and all three of them oiled themselves slick with lotion and stretched out on loungers to begin the tanning top-up process.

Donaldson retired to his room, which had a balcony overlooking the pool. He settled down and watched.

The Russians did not move for several hours, other than to replenish their drinks and have lunch at the poolside bar.

Just after midday Donaldson received a text: *Team arrived.*

Which meant that, unless urgently deployed elsewhere, a team of four former Special Forces personnel, now part of the Special Operations Unit of the FBI that Donaldson had managed to cajole his boss into authorizing, was at his disposal for forty-eight hours and not a minute longer.

He smiled grimly, then made a phone call to set up some facilities in which the heavy-handed plan he was formulating in his brain would be played out.

The next morning was essentially a repeat of the previous one, with the three Russian men appearing for a rowdy late breakfast accompanied by three different escorts, but with the exception that two taxis later turned up, one for the girls and one for Sokolov's two mates who were then all whisked away, leaving Sokolov on his own.

'Boo-hoo for you,' Donaldson whispered.

This was the moment, then, for a little prayer from Donaldson who, having eaten earlier, was already in his own running gear on the terrace.

If Sokolov didn't show for this morning's run, he would have to do some very quick re-thinking, most likely involving some very unpleasant scenes in the hotel, which he would prefer to avoid.

But Sokolov appeared and Donaldson breathed a sigh of relief and sent a quick text. He gave Sokolov a minute to get going along the path and then settled into an easy jog in his wake.

The path ran and twisted along the coastline with a string of decent hotels between it and the main road and at some points came very close to the road itself, which gave Donaldson's specially deployed team the opportunity to park their Peugeot van in a small car park adjacent to the path. Having received the warning text from Donaldson, they were ready to swarm out of the sliding door, pounce on the unsuspecting jogger and bundle him within seconds, hooded and bound, into the van and drive away. They were exquisitely skilled in tasks such as these, and this was easy compared to their usual ones.

Donaldson witnessed the snatch from about a hundred metres away, watched the ease with which Sokolov was taken, smiled, spun on his heels and jogged back to the hotel.

Donaldson sat down quietly at the table which was screwed to the floor. Sokolov visibly tensed, although Donaldson could not see his face as the thick black hood had not yet been removed from the detainee's head. He was sitting on a chair, also screwed to the floor; his hands were cuffed in front of him, attached by a short chain to a metal ring on the tabletop, and although Sokolov could not see anything, he could sense movement, hear breathing and other noises.

The room had a certain aroma to it.

Donaldson knew the venue had been host and witness to numerous prisoners passing through, this being a completely illegal staging post, usually for suspected terrorists, snatched in the Middle East and pausing here before onward flights to destinations that even Donaldson did not enjoy thinking about too deeply.

And it was an ideal place to have a little chat with Sokolov: a strengthened, soundproofed room in the corner of an aircraft hangar rented exclusively to the Central Intelligence Agency on the UK airbase at Akrotiri, near to Limassol.

Donaldson had been here before when he'd supervised the rendition of a terror suspect who'd been seized (as opposed to 'lawfully arrested') in Malta and who had finally ended up in Guantanamo Bay. It was just the once and had been a vicious two days that he wasn't proud of.

Now he was looking across at another hooded detainee.

Donaldson didn't speak.

He glanced around the room and his eyes lingered on the one-way mirror on the wall, on the other side of which sat the four men from the Special Ops team who had lifted Sokolov off the coastal path.

He smiled and winked.

Then he sighed loud enough for Sokolov to hear.

In Russian, Sokolov demanded, 'What's fucking going on?' He yanked on the handcuffs, rattling the chain, then began to heave against them, trying to break free. He was strong but there was no give in them. He wasn't going anywhere. 'Let me go, you bastards,' he screamed from under the hood which he tried desperately to shake off his head. 'This isn't legal.'

Donaldson allowed him to have his rant and his bid for freedom. He knew Sokolov would quickly realize he was here for the duration – a sobering insight.

Finally Sokolov subsided, slumped into angry submission and muttered, 'I know you're there, whoever you are. I'm a Russian citizen and you can't do this to me.'

'Speak English, please.'

Sokolov raised his head. Donaldson knew he was trying to see through the dense weave of the hood, which was impossible.

'*Yebat' tebya!*' he snarled. 'Fuck you!' in Russian.

Words Donaldson understood. 'This will be speeded up, one way or another, if you speak in English,' Donaldson said. In Russian he added, 'Trust me.'

'Trust you? Trust who, you fucker?' Sokolov shouted and began another fruitless bid to free himself from his cuffs and chains.

Donaldson waited patiently for the valiant effort to subside, which it finally did. Then he said in English, 'Now then, have you finished?'

Donaldson stood up and slowly began to circumnavigate Sokolov, treading quietly, but knowing the Russian would be able to sense him and seeing from his shoulders that he was tensed up like a coil, prepared for something dreadful to happen to him.

At one point, Donaldson stopped directly behind him, maybe two feet distant. Breathing quietly.

Sokolov knew he was there. Donaldson saw his shoulders quiver.

'You need to stop this. Just get on with what you have to do. Mind games mean nothing to me,' Sokolov said.

Donaldson remained silent. Then he circled once more, racking up the tension by standing behind him for a full minute again, seeing Sokolov's head twist and turn as he tried to listen; then he went back to his chair opposite and sat down.

'Mikail Sokolov . . . former soldier, now a hitman.'

'Wrong guy. So wrong.'

'Mikail Sokolov . . . amateur hitman at that.'

Sokolov didn't respond to that taunt.

'I know that several days ago you were sent to London where you put two bullets into a man's head as he lay sleeping.'

'Like I said, wrong guy,' he persisted.

'An upmarket brothel in Soho. Dean Street. Two bullets into the head of Dimitri Yenkov, a minor Russian politician, though I use the word "politician" loosely. "Gangster" might be a better description.'

Sokolov snorted with contempt. 'Don't know what the hell you're talking about.'

'I've been watching you for six months, Mikail,' Donaldson fibbed. He leaned across the table, reached out and whipped the hood off Sokolov's head.

He blinked even though the room wasn't particularly brightly lit. Then he glared at Donaldson. 'Who are you?'

'You don't need to know.'

Sokolov looked around the room, trying to work out his location, but all he could see were the inner walls of an interrogation suite of some sort which could have been located anywhere. 'Where am I?'

'Something else you don't need to know, Mikail.'

'You're American!' Sokolov declared.

Donaldson's face remained impassive.

'Fuck's going on?' Sokolov demanded. He pulled and rattled his handcuffs and glowered at Donaldson.

Who waited for the moment to wane, then said, 'I know you killed a man in London. Were sent there on that mission, but because you are lazy and overconfident and not a good criminal, you left a trail to and from the crime scene up to the point where you stepped on a plane bound for Mother Russia.'

Sokolov's nose flared as he listened to this. 'Wrong guy.'

Donaldson said, 'Please don't make me have to show you the evidence which incriminates you up to here.' He drew his hand across his throat.

'So what am I doing here? Somewhere which is obviously not a police station, talking to someone who is obviously not a cop, who has a team of *fucking mercenaries* at his disposal?' Sokolov's voice shouted out.

Once more, Donaldson waited for the anger to ebb. 'The Metropolitan Police in London have enough evidence – scientific, forensic and digital – to easily convict you of killing that man.' Donaldson was aware he was gilding the lily somewhat – he didn't really know any such thing for certain – but he continued to embellish it. 'At the scene they have DNA of the suspect, they have CCTV footage – which is why I called you an amateur – DNA of you at the passport desk at Heathrow, a partial match of a fingerprint from a glass of whisky you drank at the airport which matches a print from the crime scene . . .'

Now he was really laying it on, and because he saw the realization dawn in Sokolov's eyes and saw the man begin to wilt like a flower, he kept going mercilessly.

'You've been identified, and once the cops get hold of you in person – and they will – then take your DNA, your fingerprints, your mugshot, you'll spend at least twenty years in a high-security prison because the Brits do not like Russian assassins operating on their soil.'

Sokolov swallowed, overwhelmed by the barrage and not capable of thinking straight.

'So what do you want?' he growled. 'Why am I here?'

'I have power,' Donaldson said.

'What power?'

'The power to hand you over to the Brits via the Cypriot authorities with whom they work very closely . . . or not.'

He let the words sink in, eyeing Sokolov with amusement.

'What do you want from me?'

'What I want, Mikail, is for you to work for me.'

Sokolov laughed uproariously at this and shook his head. 'Joking? You must be. I'm guessing you want me to rat on my employers.'

'Up to a point.'

'Then you are a fool. These people are dangerous and much scarier than the British authorities.'

'I know that . . . but if you refuse, I'll hand you over right now and that is the complete end of your freedom for twenty years. Work for me, you stay free, and if you're discreet enough and savvy enough, you'll no doubt live a long, lucrative life and probably die of syphilis.'

'What do you want from me?'

'Actually, I don't want you to snitch on your employer, as such. I want you to tell me as much as you can about the crime family your employer has just linked up with.'

Sokolov blinked. 'The Bashkims?'

Donaldson nodded slightly.

'The Bashkims?' Sokolov repeated. 'They are why I'm here now, in Cyprus.'

It was Donaldson's turn to blink.

'I'm on a protection detail.'

'Enlighten me, Mikail.'

Sokolov shrugged. 'I don't know much about anything, usually. I'm a guy who fetches and carries and intimidates people, usually. Yeah, I killed that guy in London. I don't even know who he was or what he'd done – well above my paygrade, as you Yanks

always say in shitty gangster films – but I did it in the hope I'd
climb the ladder a bit. My boss was pleased. Patted me on the back,
gave me ten thousand euros, told me to chill for a few days, lie low
with this job we've got on here. Got to babysit some old guy, so
that's what I'm doing. Chillin', fuckin'. Then I'm on a round-the-
clock protection detail and guarding him in some villa on the
Akamas; running him to and from places if necessary, but from
what I've heard, he doesn't move much.'

'Old guy?' Donaldson quizzed. 'What old guy? One of your
bosses?'

'Head of the Bashkim family.'

Donaldson was puzzled and a strange taste juiced into his mouth.

'Name,' he insisted.

'Bashkim. Viktor Bashkim.'

The name of a supposedly dead man.

'Glad to see the back of him,' Sokolov said. He was at the wheel
of the Land Cruiser as the trio of vehicles moved off in unison from
the front of Paphos Airport. He glanced at his passenger, another
young Russian buck with pretensions of greatness within the
underworld but who would probably end up used and abused by
his master and then dead in a back alley. A life of crime was alluring
but only the chosen few really benefitted from it. He was as unlikely
as Sokolov to succeed, although there would be odd occasions –
such as today, when he had been given a specific job to do –
when he, like Sokolov, would fall into the trap of believing that
somebody up there liked him.

Sokolov's companion – his name was Yuri Blenkov – nodded in
agreement.

'Yes, man, at least we can chill now.'

'That we can,' Sokolov confirmed. Since his encounter with
Donaldson less than a month ago, after which he'd been hooded,
manhandled and dumped on spare land close to the hotel, he had
been living on pins. The American didn't really want much; he
wasn't overly interested in Sokolov's boss but wanted information
on the Bashkims and absolute confirmation that the protection
being given was for Viktor Bashkim (something that the Yank for
some reason didn't really seem to believe).

Sokolov recalled that part of the conversation very well – the point when he had revealed that old man Viktor was definitely the package he and others were protecting.

'You're sure about that?' Donaldson had said, though, of course, Sokolov did not know the American's name. Still didn't.

Sokolov had shrugged, nodded.

'Have you seen him?'

'No,' he'd said. 'He's holed up in a bedroom and lounge combined on the first floor of the villa. Doesn't ever move from there, I've been told. I haven't been there yet, so I don't know anything for certain, but I've been told his son is there, too. I just know it's an easy job. I like easy jobs.'

It was then that Donaldson had given Sokolov his instructions and conditions: that in exchange for information on the Bashkims and confirmation that it really was Viktor living a very cloistered life in a Cypriot villa, Donaldson would not inform the law enforcement authorities in London or Cyprus of his whereabouts, but if he did not pass on anything worthwhile, then the long arm of the British law would soon be feeling his collar to yank him back to face justice and prison walls.

Sokolov's problem was that he was only a small cog in a very large wheel, but he did try to keep his ear to the ground and pick up snippets of intel about what the Bashkims were up to, and although he personally never saw Viktor, he heard enough to confirm to Donaldson that the old man was a living, breathing entity.

However, the order to pick up Viktor and transfer him to the airport had come unexpectedly that morning.

Downtime for 'off-duty' guards was spent within the confines of a gated complex of villas in Coral Bay where the young Russian men were billeted – with direct access to the beach, an impressive fleet of vehicles and strict orders to behave themselves. Mostly it was a tedious lifestyle, sometimes fraught with the tension often associated with macho males in close proximity.

Sokolov only spent a few days here. The remainder of his time was spent working shifts around the villa, and during his stints there he saw the son, Nico, but never the old guy.

It was a crap job, but easy.

And Sokolov managed to keep to his side of the bargain with Donaldson by using an encrypted mobile phone Donaldson had given him and making a few calls and sending texts to the only number on the phone, but no photographs as use of mobiles was banned within the walls of the villa.

Sokolov was as surprised as anyone when he was turfed out of bed that morning and told to be ready to be a driver to escort the guy from the villa to the airport. He was pleased to be chosen as lead driver with Blenkov as passenger; all personnel were to be armed.

Things moved so quickly that he didn't have time to make a discreet call or send a text to Donaldson at any point before or during the drive to pick up and drop off the old man.

There was one thing, though – this was the first opportunity to actually see the man in the flesh, and Sokolov took a good look at Viktor as he was assisted into the middle car of the convoy by his daughter, who accompanied him, and his son, who did not.

Sokolov was entirely unimpressed by what he saw.

A wizened, grey-haired man, thin and almost doubled over by curvature of the spine, with a fancy walking stick (should have had a Zimmer frame, Sokolov thought), having to be almost lifted by his daughter (who Sokolov thought looked thoroughly fuckable for her age) and the son (who reminded Sokolov of Elvis Presley in his final years).

He supposed someone had to be the head of an organized crime gang or family, but Viktor Bashkim definitely looked past it. However, he also knew that power did not necessarily come with physique. Although a buff body, a six-pack and muscles like bricks did help.

While he and the other guys had been waiting with the cars, there had been some excitement because a local guy had spotted someone watching the villa and the gang was going to pile out en masse, on scramblers and with the hunting dogs, to confront him, whoever it was. That was a piece of action Sokolov would be denied but would have enjoyed being part of.

After they dropped Viktor off at the airport, Sokolov was eager to fulfil his obligation to Donaldson as he hadn't had the chance to bring him up to date with the latest development, even though he had no idea which flight Viktor would be on.

He hoped to be able to engineer some quiet time away from the others to make a call, but as he led the convoy away the airport,

Blenkov received an urgent call on his mobile: something had gone very wrong with the plan to confront the guy who'd been watching the villa.

Nico Bashkim had also been glad to see his father and sister climb into the Land Cruiser and be whisked away, though when the four scramblers and the dogs poured out of the gate up on to the hillside, he had a feeling very much like indigestion in his gut, which was exacerbated greatly when about twenty minutes later the two ridge-backs limped back into the courtyard, panting heavily, followed ten minutes later by more walking wounded and some very bad news.

Sofia Bashkim read the message on her phone and skimmed through the photographs that had just landed also, taking a seat next to her father as she did.

The old man watched, aware of her change of temperament as she scowled at what had arrived: a text from Nico and several photos taken by the pillion passenger of one of the bikers who had chased the watcher on the hill.

Most of the photos were shaky, but one was perfect and caught the face of the man as he drove a car yet looked over his shoulder at the people following him. Sofia closed her eyes momentarily in despair, then opened them and looked at Viktor who was frowning at her.

He said, 'What is it, my darling?'

She sighed deeply, wondering if it was the right thing to show him what had landed, but she knew she had to. She turned the phone around and let him see the screen, saw his watery eyes focus and then his face harden as he finally recognized the individual in the photo.

Sokolov volunteered to go out to the location on the hillside where the man had been seen hiding and watching the villa to see if there was any evidence up there that might be of help.

It was a thin excuse, but he needed the opportunity to make a call away from the others and especially away from the mayhem in the courtyard. Trying to give the impression of being busy by going up to see if the guy who'd been chased had left anything incriminating behind as he fled, he could call the number on the phone that Donaldson had given him, which was secreted down the front of his boxer shorts.

He scrambled up the slippery rocks and found the niche in which the man had been discovered by a goat.

There was nothing other than an empty, crushed, plastic water bottle.

He crouched down and looked back towards the villa, then fished out the mobile phone from his underpants – a small Nokia – switched it on, waited for it to pick up a signal, then made the call to the only number programmed in the device.

It was answered but no one spoke.

Sokolov said, 'Blue lagoon,' which was the phrase he had been told to say in order to identify himself and which also indicated that he was safe and not being coerced in any way. There was no phrase for the alternative.

A metallic-sounding voice responded, 'Contact made.' There was a series of clicks which he assumed were connections being made and broken so that the call could not be traced in any way, then Donaldson's voice came on the line. 'Speak to me.'

Sokolov suddenly felt vulnerable, this being the first ever contact he had made in close proximity to the villa and his colleagues. He wanted this to be quick. 'Today I can confirm eyeball,' he said. 'Target is as suspected.'

'Good work.'

'Only thing is he's at Paphos Airport, catching a plane somewhere; I don't know where.'

'You don't know? What use is that?'

'Hey! The job was dropped on us at the last minute – just get him to the airport; no one knows where he's flying to.'

'Is he alone?'

'He's with the female.'

'What about the other male?'

'He is still at the villa . . . and I've got to go now to get back there. The shit has hit the fan.'

'How?'

'Some guy been spotted surveilling the villa. Got chased and there could be some fatalities with our team. Not the guy. He got away in a boat.'

'A boat?'

'That's what I heard. A fishing boat.'

Sokolov heard the American chuckle.

'Look, I got to go.'

He hung up, then stood up and was in the process of sliding the phone back beside his cock when he heard a noise that sent a shimmer of fear through him: the sound of a double-action revolver being cocked, that unmistakeable metallic click of the hammer being thumbed back into place so that just the slightest amount of pressure on the trigger is required to fire the weapon.

Sokolov rotated his head slowly while raising his hands.

He looked into the muzzle of a .38-calibre, four-inch barrelled revolver in the right hand of Yuri Blenkov, aimed straight and unwavering between his eyes. Blenkov's face came into focus, his mouth a crooked smile.

'Yuri,' Sokolov whispered. 'What's—'

'I've been ordered to kill you,' Blenkov said simply but chillingly.

'Why?'

Blenkov shrugged. 'They say you were careless in London, reckless even, that you could be identified, that you could bring the police to our door.'

'That's not true.'

'Doesn't matter. I have a job to do . . . although . . .' He paused and said, 'I was told to kill you straight after I told you the reason why . . . and I would've done . . . however, I have a distinct feeling you have some explaining to do regarding the phone call I've just overheard . . . so put the phone down on the ground, turn around and let's walk back slowly; some people will be very interested in who you were speaking to.'

'It was no one of interest.'

'I'll let others be the judge of that, Mikail. Phone – on the ground.' He gestured with his gun.

Sokolov hesitated, but only briefly. He wondered if he could take Blenkov but knew the guy was ex-Russian Special Forces – experienced, tough, wily and one step up from him in the hardman league. He weighed up his chances and saw Blenkov smirk because he knew exactly what was going through his mind.

'You can try, Mikail,' he said, 'you can try.'

Sokolov nodded and slowly placed the phone on the ground. Blenkov made a circular gesture with the gun barrel. Sokolov turned and began to walk down the slope towards the villa as Blenkov scooped up the phone and slid it into his pocket, at which moment Sokolov skidded sideways and fled.

In those fleeting moments, he had weighed up his future and seen nothing good.

If he acquiesced and walked back to the villa with his hands up, he would be tortured until he confessed everything. He knew that. It was the way they operated. Maybe strung up by his ankles and beaten to within a millimetre of his life, probably with staves. The suffering would be agonizing, long and drawn-out. Even if he immediately admitted his wrongdoing, it was likely he would still be tortured, and in either scenario he would still end up with bullets shredding his brain.

So even though he knew Blenkov was fast, ruthless and a trained killer, he was willing to take his chances and make a break for freedom. If he died, he would at least know he'd tried.

He dipped, turned. And sprinted, zigzagging across the gravel-like surface. He felt as if he was running for a long time, as if all life had slowed down completely, as if he'd run a hundred metres.

In reality, he had only gone maybe fifteen before the first bullet struck him, smashing diagonally through his skull into his brain through the parietal bone when the soft-tipped bullet, designed to cause maximum damage, mushroomed as it entered the cerebrum. After a single flash of indescribable pain, there was nothing but blackness.

The second bullet, fired straight after the first, hit Sokolov at the same angle but just slightly lower through the occipital bone at the back of his head and again caused catastrophic damage.

He was dead before his knees gave way and he pivoted, then slumped to the ground.

Viktor Bashkim was completely silent for the next hour.

Sofia watched him with concern.

He was silent even when a porter appeared in the private lounge with a wheelchair for him and he sat in it as he was pushed through the airport, and when he and Sofia were transferred on to an electric buggy at one of the gates outside the terminal building to take them to the private jet waiting for them at the far end of the boarding walkway.

Even as the smiling stewardess welcomed him aboard and assisted him to his very plush seat.

Even as they taxied on to the runway, the engines powered up and the plane rumbled down the runway and rose quickly into the clear sky, he said nothing.

Finally, as the jet levelled off at 29,000 feet and he was brought a fresh cup of herbal tea, he spoke. 'Do you recognize that man?' he asked Sofia.

She had been brought a bottle of chilled champagne and caviar. She sipped the drink and said yes.

'You understand what this means, don't you?'

She nodded. 'It means Flynn and Donaldson know or suspect you are still alive, that you did not die.'

Viktor's tea was in a proper mug. He jiggled the tea bag on its piece of string, then clasped his hands around the mug, getting heat to the old joints in his hands.

'Who do we have available?' he asked.

She blew out her cheeks. 'The Tradesman?' she suggested. 'Once our meeting in England is over, we could redeploy him. He's as good as anyone.'

Viktor inhaled deeply. 'Contract him, then. Contract the Tradesman to kill Steve Flynn.'

FIVE

Two weeks later

Henry Christie found it quite ironic that he had stumbled into possibly the one of the biggest and most wide-ranging criminal conspiracies he had ever investigated, a conspiracy spanning three decades, on his first day as a civilian investigator with Lancashire Constabulary's Cold Case Unit.

On his arrival at the office door of the CCU, situated on the ground floor of the Force Major Investigation Team (FMIT) building on the headquarters campus, almost before he could draw breath (but not before he was insulted), he'd been dragged out by his new running partner, DS Debbie Blackstone, to arrest a man on suspicion of committing a rape that was ten years old.

That arrest, during the course of which the suspect's lights had been well and truly punched out by Blackstone (who, Henry discovered very quickly, was volatile in the extreme), had triggered a series of events that led Henry and Blackstone into a murky, dangerous world of murder and child abuse, and then the arrest of a number of 'prominent' citizens right across the north of England who were embroiled in the conspiracy.

The first of these arrests had been made several months ago, and Henry and Blackstone had hardly paused for breath since.

Today, the pair of them hoped to unlock the next door of the investigation – which had rather grandly been named Operation Sparrow Hawk (Henry had fought in vain for it to be called Tawny Owl, but had been firmly put in his place) – by turning up uninvited and unannounced at the office of a man who owned a string of care homes and funeral parlours across the north-west, but years before had worked at several children's homes and who, it seemed, had many awkward questions to answer.

So Henry was up, showered, dressed and eager to get on the road that morning. He had been a detective superintendent on FMIT before his retirement from the police, and because his life had moved on in the intervening years, he had been reluctant to sign on as a civilian investigator, but the decision had proved worthwhile from two main angles.

First on a personal level.

It had done him a hell of a bit of good. He had rediscovered his passion for investigating and inquiring and delving into people's innermost, dark secrets; he had also found a great – he was reluctant to classify what he had found as 'friendship', because it was more than that . . . but he supposed 'friendship' covered most bases – friendship with Debbie Blackstone whom he found infuriating, annoying, screamingly funny and very professional and dedicated; he could see she was a brilliant detective who had been dealt a lousy hand in some respects, but the two of them rubbed along roughly and smoothly in equal measures. Henry also realized this so-called friendship had saved him from descent into a bottle, though he never admitted that to anyone and only reluctantly to himself. He knew he'd been on the verge of alcoholism, but long days and nights investigating the most terrible of crimes – which might have sent others into a bottle – plus his relationship with another cop, Diane Daniels, had kept him out of this bleak pit of doom. He had a renewed purpose in life and at least for a while was revelling in it.

Second, because of the COVID pandemic relentlessly sweeping the world, he had been forced to close The Tawny Owl, the pub and country house hotel he jointly owned with his late fiancée's stepdaughter Ginny in the village of Kendleton.

In the early stages of the pandemic, the business had managed to stagger through the first lockdowns, but the latest one meant that, much to his distress, he'd finally had to furlough staff and close the doors. Although the business was debt-free, the income he received from his temporary contract with the police and his pension meant he didn't have to plunder the reserves of Th'Owl, as the place was known locally.

Like so many businesses in the hospitality sector, Henry wasn't sure if Th'Owl would survive the virus, but he was going to do his damnedest to make sure it did, if only to keep Alison's memory alive. He knew full well that if she had still been alive, there was no way she would allow a nasty little virus to defeat her.

To that end, and just to keep the place ticking over, he and Ginny converted the front door of the pub into a stable door/serving hatch so they could still provide takeaway food and drink which was permissible under the rules – just – from seven a.m. to one p.m. each day. They weren't sure if it was a viable idea. Normally, Th'Owl opened for breakfasts anyway to cater for staying guests and did a good trade with the locals, but providing a takeaway service was just a punt to see how things went.

And showing the true colours of the local community which was rallying round for everyone, it went much better than expected; business at the stable door was so brisk that one of the chefs was able to work each day and earn a full wage.

That morning, as Henry emerged from the owner's accommodation on the ground floor, he was greeted by the aroma of freshly ground coffee on the hob and bacon and sausages being grilled.

It was seven fifteen.

He put his head around the kitchen door and gave James the chef a quick wave.

'How are we doing?'

'Busy, busy, busy,' the tall, red-haired lad replied. 'Usual for you, boss?'

Henry should have hesitated.

Since Operation Sparrow Hawk had begun, he had fallen into the easy trap of grabbing a sausage bap and a coffee on his way out every morning, instead of maybe having a bowl of granola – but he didn't. Although the good voice in him pleaded, *No, don't do this*, the devil one beat it ruthlessly into submission again.

'Absolutely, James.' Henry smiled. 'I'll grab a coffee if you can pass the food to me outside?'

James nodded.

Henry walked on, poured a coffee into a disposable cup and went to the door where Ginny was taking an order from two game-keepers who worked on a nearby estate, two regular customers.

She turned with the order on a pad and the card reader in her hand, almost crashing into Henry who had come up on her blind side.

'Morning, sweetie.' He kissed her proffered cheek.

'Mornin', Pops,' she said, making him feel a darn sight older than he was, but also sending a nice, warm glow through him. Since Alison had died in such tragic circumstances, Ginny had called Henry 'Dad' or 'Pops'. He had two 'real' daughters of his own who lived away, but he loved it that Ginny could look on him as a father figure, although he did his best not to give her too much wise, man-centric advice.

'Busy, I see,' he said for conversation's sake.

'Usual crowd so far.' She made to sidestep him but paused mid-move and frowned. 'Diane wasn't here last night?'

His mouth tightened and he shook his head; Ginny could tell it wasn't something he wished to expand on.

She gave him a worried smile, then completed her manoeuvre and headed for the kitchen with the order. Henry let himself through the stable door on to the front terrace and nodded at the gamekeepers – twin brothers, both dressed as though they'd just stepped out of a James Herriot novel – and they greeted him pleasantly. He chatted to them as he awaited his breakfast, and when it came, he made his way to the low front wall and sat on it. All the furniture from the terrace had been removed because of COVID regulations so that customers were less inclined to hang about and mingle and spread disease.

He took a drink of coffee, then a bite of sandwich and thought about Diane Daniels. Their relationship seemed to be cooling off slightly following her successful convalescence from serious gunshot wounds which had put her off work for several months, and now her return to work as a detective sergeant in FMIT. Their relationship – oh, how Henry despised that word – seemed to have gone off the boil, but Henry was trying not to be too upset. She was younger than him and he wouldn't blame her if she wanted to move on. What they'd had together had been good, and he would have no regrets if it didn't work out. She was spending more and more time at her flat in Lancaster, which was an easier commute than having to travel out to the far reaches of Kendleton, way out in the moors to the east of Lancaster.

He was sad but philosophical.

As he sipped and ate, his eyes roved over the scene in front of him, out across Kendleton's village green towards the stream that ran through the village, and then the rise of woodland behind that.

There was a chill to the day and not much was moving. The village was in lockdown and most residents had hunkered down just to get through it all.

He saw a grey van parked further down the road, facing towards the village. Henry didn't pay it much heed even as a white guy in his mid-thirties climbed out. He was dressed in a hoodie and dark cargo pants that seemed to be nothing but pockets, steel toecap safety boots on his feet. There was an empty tool belt around his waist.

His hoodie was pulled up over his head and over a camouflage-patterned baseball cap with the peak tugged down to his eyebrows and he was wearing a black face mask, so only his eyes were visible and they were in shadow.

He walked towards Henry and nodded. 'OK, mate?'

'Good, thanks.'

The guy had a folded map in his hands. 'This Kendleton?' he asked.

'Yep.'

'My satnav's goosed and I seem to have lost my way a bit,' he said through the fabric of the mask. Henry had to tilt his head slightly to hear, which was another of those things that were part of the 'new normal' of COVID: people seemingly mumbling. The guy twirled the map in his hands and squinted at it.

'What are you after?' Henry asked.

'Simpkin Lodge?' the van man said. 'I think.'

'Hmm, doesn't mean anything to me.' Henry gestured towards the gamekeepers at the stable door, just being served. 'Those guys might know.'

'No, I know – it's Simpson Hall, not Simpkin Lodge,' the guy corrected himself.

'Oh, yeah, I know where that is. You're on the right road.'

Simpson Hall was a huge, isolated mansion that had been converted into an exclusive spa hotel and retreat, set in a few acres about four miles on the other side of Kendleton on the outskirts of the next village, Thornwell. It was very pricey and a bit snobby. Henry had never ventured there or had any interest in that sort of place, although he happily had a stack of their fliers in among all the other tourist information leaflets in a rack in the foyer of Th'Owl.

Henry gave the man directions, then asked, 'Got a job on there?'

'I do.'

'I thought they were all closed up like everyone else in that sector?'

The guy shrugged. 'Dunno . . . got a plumbing issue to sort is all I know . . . leaky pipes or something.' He looked beyond Henry at The Tawny Owl. 'This your place, then?'

'It is.'

'And you're open?'

'Takeaway only.'

'In that case, I might indulge . . . be rude not to.'

'We'd welcome your custom.'

The man walked up and across the terrace to the stable door, passing the gamekeepers who were moving away with their purchases.

Henry looked at the van he had arrived in. It was too far away and parked at such an angle that it was not possible for him to work out the lettering on the side of it, but he could see a mobile phone number across one of the rear doors. He wasn't really interested, though, and what interest he did have was terminated when his own mobile phone rang and he answered it.

Before he could speak, a female voice said, 'Is that the Old Guy?'

'Morning, Debbie, so nice to hear your dulcet tones,' Henry said with a smirk. 'What's your ETA?'

'Well, unless I've taken a wrong turn, which is highly likely on these stupid roads, ten minutes at most.'

'I'm ready and waiting.'

'Well, be ready and waiting with a bacon sarnie and a coffee for me, please. I've had no brekkie and I'm famished.'

'Your wish is my comm—'

The line went dead before he could finish. He smiled and shook his head, no longer quite so exasperated by the abrupt manner of one of the most charismatic people he'd ever met.

Then, suddenly, his eyes caught a movement in the trees on the other side of the stream as a herd of red deer burst spectacularly through the tree line, a large group of females led by a huge, muscular stag, as though they were being pursued by a pack of hounds.

As he still had his phone in his hand, Henry quickly selected the camera mode and started to video the herd – which wasn't being chased by anything – as they slowed down and began to canter brazenly down the main road into the village. Henry followed their progress with his camera, becoming slightly irritated as they went out of sight behind the parked van for a few moments, then reappeared and, still led by the magnificent stag, disappeared into the village around the curve in the road.

'Quite a sight.'

Henry stopped recording and turned to the guy who'd got his food and drink and was now standing just behind Henry, face mask still on, baseball cap still pulled down, hoodie on, eyes in shadow.

'Regulars,' Henry said. 'Even more so since the pandemic . . . get lots of sheep, too. And goats.'

The man's eyes seemed to be weighing Henry up.

'Everything OK?' Henry asked.

The man hesitated. 'Yep, guess so.' He raised his food, coffee in one hand, breakfast sandwich in the other, and said, 'Thanks for these; they look good.'

'Any time.'

He walked past Henry and climbed into his van just as two more deer emerged from the trees and began to trot across the green, stragglers hurrying to catch up with the rest of the herd. Henry still had his phone on video record, so he focused in and followed the trail of these animals as they too disappeared into the village.

Bennett had been busy dealing with the legitimate side of his business when the call came and one of the phones in his pocket began to vibrate silently. He could tell which phone it was – the old-style Nokia, which would be destroyed after contact in order to maintain security and integrity.

He would have liked to answer it immediately, but at that moment he had two elderly ladies sitting across from him, socially distanced and wearing face masks, as was he, both crying their eyes out at the loss of a loved one.

Bennett sat and listened, allowing them their grief.

He was dressed in a black suit and tie, white shirt, highly polished black shoes – a supreme example of his profession.

'He was everything to us,' one of the women sobbed, almost gagging on her tears, finding it hard to breathe properly behind her face mask. She was eighty years old and her sister, a couple of years younger, sat alongside her. 'We thought he'd be with us forever, see us out.'

Bennett leaned forward and rested his forearms on the highly polished table between him and his clients.

As his phone ceased vibrating, he said, sounding genuine, 'I am so very sorry for your loss.' His voice was solemn and caring. 'I am truly grieving with you.' He then held the palm of his hand over his heart, knowing how effective the combination of his words and this gesture were. Empathy, sympathy and just a touch of firmness rolled into one. The customers fell for it every time.

The oldest sister pushed an A4-sized laminated photograph across to him. With the leather-gloved tip of his forefinger, he drew it to him and looked with sadness at the professionally taken image.

A family group with Leonard, the deceased, sitting between the two women in a posed picture. Leonard looked dignified yet slightly dim, Bennett thought. Maybe not the sharpest of blades but good, loyal and decent. He would have had a good life, although, Bennett thought, he probably gaslighted these two old biddies remorselessly.

'He was so good looking, too,' the younger sister sobbed, and at that point Bennett did have to stifle a giggle when the old lady's top set of false teeth dropped with a clatter onto her lower set and she had to thumb them back into place.

'Yes, yes,' Bennett agreed as the phone began to vibrate yet again. 'And so big.'

'Huge, yes,' she said.

The older sister said, 'If possible, we would like to have this photograph on the coffin when he is cremated. Would that be possible, Mr Bennett?'

'Of course it would. It would be my pleasure.'

There was then a moment of awkward hesitation. Both ladies looked at him expectantly.

He pretended to be at odds with himself, but then said, 'Before we move on, could I just trouble you with the mundane matter of payment? And once that is done, we can move on at your own pace.'

There was a wireless card reader on the side of the table which Bennett reached for. He entered a figure and held out the device.

The older woman rooted out her debit card from the deep recess of her handbag, pushed it unsteadily into the slot and entered her PIN with a bony finger, not even checking the amount. Bennett ran a receipt off, which he handed to her, folded, knowing he had overcharged her for the service but that the written invoice would actually reflect this inflated amount as if it was the amount originally agreed on. He knew there would be no quibbles and smirked slightly as he placed the card machine to one side: even the legitimate side of his business had some perks.

'Now then, ladies, I know this will be an emotional moment for you both . . .'

In response, their mouths began to wobble again.

He went on, 'But would you like to see Leonard?'

The two ladies gulped in unison.

'Have . . . have you fixed him?' the older sister asked tentatively. 'He was a mess.'

'I have. Trust me – he's as good as new,' Bennett reassured them and pushed himself slowly to his feet. He walked across to the interior wall in which a large window had been constructed, currently covered by a pair of deep-purple, crushed-velvet curtains. Bennett touched a button on the wall and sombre, quiet mood music began to pipe softly through the PA system and the drapes slowly opened.

The women had joined him.

As the curtains parted, they revealed a room beyond the glass, small, subtly lit, just bright enough to illuminate the body in the coffin located under the window.

Both ladies gasped and clamped their hands to their mouths.

Bennett watched them slyly and with smugness at his own undoubted skills.

Leonard had truly been a mess in death.

He had, literally, been hit by a bus. His head had been stove in, bashed flat almost beyond recognition as it went under the front offside wheel of the vehicle. His body, too, had been mangled and flattened.

This had been one of Bennett's most challenging reconstructions and he was damnably proud of it, knew he'd done an awesome job, well worth the extra hundred he'd overcharged the women.

Leonard, their beloved Irish wolfhound, one of the biggest, lankiest dogs going, had been restored to almost pristine, lifelike condition. Bennett's work was masterful, like constructing a complex Airfix model, piecing the shattered bones back together, removing, then replacing the skin and recreating Leonard.

'You have done a wonderful job, Mr Bennett,' the younger of the two complimented him.

'Thank you. It was tricky, I admit . . . but with love, care and devotion, I hope I have done you proud.'

And not only that, he thought, the extra-sized coffin had been specially constructed – although to be fair, it was made of thick cardboard and treated and painted to look like expensive mahogany, and its furniture, the handles and edgings, were cheap brass, but charged as gold plate.

He smiled sadly.

'You have done us, done Leonard, proud,' the older sister cooed. 'You are a genius and we will be forever in your debt.'

Bennett smiled ingratiatingly, taking the praise as he also wondered how much these women had in their joint bank account. Because little did they know that after the dust had settled from the cremation of Leonard, he would empty that bank account. The card reader he used also read the account number and PIN, and he himself had also memorized the three-digit security number on the back of the piece of plastic.

In his experience, elderly pet owners, usually widows, often had bank accounts stuffed with cash, ripe for pillaging.

'Now,' he said, 'shall we proceed with the ceremony?'

He led the ladies through to the small but perfectly formed chapel which could seat up to thirty people if necessary, which was handy if the deceased pet had been a popular animal, but only the two were present that day for Leonard, who, Bennett guessed, was probably a curmudgeonly old bastard of a hound.

Bennett wheeled the open coffin through from the viewing room, giving the ladies one last glimpse of their beloved pet.

He then led the service, delivering a heartfelt eulogy based on a chat he'd had with the sisters previously. He was glad to see more tears tumbling down their wrinkled faces. He did hurry the whole thing on a little and finally ushered them out into their waiting taxi, then went back into the chapel and hefted Leonard in his coffin from the gurney on to the conveyor belt that would take him through and deposit him in the incinerator, the fierce burners of which were already fired up.

His phone vibrated again. This time he answered it.

'You have reached Bennett's Pet Crematorium,' he said.

'Is that the Tradesman?' the voice at the other end said.

'As you know, it is.'

'So why haven't you been answering?'

'I was dealing with customers.'

'Me and my family are your customers.'

'I know that . . . so what can I do for you, Sofia?'

The pet cemetery and crematorium covered four acres of land, situated to the north of Preston, Lancashire, off junction 32 of the M6. It was nicely landscaped and the crematorium building itself was a single-storey red-brick complex with the incinerator at the back of the small chapel.

Further behind in a fenced compound, surrounded also by a high hedge, was Bennett's garage and workshop in which he kept his pet hearse and all the tools required to keep the cemetery grounds in tiptop shape, such as ride-on lawnmowers, a quad bike and other gardening and mechanical tools.

Attached to this prefabricated workshop was another large garage with a small flat above which could only be accessed via the first workshop.

Following his phone call and after collecting Leonard's ashes which would be pulverized and placed into the chosen urn, this second garage was Bennett's destination. Before he entered, he removed his smart suit and hung it in a suit protector and changed into a pair of overalls.

The second garage was a huge space, divided into two distinct halves, one of which was a traditional-style workshop with a vehicle ramp, and the other half, used as a paint shop, was partitioned off by a plastic screen. Standing inside that section was a Ford Transit van he had stolen several nights previously from outside a house in Longridge, a white one bearing the logo of a plumbing company.

Bennett's mouth twitched as he examined the vehicle, a little frustrated he didn't have as much time as he would have liked to prepare it.

But needs must.

When the boss called, he had to jump as high as she demanded.

The respray he'd done in a light grey had taken him about four hours the evening before and, if he was honest, it probably needed another coat and touch up. He walked slowly around the vehicle, examining it critically, and although he wasn't completely satisfied by his workmanship, he realized it would have to suffice. Only a very close examination would reveal the respray, and he had no intention of getting himself in a position where anyone, such as a cop, would feel the need to look at the van.

He got to work replacing the number plates, using a pair which actually matched a Transit van registered in Blackpool, so, again, if a cop checked it on the Police National Computer, it would, on the surface, appear to be legitimate.

After this he applied pre-prepared vinyl decals for each side of the van which declared the vehicle belonged to a multi-skilled tradesman, who was a plumber, electrician and joiner, and gave the mobile number for this person, plus a decal for one of the rear doors which also gave the mobile number, which was false.

What wasn't fake, though, was that as well as being the owner and director of a pet crematorium, Bennett – not his real name –

was actually qualified in all these trades and had genuine certificates to prove it, again not in his real name.

He was also a handyman on retainer for the Bashkim crime family and was now, following the phone call, prepping to do a little job for them which, knowing the Bashkims, would probably lead to more lucrative work. They were good paymasters and he was a good employee.

The van was ready to go by ten that evening, and after eating a lone, microwaved supper and watching some TV, he bedded down in the flat over the workshop and slept as soundly as he had ever done.

He was on the road just after six a.m., heading north on the M6 from junction 32. It was only then that he mentally kicked himself when he discovered that the satnav in the stolen van wasn't working properly. That meant, unless he turned back to get his own plug-in one – which would be a real faff now he was on the motorway – he would have to rely on memory and the scruffy map he'd found folded up in the glove compartment. His own phone did not have a satnav app on it for two reasons. First, it was an old-style Nokia which could only be used for making and receiving calls and texts, and second, he knew if he did have a phone with a built-in satnav and things went wrong, it could provide useful evidence to the authorities as to where he had been.

So the map it was, but even with its assistance, once he left the motorway and found himself driving along the tight, winding roads in the countryside to the east of Lancaster, he was pretty much lost, so it was with some relief that he came across the pub called The Tawny Owl in the village of Kendleton, open and selling takeaway food and drink. He didn't really want to stop and ask for directions as any unplanned contact was a risk, but as always with most un-familiar journeys, he knew the last few miles were the most complex.

And he was hungry – but after his brief chat with the guy who'd been sitting on the front wall of the pub and who turned out to be the owner of the place, Bennett felt slightly uncomfortable as he waited for his food order and saw the guy take out his phone and begin to film the herd of deer strolling into the village. Bennett didn't like it because it meant that his van was caught in the sweep of the footage, and when he set off, he couldn't stop himself from looking in the door mirror at the guy who was filming more fucking deer walking past his van.

Bennett spent a great deal of his life avoiding technology that recorded his image and his whereabouts, so it particularly galled him that, by bad luck, a herd of deer sauntered past, some old guy decided to video them and in so doing included the van.

It made him feel very vulnerable and wasn't the best start to this job. It was another thing he'd have to sort out. But not now. There was somewhere he needed to be.

Henry watched the van disappear around the bend in the wake of the deer, but his attention was diverted by the sound of a car approaching fast down the road into the village, being screwed through the gears.

His lips pursed as the car came into view; although he didn't recognize it, he knew exactly who was driving.

He slotted his phone into his jacket pocket, stood up and brushed himself down as the vehicle, a Vauxhall Astra, screeched through the gates of the cark park, swerved dramatically and skidded to a halt in front of him. Then, just as in every James Bond film Henry had ever seen, the passenger door was flung open and the Bond girl at the wheel said, 'Get in!'

Except he was no James Bond and DS Debbie Blackstone was definitely no Bond girl, apart from the fact she was as tough as nails and could deliver any deserving male a vicious kick in the groin area courtesy of her kung fu training. And, although she would deny this, she was strikingly attractive.

Henry stood back and surveyed the car.

He'd expected her to arrive in her old, restored Mini Cooper, but instead . . . 'What the heck is this?' he demanded.

'Pool car . . . we're on a journey, let 'em pay, I say,' she said, referring to the constabulary. 'Now gerr-in!'

'You wanted a sandwich,' he reminded her.

'Oh, yeah – go get me one . . . and a coffee.'

Henry complied and returned five minutes later. Even before he'd closed the car door, Blackstone had put her foot down and slammed him back against the seat, making it a challenge to keep a grip on the food and drink and also pull on his seatbelt.

'Let's go and upset someone we've never met before,' she said gleefully. 'You up for it?'

'Sure am,' he said.

SIX

'Uh, yeah – plumbing issue, mate.' Bennett lowered the driver's door window so he could speak to the guy at the main gate of Simpson Hall which, in the end, he had found relatively easily on the fringe of the next village along from Kendleton, a place not much more than a hamlet called Thornwell.

He was still cursing himself for having stopped at the pub in Kendleton, and although he was pretty sure there was no damage done, you could never tell these things. *That guy!* He grimaced, visualizing the man outside the pub.

The main gates to the hall were closed and he had driven the nose of the van right up to them and honked the horn.

Through the intricate mesh of the wrought ironwork, he could see the hall in the distance at the end of a sweeping, English Rose gravel driveway.

A man appeared at the front door of the hall and sauntered unhurriedly down the drive. He was late twenties, squat, muscular, hair shaved to the skull, but with a goatee beard that Bennett could visualize removing with a knife like taking a scalp.

'What?' Goatee asked. He was wearing tight jeans and a T-shirt over a powerfully built body that reeked of steroids, with muscles that looked as though they could be popped by a pin.

When Bennett responded, the bluff began.

'Plumbing issue?' Goatee said.

'Lockdown, I'd guess. Things not being used, seizing up,' Bennett conjectured. 'Apparently, the boiler's clogged up and I've been asked to service the whole system, bleeding radiators and all that' – he shrugged – 'just to make sure it's all tickety-boo.'

'Who asked yuh?'

Bennett made a show of reaching across the dash to pick up a clipboard on which was pinned a piece of paper, his worksheet. 'Gorst, Albert Gorst . . . he owns the place, I'm told? A guy called Max Janus phoned on his behalf.' He put the clipboard down and smiled at Goatee.

'Haven't heard anything about this.'

Bennett shrugged. 'And? Not my problem, mate. I've been called out – which is a hundred quid without me even doing a thing – and here I am. Call Mr Janus if you want.'

This, Bennett knew, was the crunch moment, the make or break when the bluff would either be called or be successful. Goatee mulled things over quickly and came to a conclusion.

'Yeah, well, whatever. But we're gonna have to search the van?'

'Really? Like for guns or something? You got royalty coming?'

'You could say that. I'll open the gates, you drive in and stop, OK?'

Bennett nodded. 'Whatev.'

The guy looked up to a CCTV camera on the gatepost and made a swirling gesture with his finger, obviously to someone inside the hall watching, and the gates began to creep open. Bennett had already seen the camera and ensured he kept his face well back inside his van and out of reach of the lens. He drove through, stopped – checked the camera hadn't rotated to follow him: it hadn't – got out and opened the sliding side door to allow Goatee access. He peered in and saw a vehicle crammed with toolboxes and drawers and was, from the expression on his face, immediately struck by the enormity of actually having to search, or at least rummage, through them. Bennett saw the look but didn't betray any satisfaction from it, even though he felt it.

Goatee gave a long, 'Hmm . . .'

'Tools of the trade, every eventuality catered for,' Bennett said, which was true, particularly in view of the fact that even more tools of his trade were secreted in a hidden compartment under the floor pan of the van.

'How long are you gonna be?' Goatee asked him.

Another shrug. 'Couple of hours, I expect.'

'OK. Drive around the back and go in from there . . . there's a boiler room or something under the kitchen.' He waved him away.

'Good place to start,' Bennett agreed, got back into the van and set off.

Since managing to flee from pursuing hounds and angry armed men on scrambler bikes, Steve Flynn and Molly Cartwright sailed relentlessly across the Mediterranean, finally reaching Ibiza, where they moored in the marina at Santa Eulalia. Drained physically and mentally, both fell into a long, deep sleep.

Over the course of the journey, Flynn had tried unsuccessfully to re-contact Karl Donaldson, but the American seemed to have gone off-grid, much to Flynn's abject frustration and growing anger, especially after he felt he'd been used, then discarded.

After a long night's sleep, Flynn and Molly awoke to a beautiful day on the island and sauntered into town for breakfast at a back-street café before returning to the boat to give it a long, deep clean after the recent voyages.

Flynn was at a loss as he worked hard, hosing and scrubbing, because the revelation, confirmed by his own fleeting sighting, that old man Bashkim was indeed still alive rocked him to his core. The man whose family had brought and wrought so much havoc and bloodshed to Flynn's life by not only murdering Maria Santiago but also having killed Flynn's beloved crew member Jose, plus his friend Adam Castle and Adam's sister Karen.

The Bashkims were simply a whirlwind of violence, and Flynn – no stranger to violence himself – hadn't been sure he could get his own life back on track, but the thought that Viktor had been dead, had paid for his crimes, went some way towards it; plus his relationship with Molly, which though it had started badly when she had Tasered him in a chemist's shop, had since blossomed. Although he had dithered with saying so, he pretty much knew he was in love with her.

But now . . . Viktor was alive, or so it seemed.

Old, but still kicking, still king of a vast crime syndicate, probably still dishing out death and retribution. And Flynn, once more, wanted him dead. He needed to have that horrific wound, which had just been reopened, sutured again.

He knew he needed Donaldson's help on this, although he also realized that because of the way things had panned out in Cyprus, Viktor himself would now know that Flynn had discovered he was still breathing and any element of surprise would have vanished.

Viktor would be on his guard. And it wouldn't surprise Flynn to learn that the old man might even contract someone to come for him again.

'Steve!'

Flynn shook himself out of this muddled contemplation in which he was now imagining slicing Viktor's scrawny neck in half, when he was in fact hosing down *Faye*'s foredeck. He came back to reality with a jolt and looked through the window at Molly who was in the cockpit.

'You're going to wash the deck away,' she admonished him.

He turned off the hose. 'Sorry.'

The boat was definitely pristine again and he began to roll up the hose, crouching as he edged along the boat towards the rear deck where the hose was secured on the jetty.

It was when he looked up that he noticed a man standing there with his arms folded across his broad chest. A big guy, good looking; Flynn had known him for more than ten years now and, yes, he may have aged – Flynn wasn't sure, but he guessed he was into his fifties now – but with age had come a ruggedness and, if anything, Flynn had to reluctantly admit, Karl Donaldson was even more fucking handsome than ever.

Flynn stood slowly upright, aware that Molly was now standing behind him.

'*Now* you show up,' Flynn said.

'Let's go eat,' Donaldson said.

'You sure as hell left a trail of destruction behind you,' Donaldson said appreciatively. 'Dead guy on the road for one thing.'

Flynn's mouth twitched at the news. They had been hunting him, so you reap what you sow, he thought, but causing a death still left a taste like petrol at the back of his mouth.

'Do the cops want to talk to me?'

Donaldson shook his head. 'I've been out there, spoken to people and calmed the waters in respect of law enforcement. At the moment it's just a couple of tragic biking accidents.'

'What? Guys on motorbikes, armed with guns, trying to pursue an innocent man and kill him? Those sorts of tragic accidents?'

Donaldson grinned at Flynn's tirade. 'As no other witnesses have come forward, they'll just remain tragic accidents, particularly as the car which the biker collided with was unregistered . . . Anyway, the cops in Cyprus have a more pressing matter to deal with.'

'Such as?'

The three of them were seated on the front terrace of a restaurant overlooking the marina, one very glad of any business. They were eating paella.

'Another body was found close to the villa,' Donaldson said.

Flynn asked, 'Whose body?'

Donaldson sighed. 'My informant. One of the guards. He must have got careless.'

'Shit.' Flynn dropped his fork with a clang and sat back.

'And the villa's now deserted,' Donaldson added. 'I took a chance, went for a look-see,' he said, recalling his visit – this time without any sort of permission from his boss who really was at the end of her tether. He'd flown back to Cyprus from London following the phone call he'd received from Mikail Sokolov, not only because of what Mikail had told him about Viktor being driven away from the villa to the airport, but also because a short while later a silent call was made from Sokolov's encrypted phone which ended abruptly; the 'blip' had then completely disappeared from Donaldson's computer screen, which meant that because the phone was programmed to keep pulsing even if it was turned off or the battery had gone flat, it had probably been destroyed. Donaldson had instantly eliminated any contact with the phone in case it had fallen into the wrong hands. Not that anyone would have been able to backtrack the number in the phone or get anything meaningful from the SIM card, but he believed in never taking chances.

It was then a worrying waiting game.

Sokolov had been briefed that if anything went wrong, he should try to re-contact Donaldson by buying a burner phone and then calling another number which the American had left in an envelope behind a bar at a named restaurant in Coral Bay.

So he had waited.

The call never came.

It could have simply been that Sokolov had got cold feet, decided he'd had enough and disposed of the phone – and was now on his way back to Russia where he could go to ground in the underworld and be virtually untouchable.

Or things had gone seriously wrong.

Finally Donaldson knew he had to find out.

He booked himself on the next available flight to Paphos, hired a car, checked into a hotel in Coral Bay, then went for a stroll through the banana plantation with his shorts on and his rucksack on his back.

He found the villa was completely deserted, and as he strolled around the outer walls, he almost tripped up on a shallow grave covered by a low mound of rocks under which, after not too much scrabbling, he found Sokolov's body.

Laid across the dead man's chest was the phone Donaldson had given him, split into three parts, back, front, battery, with the SIM card snapped in two next to it.

Donaldson seized those items, re-covered the body and returned to his hotel.

From there he made contact with the local police and learned they were dealing with what appeared to be a fatal hit-and-run accident.

Donaldson then made an anonymous phone call to the cops on the emergency line and told them about the body at the villa, hanging up as the call taker demanded his details.

Flynn took a swig of lager. 'So we've no idea where Viktor is?'

'He boarded a private plane at Paphos with his daughter, Sofia. The plane disappeared over Russian airspace. I've been unable to chase down a flight plan, find out where it landed . . . nothing.'

'Marvellous.' Flynn rolled his eyes at Molly, but when he looked back at Donaldson, he was surprised to see him grinning. 'What's so funny?'

'Eat up,' he said mysteriously and scooped some paella from the pan on to his own plate. 'Then follow me.'

They strolled like an amiable trio, face masks on, along the quayside of the marina, which would normally have been bustling with tourists but because of COVID was eerily quiet.

'Is this ever going to stop?' Molly asked of the pandemic.

Donaldson said he doubted it. 'It likes people too much.'

On the corner where the Mirage restaurant was located at the southern end of the marina, Donaldson beckoned them to turn sharp left down the last section of the marina, at the far end of which was a fuel station for the boats near the offices of the harbour master.

In the car park, four beautiful supercars were parked up behind a barrier, angled in a line like the starting grid of the old Le Mans twenty-four-hour race. There was a McLaren, an Aston Martin, a Ferrari and a Lamborghini SUV, all stunning and expensive. Flynn, though no car aficionado, was suitably impressed.

'Nice,' he admitted. 'Is this why you've brought us here?'

'Kinda,' Donaldson said. He jerked his head and walked on, and they followed.

Flynn was more interested in the boats moored along here as this end of the marina tended to have the biggest and most expensive ones, and he would have liked to have explored some of them, but Donaldson, keeping it mysterious, beckoned them to look across the bay, pointed and said, 'There!'

Flynn's eyes followed the finger.

Several yachts were anchored in the sheltered waters of the bay, mostly of a similar size to those in the marina, with one notable exception: a very large, luxurious superyacht, deep blue in colour, large enough for a swimming pool at the stern and a helicopter landing pad atop, which at the moment was unoccupied.

Flynn frowned; Donaldson grinned. Flynn said, 'Explain.'

'Last time you saw that beast was in Malta four years ago; then it was a different colour, a kind of silvery grey. It's been repainted and refurbished since . . .'

As he spoke, Flynn's heartbeat started to quicken. He glanced at Molly whose eyes were sparkling. She, too, had seen the boat three years before.

'It didn't have a helicopter pad, or a pool . . . both fitted and installed since.'

'*Halcyon*,' Molly gasped.

'Viktor Bashkim's boat,' Flynn added.

'*Was* Viktor's boat,' Donaldson corrected him. 'As you know, it now belongs to a particularly evil Russian mafia boss.'

'Shit, yeah – who took it in exchange for providing Viktor with a security detail,' Flynn said excitedly. 'So is the old bastard on board?'

Donaldson shook his head. 'I don't know where he is.'

Flynn frowned with disappointment and exhaled an irritated sigh.

In the distance, they heard the sound of an approaching helicopter and all three turned to watch the approach from across the sea, squinting and shading their eyes, none of them expecting it to actually land on the boat.

Donaldson had taken a monocular out of his jacket pocket, put it to one eye and watched the helicopter manoeuvre and come to rest softly on the landing pad on *Halcyon*.

A door opened and a man hopped down.

Donaldson handed the monocular to Flynn. 'I might not know where Viktor is, but I know a man who does.'

Flynn focused the lens to suit his eye and watched the overweight figure of Nico Bashkim walk across the landing pad, then step down on to the rear deck and disappear into the main stateroom.

At first Goatee, the guy who had admitted Bennett into Simpson Hall, was a pain in the neck, who seemed to take his duties seriously and was determined not to let Bennett out of his sight.

Fortunately, Bennett really was a plumber, and after he had been taken down to the basement and shown where the boiler was – it was huge, old and very much on its last legs – he fired it up a few times, tutted a little and finally declared he needed to strip it right down to its brass pipes and give it a good service.

'Thing's from the ark,' Bennett commented. 'Be lucky if I've got any spares in the van for it, although I think I might.'

By this time, Goatee was bored and watched with increasing itchiness to do something else as Bennett removed the front panel to open up the 'gubbins', as he called it, of the boiler and started to unscrew various items.

Goatee watched with unfocused eyes.

'Yep, needs a proper service . . . gunked up, hasn't been touched in years.' He looked at the exposed parts with his hands on his hips as though he didn't quite know where to start. 'Twenty years would be my guess,' he ruminated.

'How long did you say this would take?'

'I said two hours, but looking at it now, three. And when I've done the service, I'll need to flush the system and bleed every radiator, too.'

Goatee came to an executive decision. 'Tell you what – I'll just leave you to get on with it, mate.'

'Gotcha.' Bennett didn't even look at him.

'I'll be in reception by the front door, feet up.'

'OK.'

Goatee left, leaving Bennett to get on with the servicing and everything else that needed doing.

He gave it half an hour of fiddling about unnecessarily with the boiler which, though old, was in perfect working order, before he started to make his way through the hall on the pretext of bleeding all the radiators but actually doing the real job he had come to do.

When he finished, he decided he would pay a short visit to the guy he'd met outside the pub earlier.

'How did you find out *Halcyon* was here, in Ibiza, and that Nico is on board?' Flynn asked Donaldson.

'Took a lot of phone calls, Internet surfing, stuff like that,' Donaldson answered. 'Plus,' he continued, 'I know people.' He tapped his nose. 'Plus, I'm FBI and that's what I do.'

He didn't elaborate further. For a moment.

'Plus,' he then added, 'I tracked *Halcyon* on Superyacht Radar,' he chuckled. 'Just on the off-chance,' he said, referring to the website that was similar to Flight Radar but instead of tracking aircraft was exclusively for big, privately owned boats. 'She was berthed in Limassol and I tracked her here . . . I was once a real field agent,' he said wistfully. 'And,' he shrugged, 'it wasn't hard.'

'Well, good job,' Flynn congratulated him, 'but it still leaves us with a problem . . . how to get hold of Nico and grill the fucker.'

'Steve!' Molly admonished him over his turn of phrase.

'Well,' he said like a child, then, 'Sorry. I do try.'

'It'll probably be a waiting game,' Donaldson said.

'And if the boat decides to leave with him on it, it'll be a chase-me game, too,' Molly said.

'According to the travel plans on the website, it's here for three days, including today,' Donaldson said. 'I also checked with the harbour master . . . all boats still have to register with him, even if they're in the bay. Nico'll come off at some stage, if only to razz around in one of those' – he jerked his thumb at the four supercars lined up – 'or go eat somewhere.'

'One of those cars?' Molly asked.

'They've been rented from a place in Ibiza Town for the use of the boat,' Donaldson told her.

'How do you know that?'

'Spoke to the owner of the Mirage,' he said, referring to the restaurant on the quayside. 'He's pretty knowledgeable about comings and goings.'

'So what's the plan?' Flynn asked. 'Sit and drink at the Mirage until he comes ashore?'

'Not such a bad plan. The cars mean he will be coming ashore, I guess. If he feels safe to do so after the incident in Cyprus. And Nico is a hedonist, don't forget. He likes the pleasures of the flesh and the belly. Admittedly, he might get both aboard, but I honestly think he'll come ashore, eat out, race the cars, show off to which-ever woman's on his arm. He won't be able to resist.'

They were having this conversation on the rear deck of Flynn's boat, kicking stuff around.

The day was getting towards evening and there was a slight chill in the air.

'It might just fall into our lap,' Donaldson said hopefully. 'Things like this often do.'

'Not in my experience,' Flynn said grumpily.

Henry Christie and Debbie Blackstone had done their homework.

Before setting off that morning, they had interviewed four people, all now middle-aged men, whose names had cropped up – with many others, of course – during the investigation into historic child abuse and murder that was Operation Sparrow Hawk. These men's names had turned up as having been missing persons in their teenage years, all four of whom had gravitated to Blackpool, the epicentre of the scandal.

Interviewing them had been tough for the men and for the two officers.

The four men had become adults in four different walks of life, and although they didn't know each other, their stories ran parallel and they all had the same sad, lost look about them either on or just below the surface: the look of a lost childhood.

And although all four had buried the past deep, when Henry and Blackstone began digging the ground, it was easy to unearth, easy to expose.

Their stories were brutal, painful and emotional.

And, with the men's permission, and the reassurance of the detectives, Henry and Blackstone went to round up the offenders

who were many and included a man in his early sixties, who, at
the time the four witnesses had been in Blackpool, would have been
in his mid-twenties. His previous existence had been as a worker in
children's homes on the Fylde, which is where he came into
contact with the missing youngsters, then as a councillor, spending
time as a planning officer, all of which put him in touch with
the two main offenders whose arrests had kickstarted Sparrow
Hawk. The allegations uncovered by Henry and Blackstone were
that he was an active conduit between those offenders and the
kids, and that he too was an abuser who used his position of trust
to carry out sexual assaults and may even have been involved in the
actual disappearance of children.

Either way, he had a lot of unpleasant questions to answer and
the fact he was now a successful businessman did not in any way
deter them from knocking on his office door, even though it was
the office of a funeral director.

'So run it past me again, Old Guy,' Blackstone had said to
Henry as she drove him in the grim pool car.

Henry sifted through the papers from the file on his knees.

'Blackpool born . . . and educated . . . looks like he worked in
the kitchens in a few of the children's homes in the region . . . uh
. . . went into the undertaking trade, first as an apprentice ghoul . . .
then took over a small undertaker's on the death of the owner
. . . then built up a string of them across the north and also moved
into care homes for the elderly, got over a dozen of them . . .'

'Jeepers,' Blackstone said, 'the perfect business model!'

'Isn't it just! That said, he seems to be a pillar of the community
at this moment in time, still involved in council work, and was even
Mayor of Blackpool last year.'

'None of which interests us.'

'No, you're right . . . it's what he was up to thirty-odd years ago
that bothers us, and whether it's still happening.'

'Best go ask him, then,' Blackstone said grimly.

She drove away from Kendleton, across and through Lancaster
and then south on the A563 towards Glasson Dock, but turned off
on to a driveway leading to a newly built chapel of rest where they
knew the man they wished to interview would be that morning, a
fact established by a couple of cheeky phone calls the previous day.

She drew in behind a line of four hearses and the two of them

went into the office. She flashed her warrant card to the young
woman behind the counter and Henry flashed his ID as he no
longer possessed a warrant card, being a civilian. Blackstone asked
to see the owner.

'Is he expecting you?' the woman inquired.

'No . . . surprise visit,' Blackstone said.

'One second.' The woman stood up and went through the door
of an office behind her desk and closed it softly. Henry and
Blackstone heard muted voices.

A few moments later, the woman came back out followed by a
man dressed in a sombre black suit.

'Officers? What can I do for you?' he asked pleasantly enough.

'Are you Albert Gorst?' Blackstone asked.

He confirmed it and then his demeanour changed somewhat when
she explained why two detectives had come to see him and that he
had no choice but to accompany them to Blackpool police station
for questioning. He was arrested when their patience ran out.

After a long day of questioning the man, it was eleven p.m. by
the time Blackstone dropped Henry back at The Tawny Owl, having
arranged to meet at Blackpool nick early the next morning for a
further round of interviews with Gorst, who so far had admitted
nothing and was proving to be much more difficult to nail down
than they had anticipated. But he wasn't going anywhere. On the
way back to drop Henry off, they had discussed the next day's
interview strategy in detail. They were sure they had a serious
offender in their grasp but knew that everything depended on a
confession, which they were determined to get.

Henry watched Debbie drive away, revving the engine of the
pool car for all it was worth in typical Blackstone fashion – OTT
and outrageous. Henry wondered if the car would survive its
encounter with her as pool cars, almost by definition, were clapped-
out standbys.

He liked Blackstone a lot, and had he still been a detective
superintendent, he would have fought tooth and nail to get her
on to his squad.

The noise of the car engine faded into the distance. Henry turned
to the door of Th'Owl, stretching and rolling his aching shoulders,
looking forward to a Jack Daniel's nightcap. He never got to the
door. He was struck from behind: one hard, well-aimed blow to

the crown of his head. He slumped, stunned, on to both knees as though he was praying at the altar, and then his world went black as he pitched face down.

SEVEN

Henry swirled back to consciousness several times, drifting back and forth in a sickening stupor until he finally came to properly to find his right eyelid being thumbed open and a bright torch beam being shone into his pupil, which actually hurt.

Beyond the torch was a man wearing a surgical mask and cap.

'Ah, you're back with us,' said the man, who was also wearing full protective equipment from his neck down to his shins.

'Who's "us"?' Henry asked, trying to sit up and realizing the answer to his question was that he was on a trolley in a curtained cubicle in the Accident and Emergency department at Royal Lancaster Infirmary and the guy peering into his skull via his eyes was, he hoped, a doctor. 'Don't answer that,' Henry said, pushing himself upright, then getting a swathe of agony like an electrical current zapping through his brain. 'Woaw!' he said and slowly eased himself back down into a prone position, rested his head on the pillow and closed his eyes in order to encourage the pain to subside, which it began to do. 'How did I get here? I don't remember,' he said.

'I brought you.'

His eyes shot open again, this time to reveal Diane Daniels standing worriedly over him, the doctor having taken a sidestep.

'Hey,' she said softly.

'Diane,' he said, his voice croaking, 'I thought . . .'

'Don't think. It's not your strong point.'

'But?'

She leaned over and placed the tip of her forefinger on his lips, then bent over even closer and kissed him gently on the cheek. It was a nice feeling.

'I found you out cold at the front of the pub. Me and Ginny manhandled you, very gently obviously, into the back seat of my car and we drove here. Quicker than calling an ambulance. She drove. I had your head on my lap. We thought you'd had a heart attack at first.'

'I got whacked from behind. Didn't see or hear a thing.'

'We know . . . the blood from the cut on the back of your head was a clue . . . and it's all over my trousers.'

'Sorry.'

'Just glad you're OK . . . but you need an X-ray.' She turned to speak to the doctor as the cubicle curtain was drawn back and Ginny stepped in, showing the relief on her face.

Despite the hospital being at breaking point with COVID admissions and the A & E department being like an ants' nest of furious, unrelenting activity, Henry was wheeled speedily through all this on a wheelchair to the X-ray department where he was dealt with quickly and returned to A & E to receive the verdict, which also came quickly.

No sign of a fracture. He was just going to have a sore, swollen head for about a week. A nurse cleaned him up and closed the cut with butterfly stitches.

As this happened, his brain was getting clearer by the minute.

He recalled being dropped off by Blackstone, watching her race away, then turning to walk to the front door and then, wham! – nothing. Whoever hit him had presumably been lying in wait.

He was still wearing the clothes he'd been attacked in, with blood all over his jacket shoulders and the collar of his shirt, so as the nurse who had treated him withdrew, he sat up, dangling his legs off the bed, and patted down his pockets.

Diane came into the cubicle as he was doing this.

'Hi, you feeling OK?'

He stopped his search and looked at her quizzically. 'So you found me? Which means you were either at or coming back to Th'Owl.'

'Coming back,' she said simply. 'Look, can we talk about this later? Let's get you home first, eh?'

'Yeah, OK.' Henry slid his hand into his jacket pocket, pulled out his wallet and examined the contents, which appeared to be intact. He pursed his lips. 'Doesn't look like a robbery,' he said, putting the wallet away and patting his pockets again. 'No phone, though. Must've slipped out.'

'Unless that's what they were after,' Diane suggested.

Henry screwed up his face. 'I know what you're saying, but unlikely, don't you think?'

'A warning, then? Something to do with Sparrow Hawk?'

'We've definitely upset many, many people.'

'Talking of which, I almost crashed into Debbie on the road as I drove towards Kendleton. We stopped and backed up for a quick hello.'

'Oh, nice . . . so it can't have been too long between me being assaulted and you finding me,' Henry calculated.

'Minutes at most.'

'Did you pass anyone else on the road?' he asked, knowing that the minor roads from the A583 at Caton to the village were narrow, mostly unlit and also usually deserted at that time of day, around eleven p.m.

Diane frowned, obviously retracing the journey in her mind.

'Yep – one car, possibly a van . . . I think I pulled into the side slightly and he just barrelled past me, main beam, blinding me . . . but I didn't really think about it – just one of those things on those roads. You think the offender might have driven away?'

'Unless it was a local upset because Th'Owl's not open.'

'Although it's always possible if they were in a vehicle, they could have gone one of three ways.'

'True.'

The curtain swung open again and Ginny came back in with the doctor.

'Can I go now?' Henry asked.

The doctor nodded, gave Henry an information leaflet about head injuries and said, 'I recommend you have a couple of days' rest from work, Mr Christie . . . I believe you're a police officer?'

'Civilian investigator,' Henry corrected him. 'Much more important.'

'Same thing, I suppose. Look, you've had a blow to the head; it isn't fractured, but you should take it easy for a while, and if you start feeling groggy or you're sick, get back here as soon as, OK? And use paracetamol for the pain. I presume you've reported this to the real police?'

Henry glanced at Diane. 'I'll tell Jake Niven in the morning.' He looked back at the doctor. 'He's the local bobby.'

The doctor nodded and, with a sweeping gesture of the hand, stood aside and said, 'Goodbye . . . we are somewhat busy.'

The three drove back to Kendleton in Diane's car. Henry spread out in the back seat and closed his eyes while he wondered how long it would take for him to recover from this particular bang. One thing he noticed as he got older was that everything body-wise took longer to repair.

When they drew up at The Tawny Owl, he was groggy but hauled himself out unsteadily, then linked arms with Diane as they went up the steps to the terrace and the place where he had been poleaxed. A very quick search using Diane's mini Maglite torch revealed no sign of his mobile phone, but it was still very dark and it might have skidded away under the shrubbery.

Once inside, Henry checked online and linked to the tracker site for the phone, but there was no signal from it. Its last location was at the front of the pub at exactly the time he was assaulted.

'It could still be there,' Henry said. 'I'll have another look at dawn.'

'Why so early?' Diane asked.

'Before I go to work. Got an early meet with Debbie and we still have a prisoner in the traps to deal with at Blackpool.'

'Oh no,' Ginny said. 'At the very least you're having one day off sick,' she told him forcefully.

Suddenly Henry was overwhelmingly exhausted and didn't have the energy to put up an argument.

Diane led him to bed and falling asleep with her alongside was just about the best medicine in the world.

Flynn was up early, jogging along the marina, then the promenade at Santa Eulalia.

As the bay came into view – and even though the four supercars were still parked up on the quayside, ready for the off – he had a sinking feeling when he saw that *Halcyon* was no longer anchored up in the middle of the water, but breathed a sigh of relief when he glanced sharp left along the jetty and saw that the vessel had been brought in overnight and moored in the marina.

As he turned to sprint up the slope by the Mirage to cut up on to the promenade, Flynn stopped suddenly, spun around just to get a view along the quay to the boat and noticed an SUV parked up next to *Halcyon*. Two tough-looking guys were in the front seats, probably guarding the boat and discouraging anyone from venturing too close, even though it was a public area and people had the right to stroll up most of the length of the quay, though not as far as the fuel station at the end.

That said, the two guys in the vehicle were sprawled out, heads tilted back with the peaks of their baseball caps pulled down over their eyes, possibly both asleep.

Fairly useless guards: the type he liked to see.

He turned and continued the run as far as the river mouth, then came back at an easy trot, keeping his eyes on *Halcyon* as he got closer, seeing some early morning activity on board, which looked like staff milling around, cleaning decks – the general life on board a boat of that size. He came to the end of the promenade where it turned down on to the marina and slowed to a stop, bending over, placing his hands on his knees as though he was getting his breath from the exertion of the exercise, even though a run of this length wasn't much of a test for Flynn.

It was then he heard the engine fire up on one of the supercars on the quayside. He guessed it was the Ferrari because of the primal scream of it. He hadn't seen anyone get in, but he immediately wondered if this was Nico out for a blast.

Flynn moved a few steps forward but remained half-hidden behind a lamppost while lifting one foot on to the wall and doing a warm-down stretch of the muscles, keeping an eye on the cars.

It was indeed the Ferrari.

The car moved a few feet forwards, then stalled with a kangaroo jump. It was restarted with a wild howl and edged out of the parking space with a lot of revving of the dozen cylinders.

Flynn changed his leg.

He was curious but didn't want to show himself. Although he had never been face-to-face with Nico – if that was who was in the car – he knew what he looked like and guessed that Nico might be able to ID him, too. He had to remain cautious.

The car nosed out of the car park on to the quayside in order to make its way around to the exit barrier where it could leave the environs of the port.

As the car came directly towards Flynn for just a few metres, Flynn clearly saw Nico Bashkim in the driving seat. No one else was in with him.

Flynn jerked back behind the lamppost, but seriously considered dashing across to the exit barrier, meeting Nico there, dragging him bodily out of the Ferrari and dealing with him, but even he realized this would not be the most subtle course of action.

But at least this close-up sighting confirmed what he knew, and now he and Donaldson could work through some possible options. In his heart of hearts, though, Flynn knew the bottom line was they would somehow have to organize a confrontation that Nico would have no choice but to participate in.

Henry woke with a grinding headache, disentangled himself from Diane and sat on the edge of the bed, waiting for the pain to subside. It didn't.

Accepting this, he stood up and walked unsteadily to the en suite where he looked at himself in the mirror over the wash basin, holding himself steady with both hands as he surveyed his reflection: deep, black bags under his eyes, a red patch on his forehead where, he assumed, he'd fallen on being bashed, and the swollen, shaved area at the back of his head – which he didn't recall being shaved – where the butterfly stitches had been put across the cut. All that, plus general ageing, a neck that looked as scrawny as a tortoise's and sagging man boobs did not make for a pretty picture.

He almost lost it and was about to feel sorry for himself, something that would have been an easy journey, but instead he stood upright, put his shoulders back and said, 'Right, that's not happening.'

There was a tap on the door. 'Henry? Are you OK?'

It was Diane.

'Good, thanks . . . just having an appraisal.'

'Can I come in?'

'Uh, yeah, sure.'

The door opened and Diane entered, completely naked.

Henry gulped.

She came across and slid her arms around him tenderly. 'How are you feeling?'

'Getting better with each passing second,' he admitted as her hand, palm flat to his body, slid its way from his chest downwards.

'How do you feel like making love to me?'

'Oh, go on, then, I'll give it a go.'

*   *   *

Afterwards, they lay entwined in each other's limbs.

'I'm sorry if you feel I've been ignoring you recently,' Diane said.

'I thought it was over, and I would have understood,' he admitted, trying not to bubble too much.

'Good grief, no . . . it's just that I've been feeling obliged to put the hours in, having had all that time off sick.'

'You were off sick because you got shot. It's not like you pretended to have a cold for a week.'

'I know, I know.' She propped herself on one elbow and looked at him. 'I just wanted to show I'm as good as I was before, you know? And if it feels like I've not been paying attention to you, which I haven't, then I'm sorry.'

'Been pretty busy myself.'

'I know . . . but you come back here every night, no matter what time you finish. I just went to my flat because it was easier, and I wish I hadn't done.'

'I get it, but I was starting to wonder . . .' He didn't add that what he was starting to wonder was whether she was seeing someone else.

'But, bottom line, Henry . . . love ya and don't want to lose you.' She batted her eyelashes at him and he was sure he could feel the draught from the long lashes.

'Same here, but I also get it if you want to reassess us . . . age difference and all that. It might not be a problem for you just yet, but ten years down the line when I'm in my dotage, it could be.'

The batting of eyelids stopped and became an unflinching stare. 'We'll cross that bridge when we come to it, so back off with the ageist rubbish.'

'OK,' he relented. Secretly, he thought he was being realistic. He had crept unwillingly into his sixties but she hadn't yet reached forty. Big difference when you really started doing the future maths. It was a conversation they had touched on previously and probably would again. 'So what have you been working on?' he asked her.

Even though Diane was a detective sergeant on FMIT and Operation Sparrow Hawk was being run by that department and the Cold Case Unit came under FMIT's wing, he had been based in Blackpool mostly and Diane was working from headquarters at Hutton. Their paths had rarely crossed over the last six months while at work, and Henry also knew that Diane was spending a lot of time out in far-flung divisions away from HQ dealing with some ongoing investigations.

'This 'n' that,' she said noncommittally. 'A stranger rape in Rossendale, one of a series, and two domestic murders in Blackburn.'

'Phew, best of luck with them,' he said.

'Shall we go and see if your mobile phone is on the terrace somewhere?' Diane suggested. Henry got the impression she didn't really want to discuss work.

They showered, dressed and made their way into the pub, then out through the stable door where breakfasts were being served. They searched the terrace but the phone wasn't there.

'Why just my phone?' Henry wondered out loud, not for the first time. 'Why not my wallet as well? Cash, cards in it.'

'I know. Doesn't seem to make sense,' Diane agreed as they went back inside and sat at a table in the front bow window of the dining room. 'It wasn't that expensive a phone, was it?'

'Cheapest I could get away with,' he said. Since his last phone had been destroyed, he had decided not to go down the smartphone route again and just stick to basics.

Looking out across the village green, Henry spotted Jake Niven's police Land Rover coming over the bridge. Henry had phoned him from the landline a few minutes earlier to report the assault and theft and offered Jake a free breakfast if he came and reported the incident within the next ten minutes, an offer no self-respecting cop would refuse.

He had also called Debbie Blackstone and informed her he wouldn't be in that day.

As much as he wanted to get into their prisoner's ribs, he knew he needed to stay off work to make sure there was no real damage to his head, which still throbbed despite a dose of paracetamol. Otherwise, he actually felt OK.

As he and Diane watched Jake arrive, slowing down for the herd of deer which once again, after a night on the hills, had descended into the village, Diane said, slightly dreamily, 'You know what made me realize I'd been neglecting you?'

'Do tell.'

'The video you sent me yesterday. The deer on the green, then trotting down into Kendleton. I realized how much I wanted to be here with you. The kind of stuff we should be watching together, yeah?'

'I can't disagree with that,' he said wistfully, glancing briefly at Diane with just a slight frown, but turning away when a masked-up Jake Niven entered the dining room and took a seat a respectful distance away.

'I'm here,' he said, clearly grinning behind the mask as his ears rose, but then became serious. He and Henry were good friends, and one of the last acts Henry had performed as a detective superintendent just before his retirement was to get Jake the posting as rural beat cop for Kendleton and surrounding areas, a generous thing he didn't have to do but which had probably saved Jake's career and, more importantly, his marriage. 'Are you OK, Henry?'

'Been better.'

'Sounds an odd mugging,' Jake said, eyeing Diane.

She nodded and said, 'Yep, just took his cheapo phone.'

'Which was only three-G, by the way, so whoever nicked it is going to be severely disappointed. They could have bought a new five-G if they'd used my cash or card, neither of which they took.'

'I'll take details and log it,' Jake said.

Flynn, Donaldson and Molly were discussing the problem of Nico Bashkim.

'It doesn't matter whether we know if he's on board or not; if he gets back on and *Halcyon* sails away, we're stuffed,' Molly was saying. She was fully invested in getting to Nico so the two men could speak to him regarding Viktor's current whereabouts and plans. 'I mean, we could follow him at sea, I suppose' – she looked at Flynn – 'but that boat's fuel tanks are somewhat larger than ours and we'd have to call the follow off after a relatively short distance.'

Flynn agreed. 'We'd be playing catch-up all the time,' he moaned. 'And even if we do know where the boat itself goes, it doesn't mean to say that Nico will stay on board. He could easily get on a flight somewhere and be gone, like his dad.'

They were sitting on the covered terrace of the Mirage restaurant, in shadow by the back wall. Coffees and sandwiches were on the table, from which they had a good view of the sports cars, and further along the quayside they could see the upper decks of *Halcyon* dwarfing the other boats moored alongside. The boat completely dominated the marina by being the biggest and most expensive craft in there.

At the moment, because Nico had yet to return in the Ferrari, there were just the three remaining supercars parked up.

'So we need to act quickly,' Molly said, then, 'Or not at all.'

Flynn frowned. To Donaldson, he said, 'How tough is Nico?'

'He's a playboy wuss,' the American said. 'Why?'

Flynn stood up without explanation and walked towards the sports cars, then lounged against the wall to look up the quayside before sauntering back with his hands in his pockets and taking his seat.

'What's going on in your head?' Molly asked suspiciously.

His lips pursed. 'He doesn't have any bodyguards with him, and by the looks of things, the two guys who were in the SUV parked up by the boat are not there at the moment.'

'We'd have to move damn fast,' Donaldson said, now imaging what Flynn was suggesting.

'Hang on, hang on,' Molly said urgently, getting the drift. 'You're saying we snatch him now? When he gets back.'

Flynn gave her a wicked smile that worried her.

Molly's head dropped into the palms of her hands, a gesture of disbelief.

'We'd have to be quick,' Donaldson said. 'Probably need a bin bag to go over his head.'

Molly looked up between her hands. 'And *you* would have to be invisible,' she said to Flynn. 'People around here know you. We've spent months here on and off – and you're actually thinking about kidnapping someone from the biggest, most expensive boat in the marina, a boat every tourist walking by is gawping at.' Her head began to shake slowly from side to side.

'We'd have to do it really quick,' Flynn said as though he hadn't heard her.

'You, sir, are an idiot and I'm having nothing to do with this.'

Molly stood up to leave.

Flynn's hand shot out and he laid it gently on top of hers.

'It's not like he won't shout, or struggle, or fight. Somehow you'll have to get the Ferrari keys off him and hold him down if you haven't managed to punch his lights out, and then drive away . . . all within a matter of seconds . . . in public. Too many imponderables . . . Jeez!'

'I'm kidding,' Flynn said.

'Oh, you bastard, you had me going then.' She sat back down and snatched her hand from under Flynn's. 'Why don't you just ask him?' she suggested. 'Nicely.'

Flynn and Donaldson eyed each other with arched eyebrows as they heard, in the distance, the unmistakeable scream of the Ferrari engine, a noise that drowned out the sound of all other vehicles as Nico revved the engine mercilessly; a few moments later, a beer delivery truck came into view along the quay with the Ferrari having to creep behind it, Nico at the wheel, jabbing his foot down on the accelerator, gesturing impatiently at the truck which stopped in the small turning circle by the Mirage, giving Nico just enough room to spin left with a dramatic squeal of tyres on the smooth surface.

Flynn and Donaldson got to their feet.

Molly braced herself for the worst as the two men moved towards the car, but by the time they had reached the quayside, Nico had sped alongside *Halcyon* with a spurt of power and slithered to a halt by the boat, jumped out and tossed the keys at one of the bodyguards who was scurrying down the boarding steps, obviously surprised by Nico's early return.

Flynn was as angry as a caged tiger for the rest of that day, cooped up within the confines of his own boat. As much as he kept busy – *Faye* had never been cleaner, the woodwork more polished, the engine free of accumulated oil and grease – he could not get his mind off the fact that information that would lead him to the whereabouts of Viktor Bashkim was so close to hand in the form of his louche son, and yet seemed so far away.

Donaldson had disappeared somewhere. He hadn't even told Flynn where he was shacked up, though Flynn assumed he was probably in an apartment somewhere in the resort. Molly sunned herself on the foredeck but became so cross with Flynn and his banging around that finally, and in a huff, she pulled on a pair of shorts and crop top and announced she was going for a mooch around to see if any of the shops were actually open.

Flynn finally finished his cleaning flurry and, after a shower, sat on the fighting chair with a cold can of lager in hand, brooding.

He was still amazed at how affected he was to learn Viktor was alive. Up to that point, he thought he had dealt with Maria Santiago's death. It seemed he hadn't.

Flynn had never asked to become involved in any sort of conflict with the Bashkims. They were the ones who had moved in on him and tried to overwhelm and control him. Others might have capitulated or run away, but that wasn't how Flynn did things. Never was, never would be.

He took a long, cool swig of his lager.

It tasted good and helped to chill his heart a little as he pondered over Nico and how to get his hands around his neck and begin to slowly throttle the life out of him while asking him nice questions.

His mobile phone rang: Molly. He heard gasping breath and hurried footsteps. 'Flynnie?'

'Hey, Moll . . . what's going on?'

'He's out! Bastard's out, strolling along the marina, got a floozy on one arm . . .'

'Hey? Who? What?'

'Nico . . . he's out for a bloody stroll,' she said urgently. 'No bodyguards I can see, walking past our jetty . . . now!'

Flynn rocked out of the fighting chair, shot to his feet, leapt across to the jetty and looked down towards the security gates on the quayside only to see Molly walking past, gesticulating and pointing with one hand, the other holding her phone to her ear. She was saying, 'He's just ahead of me now.'

Flynn sprinted down the jetty, swung out through the gate and caught up with Molly, sliding an arm around her waist.

Ahead, strolling along like two lovers on a romantic break, were Nico and a woman.

Flynn called Donaldson.

EIGHT

F lynn and Molly also sauntered along like a couple in love, keeping a respectful distance behind Nico and the woman.

They walked to the northern end of the marina, then continued on towards the Hotel Ses Estaques, located just beyond the boat repair yard, and along the public path that sliced across the front of the hotel towards a tiny, rocky bay. At the far side of the bay was a restaurant set among trees, with a raised terrace, in front of which was a gentle sloping area dotted with Balinese beds and sofas, a perfect romantic location with great views across to Santa Eulalia. Flynn had been here a few times, most significantly with Maria Santiago when they'd spent some time in Ibiza before her death.

The Ses Estaques was closed due to the pandemic, the swimming pool drained and empty, sun loungers stacked and chained up. Looking across at the restaurant, which belonged to the hotel, Flynn could see there were signs of activity, some members of staff milling around, and he wondered if it was still open and that maybe this was Nico's destination.

As Flynn walked past the hotel, he spotted several beer bottles scattered around the sandy ground and guessed this was probably an area where local youths gathered for a bit of social interaction away from the prying eyes of the cops. Seeing the bottles gave him an idea.

He scooped one up.

Money, and maybe intimidation, talked, Flynn guessed as he and Molly dawdled on the rocky seafront close to the hotel and from a discreet distance watched as Nico and the woman were greeted at the restaurant which, it seemed, was open only for them.

They were welcomed with extravagant gestures by the face-masked manager, who seemed to be bowing and scraping and arse-licking, and he led them up on to the terrace where only one table was set up for dining.

It was clearly a prearranged visit.

Flynn watched even more cynically when a police patrol car rolled slowly into the turning circle close to the restaurant, doing a slow three-sixty sweep, stopping briefly while the cop at the wheel opened her window.

Nico had spotted the cop car, too.

He gave it a short 'All well here' kind of wave, and the female cop responded with a quick salute and drove on.

'Cops in pocket,' Flynn muttered.

'Always helps,' Molly said.

Nico and the woman took their seats and began to scan the menus while a wine waiter arrived with a bottle in a chiller bucket which was placed by the table and then opened.

Flynn looked at the empty bottle of beer in his hand, then, holding it by the neck, he firmly tapped the body of the bottle against a rock until it crumbled and broke, leaving the bottle neck in his hand. Molly watched, puzzled, as he continued to chip gently away at the broken shoulder of the neck, blunting the jagged edge until what remained was a short tube of glass that he slid over his ring finger; if he'd been a guitarist, he could well have performed some blues bottleneck slide.

But he wasn't. He possessed no musical ability and he had a whole different plan to playing guitar with a broken bottleneck.

Ten minutes later, Donaldson joined Flynn and Molly as they sat on the rocks at the front of the hotel. Although he didn't expect Nico to be able to identify him from that distance, especially as he was wearing a face mask, he kept his back to him, sneaking an occasional glance over his shoulder to check how the meal was progressing.

'Well spotted,' he congratulated Molly.

She nodded and grinned.

'What are you thinking?' he asked Flynn.

'Haul him back to my boat, attach him to a rope, set sail and drag him in our wake like a fish on a hook. Then ask him a few questions.'

Donaldson shrugged. 'That would be fun.' Then he asked, 'Are you armed?'

Flynn said no. He didn't make a habit of walking through the streets of a friendly town packing heat. His gun was now safely and securely stowed in the secret compartment in *Faye*'s engine block.

Instead, he said, 'But I have got this.'

He held up the broken bottleneck fashioned from the beer bottle.

'Looks dangerous,' Donaldson said, mocking him.

'Danger,' Flynn said enigmatically, 'is in the eye of the beholder.'

The meal was excellent, one of the best Nico had ever eaten, and he particularly enjoyed it on dry land. While life aboard a luxurious motor yacht was fantastic, eating without any sort of movement below was always a much better experience.

He sat back, sated, satisfied, looking at the lady who was accompanying him.

She had eaten like a sparrow, literally pecked at her food and left most of it, which annoyed Nico slightly. He didn't care too much. She was paid to be with him but eating wasn't part of the contract. Escort duties, including great sex (which also involved not giggling or rolling her eyes when he couldn't get an erection, something that was happening far too often these days), were.

But he was happy enough overall. Life was pretty good to him mainly, although his big regret was actually double-crossing that FBI agent, not because of the con trick he had pulled – that was very satisfying – but because the result was that Viktor was still alive and kicking and had chosen Sofia instead of him.

The woman across the table from him – he was sure she'd had a lot of work done to her face and other parts of her body (to great effect, Nico thought; in particular, the vaginal tightening surgery had worked extremely well) – said, as per her script, 'When are we going back to the boat? I'm as horny as hell.' She spoke with a strange but seductive accent that mixed Ukraine with mid-Atlantic.

'I'm having another bottle of wine,' Nico said. He indicated with a gesture of his finger for the waiter to bring along another bottle.

'In that case, I need to piss,' the woman said.

'Lovely,' Nico said.

They had slowly approached the restaurant, dilly-dallying at the water's edge, lobbing and skimming stones into and across the gentle sea, not drawing any undue attention to themselves.

When they spotted the woman rise from her seat across from Nico, they speeded up their approach.

As the restaurant was outdoors, there was no issue with entering it, although there was a rickety gate at the bottom of the steps leading up to the terrace where the tables were set.

Donaldson led, then Flynn, then Molly.

Molly veered left and followed Nico's lady friend to the toilets.

The two men made a beeline for Nico's table, taking advantage of the fact that his back was towards them and he had no idea he was about to be ambushed.

A waiter saw them coming though and made a feeble attempt to approach and challenge but Donaldson made an 'uh-uh' gesture with a waggle of his forefinger and shook his head almost imperceptibly but conveying his meaning: *Don't even think about interfering.* It was received and understood.

A moment later, Donaldson was seated on the chair just vacated by the woman.

Nico said, 'What the hell?'

Flynn came up behind him and pushed the top of his newly fashioned bottleneck-cum-gun barrel into the back of Nico's neck, just below his jet-black hairline, replicating the feel of a large-calibre muzzle being screwed into his skin at the point where his skull rocked on his spine. 'Stay fucking still or I'll blow your stupid head all over your dessert,' Flynn growled.

Nico tensed instantly and instinctively knew to place the palms of his hands flat down on the table and thereby signal through his terrified body language there would be no trouble.

Donaldson had judged the measure of the man perfectly. Nico certainly had the ability to kill or hurt people, but at heart he was a coward.

He stared across the table at Donaldson, whom he had yet to recognize, and swallowed slowly and deeply as he waited for the finger on the trigger to be squeezed.

Donaldson eyed him for a moment, then, with the tip of his forefinger, eased down his COVID face mask to reveal his features and watched Nico's eyes grow even more wild with terror before he lost it. His head slumped into his hands and he emitted a groan before raising his face again, stretching his features.

'You!' he said.

'Me,' Donaldson confirmed. 'And standing behind you is Steve Flynn ready to shoot you like the snivelling shit you are, Nico.'

Nico nodded slowly. His nostrils were permanently dilated, his breathing suddenly short and laboured. His heart thudded and he wondered if it was going to stop. He expected that after years of good living, rich food, alcohol, cocaine and now pure terror, it could easily do just that.

He licked his dry lips.

Donaldson crossed his legs casually and leaned on the table.

Nico stared at him, too petrified to move.

Behind him, Flynn reapplied the 'muzzle' of the beer bottle into Nico's skin and twisted.

Then Nico's eyes blinked slowly.

'You did the dirty on me, Nico,' Donaldson said casually. 'Did you really think you would never see me again?'

Now the Albanian's Adam's apple rose and fell with a 'glug', but he made no reply.

Donaldson arched his eyebrows, trying to elicit a response.

'No,' Nico said thinly.

'And as for Mr Flynn behind you . . . he is fuming.'

'About what?'

Donaldson chuckled. 'That your daddy is still alive. You know, the man who ordered the decapitation of his girlfriend?'

Just so Nico understood how furious he was, Flynn twisted the bottleneck again.

'If I give him the word, the nod, and I move to one side, your throat is going to be all over this table when he pulls that trigger. You know that, don't you? Soft-tipped bullets make very big, messy holes.'

'Yes.'

'So, is Viktor on board with you?'

'No.'

'Where is he, then?'

'If I tell you, you'll kill me.'

'Maybe.' Donaldson pointed at him. 'You certainly deserve it.'

'I know. But he is my father.'

'Ah, you Albanians and family.' Donaldson smirked, then leaned forward sharply, making Nico jump. 'It's not family, Nico. It's power. It's money. It's destroying people. It has nothing to do with family, you hypocritical asshole.' He leaned back. 'So, do you now run the Bashkim family business? Did it all work out for you?' Donaldson smiled at the question.

'No.'

'Didn't think so. Viktor would never let a pleasure-seeking lush like you take the reins, would he? Not while he still breathed air into his lungs.'

An expression of disgust came over Nico's face. Donaldson tried to read it and decided the revulsion was aimed inwardly at himself.

Nico said, 'My sister, Sofia . . . she runs things . . . will take it all over.'

That confirmed one of the rumours that Donaldson had heard: the father was still the figurehead for the moment; the daughter from the shadows, about whom he knew very little, was the engine, the driving force.

'OK,' Donaldson said. 'Where is he and what is he doing?'

Moments later, Flynn backed off and walked quickly to the ladies' toilets where he found Molly standing at the door of one of the cubicles, inside of which Nico's woman was sitting on the loo. The two seemed to be chatting amiably enough in spite of the fact that Molly's task was to keep her pinned down and quiet while Flynn and Donaldson dealt with Nico as quickly as possible without too much disruption or having to shoot him with a bottleneck.

As it transpired, the woman – who was called Lulu – had been quite accepting of the situation, probably because in the circles in which she moved, such events were not unheard of. She knew it was best to comply rather than face the possibility of getting a bullet in her own brain.

Flynn beckoned Molly to move.

'Bye, Lulu,' she said to the woman on the toilet.

'Bye.'

Once they were out, they joined Donaldson and were heading back towards Santa Eulalia having given Nico strict instructions to remain seated and not to look around for at least five minutes. He was happy to comply. He was still alive and there was every chance Donaldson would get to his father and take him out of the picture for good; then he, Nico, would move against Sofia and put her in the ground where she belonged.

Instead of moving, he ordered more wine as Lulu resumed her seat opposite, quite amazed to see him in one piece.

'How did it go?' Molly asked as she and the men jogged past the Ses Estaques, Flynn flinging the bottleneck into a litter bin.

'Good,' Donaldson said. 'How did it go with the companion?'

'It was almost as though she expected something like this to happen at some stage. She sat, waited and we chatted . . . she told me all about her fanny-tuck.'

Flynn shot Molly an astonished look. 'You girls!'

Molly said, 'So where do we go from here?'

When Flynn answered, she almost tripped over.

Nico guzzled two more bottles of wine and even paid a visit to the men's room where he treated himself to four lines of high-quality cocaine, two for each nostril, snorted up from the lid of the toilet cistern through a designer straw made of fine china. After about an hour, when it was obvious from the uncomfortable behaviour of the very worried staff of the restaurant that they wanted to see the back of him, he jerked his thumb for the bill, paid double and began to walk back to the marina, arms linked with Lulu.

In some ways, he was glad, almost relieved, that Donaldson had tracked him down, although he hadn't been keen on Flynn standing behind with a gun screwed into his neck.

His family had taken on Flynn and learned he was not a tiger to be prodded.

However, having experienced life under Viktor following the car bomb escapade, there probably hadn't been one single day that Nico did not regret doing the dirty on the FBI man. Yes, it had been a good scam and it had saved his father's life – but at what cost to himself?

To become, once again, the runt of the litter.

Overlooked, bypassed, sneered at, just because he didn't have the killer instinct that had raised the Bashkims way above most other crime families emerging from Albania. Yes, he could kill if he had to, order killings if he had to, but, deep down, he hated it.

Yet the thought of taking over the business had always been present in his mind. He was sure he could have done it given the chance, but Viktor wasn't.

Sofia, though . . . now she had what it took, even though she had kept the family at arm's length for the past twenty years. Viktor could see the ruthlessness in her, which was why he lured her back into the fold after Aleksander had been killed and convinced her this was her destiny.

And Nico had to bear the pain of watching from the sidelines. The runt.

So when Donaldson sat down in front of him, Flynn behind, he was more than agreeable to tell them exactly where Viktor and Sofia were, what they were up to, in the knowledge that once Donaldson knew this, Viktor's real demise probably wouldn't be far behind.

The expression on Nico's once handsome but now slightly chubby face turned to a self-satisfied smirk as he strolled along with Lulu, who seemed completely unaffected by her experience in the toilets.

On reaching the marina, Nico popped a Viagra pill and took his time as he strolled along. At one point he stopped at the water's edge, taking in the view of the boats moored alongside the jetties, the moon rising, and, in the water itself, a shoal of fish fighting for bits of bread a kid was chucking in for them, making the water bubble frantically.

He inhaled deeply, now happy about his future.

Donaldson and Flynn could take care of his father; he would take care of Sofia.

Standing there, a grim smile came to his face as he imagined his hands encircling her neck and squeezing the life out of her, making her eyes pop.

But then something changed and his hand shot up to his own throat.

That feeling in his chest, the one he'd experienced when initially facing Donaldson, returned with a vengeance. His heart began pounding wildly with no discernible rhythm, all over the place, and suddenly he was drenched heavily in sweat. He went very pale as a searing pain radiated up from his ribcage, out across his left shoulder and shot down his arm to his fingers, which felt as though he had thrust them into a raging inferno.

He gasped and turned to Lulu who, shocked by his change of appearance, backed away with her mouth open.

'Darling? What is the matter?' she asked with her hand to her mouth (she was contracted to call him 'darling' as well as other lovey-dovey terms in English, Albanian and French).

Then all those fleeting worries about how his hedonistic lifestyle might have affected his health came home to roost with a second, overwhelming surge of agony.

Clutching his chest, tearing at his shirt, Nico crashed down to his knees and then pitched head first into the waters of the marina, terrifying and scattering the shoal of feeding fish.

NINE

H enry Christie spent the day of his sick leave pottering around The Tawny Owl, doing one or two easy chores that would probably never have been done in normal times but which, due to the pandemic, stared him in the face. He also spent a lot of time fending off calls from Debbie Blackstone who ribbed him mercilessly about being old and unfit for the job and that maybe he should call it quits.

Although she was mocking him, there was an underlying seriousness to her jibes which she didn't mean but which Henry, feeling sensitive and vulnerable after being whacked on the head, took to heart a little too much.

At the end of Blackstone's working day, she called less upbeat and began the conversation a little contrite by saying, 'Look, I didn't mean all that stuff I said earlier, you know.' Henry almost thanked her, but Blackstone tarnished the moment slightly when she added, 'Yeah, you're old and fragile and all that, but I do hope you're OK because you're the best partner I've ever had, y'know; these last few months have saved me and you know that . . .' She paused.

Henry said, 'You know I'm smirking, don't you?'

'In that case, fuck off, you old trout. I'm baring my soul here!'

She hung up abruptly. Then rang back almost immediately. 'You wiped that smug look off your chops?' she demanded.

'I have.' He hadn't. However, he added, 'And, without doubt, you are the best partner I've ever had.' He meant it.

'Soft arse,' she said.

'Me all over.'

'Back at work tomorrow?'

'Reckon so . . . and, after all that preamble, how did you go on today with Gorst?'

'Um.'

'What?' Henry asked dubiously.

'He got "briefed up" . . . that there Hortense Thorogood . . . biatch!'

'Oh.'

Hortense Thorogood was a name designed to send shivers down the spines of most detectives. She was one of Blackpool's top defence solicitors – scared of no one and known to be quite intimidating. Henry had come across her numerous times over the years when he'd been a detective in Blackpool, and also on FMIT, and had given as good as he got. They had a mutual respect for each other, though neither gave any quarter.

That said, she had done Henry a very big off-the-record favour recently, and although their professional relationship would be no different, Henry had a grudging new respect for her.

He heard Blackstone sigh irritably, then say, 'She waded in with her usual panache, browbeat the shit out of the custody sergeant, then the duty inspector, then the divisional super – all male by the way – who all rolled over like puppies and let her . . . well, you know where I'm going with that. Anyway, she maybe has a point,' Blackstone relented. 'She said we were just fishing, making speculative arrests based on no real evidence whatsoever, insisted that I reveal what evidence we had, and to be fair she might be right. We locked Gorst up on circumstantial, mainly, and we didn't really get our ducks in a line. Plus, apparently, Gorst had an important business meeting to attend tomorrow . . . so he went.'

'OK,' Henry said. 'That doesn't mean we don't get another crack at him, Debs. Let's reassess where we are with him and next time go armed with statements that nail him to the wall. It's one of the problems with enquiries of this nature, going back years. You get setbacks. Nature of the game.'

'Yeah, yeah, I get it,' she said despondently. 'Just frustrating.'

'It is . . . but lesson learned. Let's go back to square one with him, because I'm sure that he has real questions to answer; it's just a matter of us doing our job even better.'

'I thought you'd be mad.'

'I am mad . . . but now I want to get even, as they say.'

'I feel better now.'

Henry toyed with the idea of coming back with a witty, scathing riposte, but decided against it, picking up how badly she was taking it.

'I'm back tomorrow. What say we have a heads-together?'

'I'll be there.'

They hung up and Henry shook his head, feeling the frustration inside. It was unlikely that anyone arrested so many years later would just crumble, especially without any real evidence presented to them. He and Blackstone would just have to find it now.

Diane arrived back shortly after he finished the call, having taken an 'ED' – Early Dart – for once, and she and Henry chilled out in front of the TV for most of the evening. He thought she seemed a little distracted and distant, but she didn't seem to want to open up, so he didn't push anything.

In the morning, despite a slight throbbing at the back of his head from the blow, he felt good and ready to get stuck back into work. He was up at six thirty, discovering that Diane had already left without waking him.

He scoffed some granola for a change, but although the morning was cool and there was a light drizzle, he still wandered out on to the front terrace with his coffee and watched what life there was go by.

Very few people were knocking around. Even the gamekeepers hadn't turned up for breakfast, and apart from the sound of Jake Niven's Land Rover in the distance, getting closer, the village was silent.

Niven came into view as he had done from the same direction the previous day, from his house, across the bridge and stopping in the car park in front of Henry. He sauntered across, sipping his morning brew from a thermal cup.

'Morning, Henry. How are you feeling?'

Henry touched the back of his head tenderly, feeling the wound over the dressing that was still in place. A couple of paracetamol tablets had started to dull the pain slightly. 'OK, I guess. Have you got anything for me?'

'Nah. I asked around the village, but no one saw anything unusual – not that there was anyone out and about at that time of night anyway. Everyone's locked down . . . I never asked you, by the way – did you hear a vehicle or anything when you got hit, just before or after?'

'Not that I remember. Not to say there wasn't one.' Henry shrugged, sipped his coffee and thought about it, as he had been doing since the incident, but nothing came to mind. He shook his head.

'Someone lying in wait, then? Which is creepy and very worrying,' Jake suggested.

'Very.'

'Someone from an old case?'

'Want me to compile a list?'

'True . . . you've upset so many people over the years.'

'It's the phone thing – why just the phone? I don't get it, unless whoever it was panicked.' He sipped his coffee, knowing he would need another before setting off for work just to keep his caffeine levels up.

The two men became silent until finally Henry said, 'I need to get going. Oh, by the way, I've commandeered Ginny's phone . . . you know her number, don't you?'

Jake nodded. He did.

Henry asked, 'You busy today?'

'Ticking over. COVID patrol.' Jake screwed up his face. Like all cops, he did not enjoy the extra pressure on the job because of the pandemic, having to make decisions that were at best unpopular and sometimes led to violence directed at him and his colleagues.

'Refill?' Henry held out his hand for Jake's mug.

Ten minutes later, he was on the road out of Kendleton.

'Jesus H! Watch out!' Albert Gorst screamed as the car in which he was travelling as a front-seat passenger, and which was hurtling far too quickly along narrow country roads, lurched violently to the right as the driver narrowly avoided colliding with the magnificent red deer stag that had suddenly burst through the hedge on the nearside and leapt into the middle of the road, causing the driver to take avoiding action.

As soon as the beast landed, it vaulted across the drainage channel on the other side and disappeared into a field.

Gorst scowled at his driver, a man called Max Janus who, despite his vast experience as a security escort driver, had almost been blindsided by the animal.

'Christ, Max!'

'Country roads, boss,' Janus replied, gripping the wheel of the Bentley Bentayga, a bulky car, the size of which belied its nimbleness when required. Janus had actually enjoyed the moment, the test of his long-dormant skills, and the instant surge of adrenalin. 'More hidden dangers than a motorway.'

Gorst swore again and spun in his seat to check over his shoulder at his wife Melanie, who hadn't seen anything, just experienced being hurled from side to side and back again. She didn't even spill her drink – a very large vodka with a touch of tonic – in an insulated travel mug. Although it was only seven thirty in the morning, she was already half-cut and determined to spend the rest of the day in that state.

'You OK, dear?' Gorst asked.

'Why shouldn't I be?' she asked with a lopsided grin.

'Oh, no reason.'

Gorst looked beyond her, out through the back window, and saw that the vehicle behind, a white Range Rover with four dark figures on board, seemed unaffected by the sudden appearance of the indigenous wildlife. He spun back with a further passing gaze at his sozzled wife who caught the roll of his eyes with a sneer of her own, and faced the front again just as the Bentley rounded a tight bend, still at speed, hogging the centre of the road, this time to be faced with a car coming in the opposite direction which, while travelling more sedately, was on the correct side of the road as much as it could be, bearing in mind the narrowness of the road itself.

Fortunately, the road did widen slightly at that point and the driver of the oncoming vehicle was able to veer sideways and slam on the brakes as the Bentley and the Range Rover barged their way through and were gone.

Henry didn't even have time to swear out loud as the massive Bentley SUV came around the bend, straddling the centre of the road, not making any effort to pull to one side. Instinctively, he yanked the steering wheel of his Audi down to the left where, fortunately, the road widened slightly, giving just enough room for the big car, which was followed by another big one, to pass without any sort of collision.

Henry estimated there was maybe four inches between the

vehicles and he was lucky not to have his door mirror ripped off. The incident was over in a blur but, like all such encounters, it slowed right down in time and mind, and Henry saw it all clearly like an action replay (he wasn't sure if 'action replays' still existed, as he hadn't watched a game of football on TV since he was in his teens). He saw the silhouette of the Bentley driver, fleeting yet precise, and got the impression there was someone in the passenger seat and in the rear; when the second car zoomed past, he definitely saw two men in the front seats, two in the back, but in no great detail.

'Absolute . . .' He was going to swear as he watched the cars disappear in his rear-view mirror but didn't. He took a breath and dialled Jake Niven's number via Bluetooth and connected quickly.

'Hi, Henry.'

'Jake, where are you, mate?'

'Just driving towards Thornwell. Problem?'

'Well, something and nothing, I suppose . . . Just been almost forced off the Caton Road by two big four-by-fours in tandem, steaming through, not giving a shit. Just wondered if you were in a position to pull them over and have a word . . . but if you're not, it doesn't matter – no harm done. I didn't get reg numbers by the way, but the lead one was a blue Bentley Bentayga and the second was a white Range Rover.' Henry might not have known his football, but he knew his cars. 'They're very noticeable.'

'I'll keep an eye out,' Jake promised.

Henry ended the call and decided to concentrate on his driving but also apply his mind to working out how to get enough evidence together that a re-arrest of Albert Gorst would be viable.

He hated letting people go when he believed they were guilty of crimes of the nature he and Blackstone were investigating.

'Just get us there in one piece, will you?' Gorst demanded of his driver.

'Sorry, boss,' Janus replied. 'These piggin' roads – you never know what's behind the next damn bend.'

He reduced the speed of the Bentley as they descended into Kendleton, passed The Tawny Owl heading towards Thornwell and adopted a more sedate pace, much more suited to a luxurious car such as the Bentley.

Gorst was on the Bluetooth connection, calling ahead. 'Five minutes away,' he said to the man on the other end of the line, looked at Janus and grunted, 'Bastards better have the place ready.'

But coming in the opposite direction was Jake Niven in his police Land Rover who, having had the call from Henry, had done a six-point turn in his unwieldy cop car and headed back to Kendleton in the hope of bumping into the vehicles that had made Henry swerve to a stop. He had only done so, really, for something to do, but had struck lucky as he came face-to-face with the two vehicles, flashing them to stop with his headlights and sticking his arm out of the window and flapping it up and down.

'What do you think, boss?' Janus asked. 'Ignore him?'

'Ugh – pull in. We don't want a friggin' drama, do we? Not today, anyway.' Gorst shook his head with annoyance.

'What about the guys behind?'

'Up to them, innit?'

Both cars passed with Jake still me-mawing them to pull over and he executed another laborious about-turn as both actually pulled in for him.

Gorst was on the phone to the following vehicle. 'Guys, be nice – no scenes, OK? Just roll with the punches.'

Jake drew in behind and slid out of the Land Rover, fitting his face mask and pulling on his chequered baseball cap. He sauntered past the Range Rover, telling the driver he would be with him next.

He walked to the driver's window of the Bentley and Janus opened it.

'Morning, gents,' Jake said, then stooped slightly to get a view over the driver's shoulder at the woman in the back, and added, 'And lady. Can I ask what you're doing around here?'

'How is that your business?' Janus snapped, but Gorst laid a hand on his arm. Janus nodded, then said, 'We've got a property we need to visit. This is my boss, Mr Gorst, and that's his wife in the back. We need to check on its condition – see if any repairs need doing.'

'Which property?'

'Simpson Hall, Officer,' Gorst cut in, leaning slightly across Janus. 'It's business.'

'And is your journey essential?'

'Absolutely. I know we're all restricted by the pandemic, but my property needs to be checked and any repairs done. If I leave it any longer . . .' Gorst shrugged. 'It'll cost double.'

'Is that the spa place, Simpson Hall?' Jake asked. 'And the wedding venue?'

'It is.'

'And these guys behind?' Jake jerked his thumb at the Range Rover. 'They with you?'

'They're my workmen. We work as a team, a bubble, so you've no need to worry – all COVID tested, et cetera.'

Jake nodded thoughtfully, weighing it all up. 'I've had a report from a motorist back up on the road out of the village that you almost forced him off.'

Janus shook his head. 'I can explain. A fucking deer jumped out in front of me. I swerved, missed the brute, and next thing there's this guy heading towards us – in the middle of the damn road, I might add – and it was just a bit of over-correction on my part.' Janus lifted his hands off the steering wheel. 'Nothing to see here, Officer.'

Jake's mouth twisted, not completely believing this. 'Doesn't quite match the story I have.'

Janus's head turned slowly to him and his eyes settled on Jake like a cobra on a mouse.

Jake felt a quiver go through him. He knew a tough guy when he saw one – and not one of those Friday-nighters swaggering through the city centre, but a real one – and this guy oozed it. The man next to him – Gorst – obviously knew his driver didn't particularly like being challenged, and he placed a calming hand on Janus's arm again.

'We're sorry, Officer. We really did swerve to avoid a deer, and if it hadn't been for Max's reactions, you'd be attending a serious accident now, not a near miss with no real harm done. Just a driving incident.'

Jake was not one to be intimidated or have the wool pulled over his eyes, and he was not worried by the dangerous look from the driver, nor completely taken in by the people in these two cars.

Despite the obvious high value of the two cars, there was something not quite right, but he couldn't put his finger on it. Neither, he thought, did he have just cause to give them a full shakedown.

He took a decision. 'Right . . . I need details of both drivers and I want to see driving licences, please . . .'

'You must be joking,' Janus said, simmering. 'What power do you have?'

'That would be the power of a constable in uniform to demand to see such documents from the driver of a vehicle on a public road. *That* would be the power.'

'Well, you can . . .'

'Can what, sir?'

'Max,' the passenger intervened, 'just do as he says.'

Janus inhaled deeply, trying to control himself.

Jake smiled nicely at him.

But then his police radio chirped up urgently. '*Report of a two-vehicle accident on Moor Road, Kendleton, near to the junction of Lune Lane . . . sounds serious, air ambulance en route . . . can you attend and cover the scene until traffic arrive . . . ETA twenty minutes from Lancaster.*'

'Roger that,' Jake replied.

He bent slightly forwards so his face was level with the driver's but maintained his distance and said, 'I have an urgent job to go to, so take this as a warning about your driving. These roads are narrow and can be hazardous, so you need to take care.'

'Yes, Officer, we understand,' the passenger said.

Janus just tightened his jawline at the mini lecture from the cop.

'Forget the documents, but I'm going to need some details, then I'll take photos of your registration numbers,' Jake said, taking out his phone.

'Be my guest,' Gorst said.

Jake smiled nicely at him and quickly took down the information he needed. He then walked to the front of the Bentley and took a photograph which included the number plate and front passengers, then walked around and did the same with the Range Rover, stepped away and, with a sweeping hand gesture, gave the two vehicles permission to carry on.

Just as he knew it would, the Bentley surged away from a standing start, wilfully disregarding the warning about speed.

The Range Rover followed.

Jake watched them disappear into the village with the premonition that he might well bump into these characters again at some point. Then he jumped into his car and, blue-lighting it, raced towards the scene of the accident, which turned out to be fatal and would keep him tied up for the remainder of the day.

TEN

Viktor Bashkim had been completely silent, brooding and constantly perusing the photographs on Sofia's mobile phone of Steve Flynn, looking over his shoulder while being pursued from the villa in Cyprus. He had said nothing on the flight out of Cyprus on the private jet owned by the head of the Lyubery mafia who had been providing him with protection for four years.

Sitting across the narrow aisle from him, trying to get some rest on the luxurious, reclining seat, Sofia watched her father with concern.

Finally, Viktor broke his silence. 'We should have hunted Flynn down anyway, not left him in abeyance. It's as simple as that. This' – he flicked his fingers angrily at the photographs on the phone – 'was always going to happen. He's resourceful and clever and dangerous, and was always going to discover I was still alive. Both he and that FBI agent should have been hunted down.'

'But that didn't happen, Father, and we are where we are.'

The old man nodded, sipped his tea, then said, 'Once we have completed these . . . these business negotiations, I want you to see it through: Flynn and Donaldson. Both must die if I am to live out the remainder of my days in peace. And that is what I want, Sofia – peace. After this, I will return to Albania and live out my years in the familiar surroundings of our traditional home. Do you understand, my dear?'

'Yes, Father.'

He sat back. 'I trust you to do it and also make your peace with Nico. He is no businessman, completely incapable of running our enterprise, even though he thinks he could. He must be given an important role of some sort to make him feel valued and have no animosity towards you or me. We must appease him.'

'I understand, Father,' Sofia agreed, knowing it would be easier said than achieved. Nico's bitter resentment was deep and unflinching – and who could really blame him? To summon her back from the life she led in the United States, where she had been hidden away for so many years, quietly acquiring knowledge and skills pertaining to business and murder, and then to take on the mantle of family head, had wounded Nico badly, and the truth was Sofia didn't now trust her brother. She could see the sheen of murder in his eyes every time he looked at her, so she knew she could never be safe while he was prowling around. She guessed that once the negotiations that she and Viktor were attending to were over and they returned to the shelter of Albania, she would have to play a waiting game; somehow keeping Nico, if not happy, then busy, while she bided her time until Viktor passed away, at which point she knew she would have to move quickly and kill Nico before he killed her.

She puffed out her cheeks at the prospect.

It would be a long, drawn-out game of chess.

The flight took over three and a half hours before the plane touched down at a small provincial airport controlled by the Lyubery on the outskirts of Moscow, Russia.

A stretch limousine awaited Viktor and Sofia, and without the formality of any customs checks, the pair was whisked away to a secluded compound in a forest overlooking a small, silver lake.

Here, Viktor and Sofia were treated like royalty, spending time with old friends and trusted business partners for two weeks, and they rested up until the next section of the journey commenced, leaving Russia first-class on a commercial flight from Moscow to Amsterdam and using false but entirely valid Russian passports.

The journey had been pre-planned and, even without the re-emergence of Steve Flynn on the scene, was designed to move the pair of them across Europe incognito.

From Amsterdam they were picked up and escorted to a private airfield where they boarded a small plane which hopped them across the North Sea to another private airfield in Lincolnshire, England.

They stayed that night in a small, discreet hotel close to Lincoln where the old man slept heavily. The following evening, paperwork arrived by courier in the shape of two more false passports.

Next day, two vehicles rolled up driven by Albanians who worked for the Bashkims in Hull, and they were driven across the breadth of the country to the north-west where they were ensconced in a small hotel on the outskirts of Preston, which, though closed due to COVID, had been 'opened' especially for them.

Even though Viktor had managed to sleep well in the course of this fairly tedious journey, he was still exhausted and all he wanted to do was sleep.

Sofia, though, was well rested, and that evening she went for a stroll along the banks of the River Ribble, during which she received a phone call to tell her that everything she had requested was in place, ready for use if required.

She was pretty sure it would be.

Henry parked next to Debbie Blackstone's restored Mini Cooper in the training school car park and walked through the landscaped woodland to the student accommodation block that had been converted years before to house the offices of the Force Major Investigation Team, the department Henry had once been joint head of as a detective superintendent prior to retirement. Under the banner of FMIT, the Cold Case Unit occupied a small, half-forgotten, very poky corner office on the ground floor.

There was a small car park for FMIT staff closer to the block, but Henry knew Blackstone parked in the training school car park simply because it took her about four minutes to walk to it, four minutes being the difference between exploding and cooling down.

Henry got it.

Some days he had left his office – which was then on the middle floor of the block – seething with fury, usually at his bosses who were located across at the 'Big House', the actual headquarters building on the far side of the sports pitches, also known as the 'Dream Factory'.

A four-minute walk might have helped cool him down.

As it happened, he didn't really have much choice in the matter. As a civilian investigator on a short-term contract, he didn't have any parking rights and had to find a space where he could.

So a four-minute walk it was.

However, the four minutes it had taken Debbie Blackstone to walk from her car to the office that morning seemed to have had no effect on her mood. As Henry tapped in the keypad code to enter the FMIT building, he could already hear her voice, even though he still had a fire door to go through and the CCU office was at the far end of the corridor.

Henry winced as he walked towards the sound of her voice.

'You can stuff that!' he heard her shout.

This was followed by a tearing sound and the sight of a desk telephone being flung out of the office door, crashing against the wall opposite and falling to the floor.

Amazingly, although ripped out of its socket, it looked as if the phone hadn't actually been damaged.

Henry peered cautiously around the door to see if it was safe for him to enter. Blackstone was standing facing the office window with her back to him, looking out.

He stooped and carefully picked up the phone, entered the office and placed it back on Blackstone's desk while keeping his eyes on her all the time. He could tell from the rise of her shoulders that she was, as ever, enraged by something.

'I need a fucking brew,' she said, not turning, but obviously aware it was Henry who had entered the room. 'I need a whisky, actually, but as I don't drink on duty, a brew will have to do!'

Henry glanced at the coffee machine which was empty and probably hadn't been rinsed since its last use.

'Something got your goat?' Henry ventured.

'Oh, you noticed, then? You really can read my mood,' she said cynically.

She spun around. Henry took in her spiked blue hair, the chequered shirt, tiny, tiny skirt, blue tights, a look finished off by Doc Marten boots with blue stars.

Six months ago, Henry would have been appalled by her appearance and the thought that any cop, let alone a detective sergeant, might look like this on duty; now he was less forthright with that rather dated view, having met and worked with Blackstone to discover she was one of the best jacks he'd ever met. Volatile as fuck, yep, but tough, single-minded, determined and just a bit clever. He'd happily work with her over any of the stuffed-shirt, rod-up-arseholes he'd come across in his police career.

'Green Frog, maybe?' he suggested.

In response, she pulled her face mask up over her nose and barged past him out of the office, snatching up a file from her desk as she went.

'I'll take that as a yes,' Henry said, following.

*   *   *

Fifteen minutes later, they were on Preston Docks and Henry had bought Blackstone a coffee from the Green Frog catering caravan on the dockside. They hadn't spoken a word on the relatively short journey from HQ, and Henry hadn't felt inclined to intrude into Blackstone's thoughts.

They were leaning on the railings overlooking Albert Edward Dock. Blackstone's apartment was on the opposite side, on the top floor of a converted warehouse.

After peeling the plastic lid off her drink and taking a sip of the hot brew, she said, almost spat, 'CPS!'

Meaning the Crown Prosecution Service.

Henry waited. Blackstone went on, 'Just browbeaten by that bitch Hortense Thorogood, and as shite rolls downhill, I've had a flea in my lughole from the detective super about being overzealous with regard to arresting Albert Gorst.'

'She is good,' Henry said of Thorogood.

'She's a twat and a muckraker,' Blackstone said.

Henry looked at Blackstone's profile as she leaned on the railings. 'Sometimes you've got to take things on the chin. Mostly, we get our way and rightly so. The way I see it, defence solicitors come in and fight for the rights of their clients while we fight for the rights of victims, and to me, while we must be fair, our side of the coin is the more important one. The problem with this case is that it's so old and we were probably a bit gung-ho with Gorst.'

Henry saw her nod. 'Yeah, he seems to be on the periphery of what we're dealing with; we know he's involved but we need to spend more time looking at him,' she said grudgingly.

'I get the feeling he was a bad man and still is, but now he gets away with things because he portrays himself as a holier-than-thou respected care-home owner and funeral director . . .'

'As I said before, the perfect business model,' Blackstone said.

'Money comes in when his customers are alive and then again when they are dead . . . it's a no-brainer when you think about it.'

'Father, you need to put this on.'

'I don't see why,' Viktor Bashkim protested.

'Because we can't be too careful.'

Sofia was holding up a covert bulletproof vest which had originally been developed for use by undercover cops, made from Kevlar to provide protection from a nine millimetre bullet, a knife or a spike. It was engineered to keep the wearer cool, ventilated and, as far as possible, comfortable.

It wasn't really manufactured to be worn by an eighty-year-old man, particularly one who didn't feel the need.

'They wouldn't dare,' Viktor insisted.

'They *shouldn't* dare,' Sofia corrected him.

Viktor smiled wickedly. 'But we dare.'

'If necessary, yes, we dare. Now, come on, old fella, let me help you with this.'

Reluctantly, he acquiesced and Sofia threaded the vest over his actual vest and pulled the Velcro straps just tight enough. Then she helped him put his shirt on, buttoning it for him and then fastening his tie before he put on his suit jacket.

She then circled him, checking that the vest wasn't too obvious.

'You'll do,' she said and kissed him on the cheek, at which moment her mobile phone rang.

They were in Viktor's bedroom at the hotel they'd stayed in overnight.

Sofia looked at her phone and didn't recognize the number. She said to Viktor, 'I'll take it out here,' and backed out of the room into the corridor to answer it.

She reappeared a few minutes later, hoping that she wasn't showing the mixed emotions she felt on hearing the news she had just received.

'Ready, Father?'

Viktor was silent for most of the journey. He and Sofia were in the back of a red Jaguar being driven swiftly, quietly, along the motorway and roads of Lancashire. Two Albanians were in the front seats.

It was in moments like these that Viktor really understood just how old he was. When he was expected to take the reins of a business he had meticulously cultivated and grown for over sixty years . . . but now he was tired.

He would really have liked to spend time pottering around a garden growing tomatoes and playing with grandchildren. He realized the latter part of this whimsical wish was unlikely to happen (though he suspected that Nico did have some bastard kids out there somewhere – the boy who couldn't control his urges yet fancied being in control of a multi-billion-euro crime organization; he also felt there was no chance of Sofia ever becoming a mother as he had yet to see any sign of maternal instincts).

He knew it was on him to make this last effort to demonstrate to others he was a true leader who could not be messed with, someone to be admired and feared in equal measure, despite his obvious fragility, while also making it known that after today it would be Sofia who ran everything – absolutely everything.

The English countryside shot by, unfocused in Viktor's eyes until he finally sat up, inhaled and asked Sofia, 'What can we expect from today?'

Albert Gorst was nervous, which was unusual for him. He had only ever met Viktor Bashkim once, almost a dozen years earlier, and had since had to deal with his minions and gofers, but this time he had insisted on dealing with the main man because so much was at stake. Things had moved on in the intervening years and old contracts were no longer valid in Gorst's opinion. In fact, they were just plain stupid and condescending, and he had had enough of shitty percentages.

He had to take control and he knew the only way to do this was by going head to head with Viktor, laying it on the line and showing him he wasn't going to be screwed over any longer.

There was a nice conference room at Simpson Hall, but since the pandemic it had not been used for almost a year. Gorst had brought it out of mothballs and employed a cleaning company to freshen it up for that day's proceedings.

On his arrival at the hall, the gates were opened by his two lackeys who'd been keeping an eye on the property for a few days and were responsible for supervising the tradespeople Gorst had contracted to bring the hall up to spec prior to the Bashkims' arrival.

According to the guys, all had done well. The rooms required had been thoroughly cleaned and prepped, and the heating system was back to working properly again. A catering firm was due in later to set up a buffet and would be back in the morning if there was a need for breakfast.

Gorst and Janus helped the inebriated Melanie Gorst out of the

Bentley and between them whisked her into the hall, up the stairs to the first floor and deposited her in the suite in which she and Gorst would be sleeping that night. It was already well stocked with booze and snacks, and Gorst hoped she would get the message and continue to drink herself into oblivion over the next twenty-four hours and keep out of sight. Melanie was usually quite amenable to that and Gorst didn't expect to see much of her.

After that, he and Janus did a walk-through of the house and were satisfied everything seemed to be in order; they completed their inspection tour in the conference room which had been set up using a big, oval-shaped teak table.

The French doors opened out on to a terrace overlooking the somewhat overgrown grounds beyond. The two men stepped out and Gorst surveyed the untended gardens with distaste. Normally, they would be neat and tidy – an ideal place for newlyweds to pose for pictures following their nuptials, which is what the hall was mostly used for, but the pandemic had scuppered that line of business. Now the grounds looked unkempt, which irked Gorst because he liked a nice garden.

'That's a shame,' he said. 'The gardens.'

'He isn't coming to check up on the landscaping.'

'True, true.'

Janus wandered back into the conference room – which was also most often used for wedding breakfasts – and leaned against a wall, his bottom against a warm radiator as he waited for Gorst to come back inside. He frowned as a nebulous thought skittered through his mind, but then it was gone and he couldn't quite retrieve it to dissect it.

The door to the conference room opened and the lackey with the goatee appeared, just as Gorst stepped back in from the garden.

'Boss, you expecting a bloody florist?' Goatee asked. 'There's one at the front door with a huge bunch of flowers.'

Sofia had to admit that the flowers were gorgeous. She received them with good grace and braced herself for the kiss on both cheeks from the slimy creep that was Albert Gorst, who reeked of body odour and cheap aftershave.

'You are so very kind,' she said, her arms sagging somewhat under the weight of the blooms.

'And you are so welcome,' Gorst said effusively before turning to Viktor Bashkim, his face breaking into what seemed a genuine smile at the old man who stood propped at an angle on his walking stick. 'And, Viktor, it is so good to meet you again. It has been too long.'

Sofia noticed two things about Gorst. First, he couldn't keep his eyes off the chunky gold necklace that hung around her neck, making her wonder if he understood its significance – that the wearer was the leader. And he didn't like it: that she was the one wearing it seemed to have thrown him.

Next, when he looked at Viktor, Sofia could tell he saw weakness. A withered old man with a cane to keep him upright, someone who would be no contest for him mentally or physically.

What Gorst didn't know was that Viktor's obvious use of the cane was deliberate. He wasn't great physically but he didn't quite need one all the time. He had decided to act weak in order to lure Gorst into a false sense of security.

An old man and his daughter: not even a contest.

Sofia could see all that in his look of triumph as he stepped towards Viktor and gave him a manly bear-hug embrace which the old man took in good part, even though it was a psychological early move by Gorst to declare that he was in charge.

Behind Gorst stood Max Janus. Sofia eyed him discreetly.

She'd done her homework on him too. Ex-Special Forces, moved on to be a close protection specialist for wealthy Arabs in the Middle East and finally, although how it happened she didn't know, working as muscle for Gorst for the last three years. Sofia knew he was a dangerous man and she would have to watch him carefully in the hours ahead, which also saddened her because she quite liked what she saw.

Such was life, she thought.

She had also quickly taken in the other muscle: four guys outside and another two wandering around inside.

If things did degenerate, she knew she would have to be good, fast and deadly, and Viktor would also have to do his thing, too.

'Come in, come in,' Gorst effused in a friendly way. So far everything had taken place in the tiled vestibule, but he beckoned them through into the vast entrance foyer of Simpson Hall where he then turned and said, 'I'm sure you guys won't be offended, but you know the drill. We need to search you.'

Sofia said, 'Works both ways, Albert.'

'Sure, sure . . . but in the meantime . . . please.'

Sofia placed her piece of hand luggage down and opened it wide.

Grinning, Janus stepped forward and rummaged through it, found nothing, then rose up and looked at Sofia with a hint of amused lust. He was going to enjoy the next bit, and so was she.

She raised her arms and Janus stepped close, face-to-face, expertly running his hands under her jacket, around her back. She felt his fingertips linger for a moment on the straps and fastenings of her bra underneath her silk blouse, at which point their eyes met and locked as he descended to a crouch, still holding her gaze while feeling down the small of her back at her waist, then across the cheeks of her arse before running his fingers down the inside of her legs, but not actually connecting with her crotch – which, if he had done, would have resulted in a smack across the head.

'Satisfied?' she asked as he stood upright.

'More than.'

Their eyes remained locked for another moment until he moved across to Viktor who opened his jacket and allowed him a brief search.

'They're clean,' Janus announced.

'What about you and your guys?' Sofia asked.

'Just take it as read,' Gorst said.

Sofia's mouth tightened to an angry line. Now it was just her and Viktor; their two escorts had been sent on their way and banished from both the grounds and the hall.

She nodded.

'Let me show you to your rooms,' Gorst said. 'I know you've had a long journey, so I assume you'll want to freshen up.' He led them to two adjoining suites on the first floor. 'And I suppose you'll be needing a nap,' he said patronizingly to Viktor.

When he had gone, Sofia knocked on the connecting door between the rooms and entered Viktor's side to find him perched on the edge of the large bed.

'If only for that last remark, darling,' he said, 'I would like to see that man dead.'

*   *   *

It turned out to be one of those uneventful days at work for Henry and Blackstone. Once Blackstone had managed to suppress her anger at her perceived failure of the day before, the pair returned to HQ where they hunkered down in the Cold Case Unit office and decided to review Operation Sparrow Hawk, what they had done and achieved, where they were up to and where they were going.

Since uncovering the conspiracy, which they had been investigating for almost five months now, their digging had uncovered a great many unpalatable facts about the extent of child abuse on the Fylde coast of Lancashire and its hinterland, going back many years.

Arrests had been made, trials and, they hoped, convictions were pending and others were likely, but Henry and Blackstone knew decisions had to be made about how far and wide the operation would continue to cast the net – that in itself wasn't their remit because the issue of costs and resources was decided above them. Either the constabulary committed itself to a much bigger investigation or a line had to be drawn and the Sparrow Hawk team had to call it quits, deal with what they had found so far and be satisfied with that.

The problem for the pair was they knew there was so much more to uncover, which would probably include murders, and where there were dead people, in particular children and young adults, neither of them wanted to let go. They were hard-wired in that respect, like Jack Russell terriers going after rats.

So they spent the whole day putting together the bones of a report explaining all this, which they intended to submit to better people than them (how they sniggered at that concept) to make a decision: enhance Sparrow Hawk and find the money and resources necessary or knock it on the head.

It was one of those between-a-rock-and-a-hard-place decisions that came with higher rank, and so be it.

By three p.m., Henry needed to call it a day. His head throbbed and he was pretty weary.

Blackstone could have kept going and she scoffed mercilessly at Henry, although secretly she'd had enough, too.

In the 'old days', they would have gone to the pub, but as pubs were a thing of the past for the time being, they decided to head home and reconvene the next morning.

*   *   *

It was just a business strategy meeting.

Nice room. Nice view.

Coffee and tea and water on tap.

Sandwiches, biscuits and cake.

All very civilized, yet with the undercurrent of greed.

And it truly was a business meeting. It's just that the business being discussed was crime, because that was how the people in that conference room made their very lucrative living.

There were several threads to their business, the main ones being the trafficking of drugs, firearms and people and the laundering of money across Europe and into and out of the cash cow that kept on giving – the United Kingdom. An easy, insatiable target.

And as a loose subsidiary of the main company that was the Bashkim Crime Organization, which had a proud history of making immense amounts of money from the suffering of others, Albert Gorst's small organization had benefitted considerably because of their links.

However.

Gorst was ambitious and restless and wished to increase his influence, which was a euphemistic way of saying he wanted more, much more, and had seen opportunity in the age of Viktor Bashkim, because ageing meant weakness; he had also heard on the grapevine of the rivalry between Sofia and Nico and the fact that Sofia was the chosen one, which to Gorst also meant weakness. Women were weak and easy to dominate, he always believed.

'So, yes,' Gorst was saying as he sipped green tea, 'we do have a very good relationship, you and I, Viktor.' His eyes jerked sideways to Sofia, who, like Viktor, was sitting on the opposite side of the oval table.

'But you are not satisfied,' Sofia said.

In spite of Gorst's insistence on directly addressing Viktor throughout their discussion and blanking out his daughter, Sofia had continually interjected and taken up the running for the Bashkim camp, much to Gorst's growing irritation.

Now Gorst looked at her properly. 'Love,' he said condescendingly, 'this is a man's game, so zip it.'

She blinked and said nothing. Gorst looked at Viktor again, who sat there quietly, patiently, not giving anything away.

Standing behind Gorst, leaning on a lukewarm radiator, was Janus, whose eyes were always on Sofia.

Gorst went on – to Viktor, 'Yes, it has been good but now it is time to move things on, Viktor. Your time is up because you are a doddering old fucker.' After two hours of bashing his head against the wall, metaphorically, Gorst had decided that enough was enough; it was time to stop beating around the bush. They'd pussy-footed for two hours, and both sides knew what was coming. 'You need new blood, old fella, a transfusion.'

Out of the corner of his eye, Gorst saw Sofia's chin rise.

Gorst went on, tapping his own chest angrily, 'I . . . I make only a tiny percentage of what you make. I'm a dog at your table, taking scraps from your plate, yet I do all the hard work. I have to set up lines of trade from lorry drivers to drug mules to rigid inflatables to county lines to rebuilding your brothels in the north of England because your previous ones were burned to the ground. I provide men and manpower. I provide a money-laundering system through my care homes and funeral services, all of which feeds back huge amounts of capital to you, Viktor. Do you hear?'

The old man stared at him, his eyes watery.

'Look,' Gorst said, trying to sound reasonable, 'I'm not trying to cut you out of this completely, Viktor . . . but I want control, I want to flip the percentages . . . simple.'

Then, almost indiscernibly, Viktor shook his head. 'That will not happen.'

'I think you're wrong there, Viktor. As we speak' – Gorst checked his watch – 'I have people all over the UK and Europe ready to move in on my say-so. On my signal, they will oust your people . . . this is my new blood . . . and this – this "transfusion" as I call it – can be done amicably or else it can be done . . . dramatically, shall we say?' Gorst stood back and folded his arms.

'In less than an hour, once I give the word, your networks will come under my control. Your knocking shops will be in my power. Your drug lines will be controlled by my people . . . do you get my drift, Viktor? Sofia?' He spoke her name with disrespect. 'Do I need to continue to explain, other than to say this has been in the planning for months? I've been getting ready for this in conjunction with some old friends of yours, by the way.'

'Old friends?' Sofia asked.

'The Toskus family. You know them well.'

A tense silence descended on the room; the only noise was the faintest rasping of Viktor's lungs as he inhaled, exhaled.

Then the old man said, 'They are our greatest enemy.'

Gorst said, 'Exactly, but I speak for them to assure you we can all work together from now on.'

'That will not happen,' Viktor stated again.

Gorst smashed his open hand on the table, leaving a damp palm print on the highly polished wood which quickly evaporated. He leaned forward menacingly. 'You are so wrong. I do the work. I want the benefits. I'm not bothered about what happens in France or Germany, or fucking Albania for that matter, but I want the UK and I'm going to have it, even if it means using your worst nightmare. I will have it, do you understand, old man?' He looked at Sofia and sneered. 'Or should I really be speaking to you? I see you're wearing the gold chain.' He pointed to her neck. 'Yeah, I know the myth, the backstory.'

'In which case you should know the reality of the strength and depth of our proud family,' she told him.

He laughed. 'Your family hardly exists now.' He wagged a finger at Viktor. 'An old man at death's door.' He pointed at Sofia. 'A daughter brought in to run a failing organization. A drunken, drugged-up son who likes getting his cock sucked more than making money? A dead son and two dead grandsons . . . you lot are nothing! Fuck all!'

His voice had risen as his contemptuous bile spewed out and the echo of those last two words hung in the air like a bad aroma.

Opposite, Viktor and Sofia sat there placidly.

Until Viktor said, 'You are a fool.'

Gorst smirked. 'I think you'll find you are the fool – an old fool, Viktor, who has had his day. You're wealthy, so my advice is take a back seat and die in clover. And as for you, missy' – he glared at Sofia – 'get yourself a husband, then get yourself knocked up before that biological clock of your counts down and goes boom.' He made an exploding gesture with his hands.

In response, Sofia said, 'I need to pee.'

The conference room door closed behind Sofia, leaving Viktor to face Gorst and Janus.

The old man held out his cup and saucer. 'Would you be kind enough to get this old man a fresh cup of tea?' he asked Janus.

Janus leaned over and took the crockery, moving away to a sideboard against the wall on which the food and drink had been laid out.

'You probably won't even feel the effects of this new paradigm,' Gorst said, leaning back in his chair. 'You have enough to live on.'

Viktor smiled as Janus came back with his refreshed brew and slid it across, then went back to the wall to lean on the radiator.

'Things change, admittedly,' Viktor conceded.

Janus watched him, sipping his own tea, as he rested his backside on the warmth coming from the radiator. It felt quite pleasant.

But then, in contrast to that heat, a sudden chill rippled through him. He stood up straight and without warning rushed to the door and yanked it open as Goatee's words rang through his mind.

Innocent-sounding words.

But now significant and possibly terrifying.

Words about the heating system working properly again.

Two of his men were lounging on chairs in the foyer and they leapt to their feet as Janus stepped out of the conference room.

'Where the fuck is she?' he demanded.

The two guys looked at each other, then one said, 'Uh, the bogs, I think.' He pointed along the ground-floor corridor. At the far end was a sign indicating toilets for men and women.

'With me – now!' Janus started to run, pulling a nine-millimetre Glock out of his waistband and thinking, *I didn't ask anyone to look at the heating.*

Sofia recognized the moment when it arrived.

It was so obvious when the meeting descended into pathetic and childish insults and name calling and, of course, the chest-beating belief on Albert Gorst's part that he could intimidate Viktor and Sofia into whimpering submission.

To Sofia's knowledge, Viktor had never given in to anything.

'I need to pee,' she had declared.

It was true: she did. But it could wait.

She had walked out of the conference room, acknowledging the two men in the foyer and giving a pleasant nod to each. She kept her walk measured, unhurried. Then, at the end of a seemingly never-ending corridor, she turned right into the ladies' toilets.

They were empty, of course, and smelled of lavender.

On the right was a row of six washbasins and on the left six toilet cubicles with floor-to-ceiling partitions, no gaps under the doors or between them, ensuring total privacy. All the doors were closed, but not locked.

She went into the one furthest away and closed the door behind her.

Fitted in the cubicle was a back-to-the-wall toilet, the cistern concealed behind the pan by a vanity unit so none of the pipework was exposed. The top of the unit was flat and had an artificial flower display on it.

Quickly removing her jacket and hanging it behind the door, Sofia lifted the flower bowl off the unit, placed it on the floor and took out an Allen key she had brought with her. It was small enough to be missed by Janus's quick search, concealed uncomfortably by the underwire of her bra. The flat top of the unit was secured to the base by four screws, one in each corner, the heads of which could only be loosened by the Allen key.

She went to work quickly, removed the screws in seconds, then lifted the lid off, placed it against the cubicle wall and peered into the cupboard space where the toilet cistern was located. She smiled as she lifted the first of the two weapons that had been left there for her by the Tradesman.

It was a Skorpion EVO3 lightweight submachine gun, originating from the Czech Republic, purposely designed for ease of use in confined spaces. It had been pre-loaded with a twenty-round magazine with nine-millimetre cartridges. There were two spare magazines and Sofia knew the weapon had been left for her with the three-round burst selection having already been set.

The second weapon was a Makarov semi-automatic pistol with an eight-round magazine inserted, the gun cocked, and a spare mag balanced on top of it.

Sofia pushed the Makarov into her waistband and spare mags into the back pockets of her jeans.

At which moment she heard the door to the toilets kicked open and Max Janus yell, 'Where are you, you fucking bitch?'

*   *   *

'Go, go!' Janus shouted, hustling his two men ahead of him, almost forcing them through the door, their weapons drawn, but neither sure what they were letting themselves in for.

They began at the first cubicle.

One stood back, crouching low, as the other flat-footed the door open with a loud clatter. The door flew back.

Empty.

'Clear, boss.' The guy turned to Janus who was still on the threshold, a double-handed grip on his pistol, aiming it at the floor.

'Well, fucking do the next one!' he screamed at the incompetence.

Which the guy did. Also empty.

'Come on, move on!' Janus screamed again at the men who then leapfrogged each other down the line of cubicle doors in a choreographed version of Russian Roulette with a six-shot revolver, only in this case the bullet chambers were doors, and when the final one was booted open they would find the loaded one occupied by a woman brandishing a Skorpion submachine gun.

Sofia knew she would have to act without hesitation. She had already counted Gorst's entourage – eight, including the man himself.

Janus was with the two of them who were working their way towards her, door by door.

That meant three guys were coming for her.

The four other guards were presumably patrolling the grounds. Their precise location at this moment did not concern her. They would either come running once the shooting started or leg it.

The important thing was that Janus had come after her, although she did not quite know why he had; something must have spooked him into action. At least she knew where he was and that he would have to be among the first to be put down: she could smell he was dangerous.

She heard the first cubicle door open.

Then the shout. Empty.

Then the next. Also empty.

Two down, four to go.

Sofia steadied herself, standing right back in the corner of the cubicle, to one side of the toilet bowl with the Skorpion in the firing position, her left hand supporting the 196-millimetre-long barrel,

fingers curled around the ribbed pattern on it and her right holding
the handle with her forefinger on the trigger.

Another toilet door kicked open.

Then another.

When they got to the fifth door, the one next to the cubicle she
was in, and they found it empty, what would happen?

Would their adrenaline be flowing so much that it would make
them rash decision makers? Because had it been her, she would
stop, back off and regroup, having worked out that the enemy was
in the last one.

She thumbed the fire selector switch to fully automatic.

When they reached the fifth door and found the cubicle unoccupied,
they did realize that if Sofia was anywhere, it would be in the next
one. One of the men held the other back by putting out an arm,
restraining him while both looked to Janus for guidance.

Which they got. Janus shouted, 'What the hell are you waiting
for? Boot it down!'

Sofia didn't bother waiting for the door to fly open.

The cubicles were constructed of pretty unsubstantial wooden
panels, MDF veneered with a plastic coating to give them a sheen
of affluence, but in reality they were just cheap boards and certainly
not an effective barrier for the first burst of machinegun fire that
ripped through them from the barrel of the Skorpion in a controlled
arc and brutally cut the two men down as they dithered on the tiled
floor space between the cubicles and the wash basins.

The bullets tore across the midriffs of both men, almost slicing
them apart.

'What the hell is that?'

In the conference room, Albert Gorst shot to his feet on hearing
the unmistakeable sound of gunfire.

This was also the moment that Viktor Bashkim came to life,
moving more quickly and with more deadly accuracy than should
be possible for a man of his age. Twisting the ornately carved silver
handle of his walking stick to unlock it, he slid the slim stiletto
blade out of the hollow tube that formed the shaft and, powering

himself up, he lunged across the tabletop at Gorst, slithering as he plunged the fine, deadly blade into Gorst's belly.

Sofia swung out of the cubicle only to see Max Janus throw himself sideways out of the toilet door back into the corridor.

Cursing, she jumped over the bleeding bodies of the two men and sprinted to the door, flicking the Skorpion back into three-shot firing mode in order to save ammunition. Even the short, controlled burst she had put into the two men had severely depleted the mag, and although she did have one spare, she knew it would be better to conserve her shooting power.

She paused at the threshold, took control of her breathing and heart rate for a second before crouching slightly and taking the chance to have a quick look into the corridor, only for Janus to do a double tap from his position. He was hiding in a doorway further down, on the opposite side. But his shots were hurried and he missed. In a change of tactics, Sofia then thumbed her weapon back to full-fire, dinked out and sprayed her remaining bullets into the wall around the point where Janus had backed himself tightly.

She dinked back into cover, releasing the magazine as she did and smoothly replacing it with the full one from her back pocket, then took a quick look along the corridor to see the door at which Janus had been hiding close softly on its pneumatic strut.

With her back tight to the wall, she edged along with the reloaded Skorpion ready to fire, back on three-shot mode again.

It had been a long time since Viktor Bashkim had stabbed anyone. He had fairly recently baseball-batted someone to death, a guy who had been strung upside down on the rear deck of the *Halcyon* when Viktor had owned the boat, and as satisfying as that had been – feeling the wood connect with bone – nothing was quite as wonderful as sticking a knife into someone's belly.

An amazing sensation.

And then withdrawing it, hearing the slurp of the blade as it came out.

And as he extracted the stiletto from Albert Gorst, Viktor heard that sickening noise and looked up to see Gorst's wide-open, disbelieving eyes, horror-struck . . . almost offended.

Viktor slid back across the table, accompanied by a spray of blood from the narrow but very deep wound.

He thumped back into his chair and watched Gorst stand there, looking at Viktor accusingly, then down at his stomach and the blood on his clothes, then clamping his right hand over the wound just as his legs turned to mush. With his left hand, he tried to remain upright, using the tabletop for support, but his palm slithered in the blood and there was no grip, no way of preventing himself sinking down to his knees, disappearing inch by inch until Viktor could only see his head.

The Albanian smiled.

Gorst toppled over with a grunt.

As Sofia reached the point where the corridor opened out into the front foyer, the front door opened and Gorst's two guys who had been on duty at the front of Simpson Hall ran in, drawn by the sound of shooting.

Sofia stepped out and shot them down.

'Four down,' she said, keeping tally, but then added one and said, 'Five,' because she knew one hundred per cent that Viktor would have gutted Gorst: old did not mean incapable.

That left two more plus Janus, who was the one she was really worried about.

Suddenly she froze, hearing the clip-clop of footsteps coming down the stairs from the first floor. A woman appeared, staggering with a bottle of vodka in one hand.

Sofia had no idea who this was.

But without hesitation, she shot her, one three-bullet burst sending her windmilling backwards a few steps, the bottle wheeling out of her hand and smashing to pieces on the floor as the woman fell back.

'Still three left by my reckoning,' Sofia said, revelling in the pulsing sensation of blood coursing through her veins.

She pirouetted, then ran to the door of the conference room, stepping in and finding a scene she fully expected: Gorst, apparently dead and bleeding on the floor, and Viktor calmly using a napkin to clean the blade of his stiletto, which he then slid back into the walking stick and twisted the handle one click to lock it in place.

As he looked at her, Sofia did not say anything but held up her left hand, her thumb holding down the little finger to indicate with the upright digits there were three targets still outstanding.

Viktor understood.

Sofia gave him a reassuring nod which was only half-completed because the two remaining guards who had been patrolling the outside of the hall at the rear suddenly appeared at the French windows, drawn by the sound of gunfire. They clustered up to the window, shading their eyes from the natural glare in order to peer inside.

'Amateurs,' Sofia said with contempt. She flicked the Skorpion back on to fully automatic and fired, emptying the whole twenty-round load into them, shattering the windows. Both staggered backwards in a synchronized zombie dance before falling down the terrace steps and disappearing from view.

Sofia discarded the Skorpion and drew the Makarov from her back pocket. 'Janus,' she said to Viktor.

He nodded. 'He's dangerous.'

She held the Makarov in a double-handed grip and wondered what her best move would be. The last thing she wanted was a cat-and-mouse chase.

On seeing his two men gunned down in the toilets – shredded – Max Janus instantly realized he could not hope to compete with Sofia's firepower unless he got lucky. His two-inch barrelled, six-shot detective special was no contest for the Skorpion, which Janus recognized as she emerged from the cubicle. He had seen and used many similar weapons when he'd been a soldier, and having been a soldier, he also knew all about valour and survival and how, very often, they were not good bedfellows.

Retreat was often the best option.

Scrambling away down the corridor, he slammed himself into a door recess and – stupidly on quick reflection – took two hasty shots at Sofia as she looked out of the toilet door, completely missing her. Even in that moment, he was furious as he found himself two bullets down, four remaining, and he needed to connect with his four remaining men who were all outside somewhere.

As he went through the door he was flattened against, Sofia unleashed a further broadside from the Skorpion and he felt the sharp sting of a bullet creasing the muscle covering his shoulder blade.

He stumbled into the main bar area of the hall, currently in mothballs due to the pandemic, his mind playing the image of that ferocious woman, deadly and focused in her mission, with a searing pain in his upper back now.

The bar itself was closed and secured by a locked drop-down mesh screen; chairs were stacked all the way along one wall with tables upended, slotted into each other like a conga line. He knew that the inner doors, one leading to a kitchen area behind the bar, one to a small office, were locked, yet there was a fire exit door on the back wall which opened on to the rear terrace that ran the whole length of the rear of the hall.

Janus ran straight across the small circular dance floor, leaving a trail of blood from his freely bleeding shoulder, and threw himself against the bar of the fire exit – which didn't budge.

He heard more firing out in the corridor.

He cursed, not even daring to imagine the havoc Sofia was wreaking. Who had she killed now? His men?

He inspected the quick-release bar and saw it was locked by a slot-in bolt, though not to prevent people getting out in case of fire but to stop unwanted intruders getting in. He flicked the bolt out, slammed the locking bar down and stepped outside to see his two guys with their faces pressed up to the French windows of the conference room.

Before he could shout, the pair became the next victims of Sofia's murderous rampage, dancing backwards like ragged puppets as the bullets ripped into them.

Even Janus, who had seen many bad things as a soldier, done many bad things, was stunned by the absolute ferocity of the shootings. Had he and his boss, Gorst, been naive to expect anything less? Gorst was, after all, proposing to overthrow the Bashkims.

Janus didn't have any time to debrief that thought as he watched the writhing bodies of the men crash down the steps. Instead, a sudden, uncontrollable rage engulfed him, which tossed aside all caution. He stormed across the terrace to the shattered windows and, with his revolver ready and in a weaver stance, twisted himself into the conference room.

*   *   *

Sofia saw him. She fired before he could even discharge one shot at her, hitting him with a double tap. Janus was flung away, dropping his gun, which skittered across the terrace.

Only one bullet from the double tap hit Janus in the right shoulder, ploughing a furrow through the outer part of his deltoid muscle but not imbedding itself in the joint. He spun around, unable to keep a grip on the gun, then, in order to stay alive, he ran across the terrace, leaping down the steps into the garden, over the bodies of his men, and diving head first into the bushes, forcing himself through the undergrowth towards a small area of woodland where he rolled behind a tree trunk. He came up on to one knee, clutching his right shoulder which was bleeding profusely.

Sofia went into hustle mode, helping Viktor to his feet and manoeuvring him gently but swiftly out of the conference room, through the foyer and out through the front doors of the hall.

She had her phone clamped to her ear.

First call: instructing her guys to get here fast. They were parked up on the road outside, waiting for this, so they were only seconds away.

Second call: instructing someone else to move in quickly.

Their car screamed through the gates and up the drive, skidding to a halt and allowing her to ease Viktor into the back seat and then run around to the opposite side, shouting instructions to the driver as she fitted Viktor's seat belt for him.

All the while, his watery, weak eyes watched her with pride.

When he was secured, she shouted, 'Go!' to the driver, then sat back, exhaling long and hard.

Viktor said, 'Now you know why I chose you over Nico.'

ELEVEN

Although it was the task of the much depleted (and, some cynics would say, non-existent) traffic department to deal with, investigate and report fatal road traffic accidents, Jake Niven's sense of duty and compassion kept him at the scene of the accident he had been deployed to attend earlier that day, not least because it was on his patch and the people involved were locals.

There was one dead, two with serious, life-threatening injuries and one person unscathed, and Jake knew them all.

Two vehicles were involved: a car and a lorry.

The car came off worst.

It was a head-on collision, the car being driven too quickly by a young buck who had just passed his test, driving a car bought for him by his father, which ended up under the front radiator grille of the lorry, a large articulated vehicle owned by a chicken farmer from Kendleton. The car was a horrendous mess.

The eighteen-year-old driver, who had not been belted up, had pitched head first through the windscreen into the front of the lorry, completely flattening his head on impact, causing instant death.

The front-seat passenger, the lad's girlfriend, was severely injured, as was their mate in the back seat, but both had been kept in place by their seat belts, the payoff being that because the car was wedged underneath the lorry, they were both trapped and had to be cut free by the fire and rescue service.

As the two survivors faded in and out of consciousness, Jake had reassured them, speaking softly, telling them he was there for them. All the while, the spectre of the driver's legs and body splayed across the mangled bonnet, while his head had been effectively minced through the lorry's radiator grille, was an unwelcome, terrible distraction as Jake and the paramedics reached in and supported the two survivors as best they could until they were cut from the car.

The road was closed for six hours. When the traffic officer dealing with it finally thought he'd got enough from the scene, both vehicles were hauled away and Jake reopened the road, having swept as much debris as he could into the gutter with a stiff brush.

It was only then he realized he hadn't eaten or drunk anything since breakfast.

Wearily, he climbed back into his Land Rover and informed the control room he had resumed mobile.

He felt numb as he drove towards Kendleton, continually running through the day's images in his mind: the accident and the way in which the emergency services had dealt brilliantly with the traumatic incident. There was a smidgen of pride in him and he was glad to have been a small part of the response . . . Then he thought, *Oh shit, Henry Christie.*

'Just driving into Kendleton,' Henry said, using the hands-free connection in his car to answer Jake's call.

'Early dart?' Jake teased him.

'Something like that.'

'I'm not far behind. Catch up with you at Th'Owl?'

'Roger, dodger.' Henry hung up and enjoyed the last couple of miles behind the wheel as he descended into the village, getting *that* view of The Tawny Owl on the other side of the village green.

Home now, and he couldn't envisage living anywhere else. He loved the peace and the setting and the people, mostly, and was desperately looking forward to a time when the pandemic had ebbed, the vaccine rolled out and everyone had been jabbed, and he could return to being mine host again.

Once more the deer were grazing on the green, but there was no sign of their macho leader who was generally shyer than the ladies he 'looked after'.

Henry smiled at the sight but knew that once normal life resumed, the deer would move back to their more traditional grazing lands on the high moors and rarely be spotted in the village. That would be a shame, but inevitable as the human race got back into gear again.

He pulled into the car park, got out and waited for Jake to arrive, which he did a short time later.

Henry watched as his friend eased himself wearily out of the battered Land Rover that he now cherished so much and saw the bloodstains on his reflective jacket.

Henry knew about the fatal accident and that Jake had been to it. He also knew, though not well, the people involved. The lorry driver was a regular at The Tawny Owl and the young lad who'd been killed and his girlfriend had just started coming to the pub before lockdown stopped everything.

'You OK, Jake?'

'Well, y'know . . . you just get on with it, don't you?'

'Suppose.' Henry shrugged, knowing there had been times in his career when getting on with it had been difficult, when the compartmentalization in his brain had come crashing down. 'Talk if you want,' he offered.

'Cheers,' Jake said, his manhood unoffended. The days of hiding emotions and feelings were long gone in the police.

'Looks like you need to freshen up.'

'A shower, a big, unhealthy tea and a hug from my missus and kids are on the agenda,' he said, 'and' – he looked down at his yellow jacket – 'a new one of these.' He smiled. 'Anyway . . . back to you.'

'Me, as in the first casualty you might have had this morning if I'd been driven off the road?'

'Yep.' Jake reached back into his car and grabbed a crumpled piece of paper which he unfolded. 'I stopped the vehicles that almost ran you off the road and had a chat.'

'Oh, nice.'

'But while I was dealing with them, I got the call to the fatal. Anyhow, the big, eff-off Bentley was being driven by a guy called Maximillian Alexander Janus – one tough-looking dude, I might add . . . had a whiff of ex-soldier about him. But he wasn't the owner. The owner was in the front passenger seat, a fella called Albert Gorst, and the car's registered to Gorst's Funeral Services in Blackpool. I checked it on PNC – no markers,' he concluded, meaning the car wasn't registered as being of interest to the police.

'Oh,' Henry said, taken aback, remembering he didn't get a decent look at the passenger, just the driver.

'Mean something?' Jake had picked up on the inflection in that short word.

'Yep – me and Debs locked him up day before yesterday.'

'Really? Sparrow Hawk?'

'One of many names emerging from the woodpile,' Henry said. 'What was he doing around here?'

'Going to Simpson Hall, which he owns, apparently.'

Henry scratched his head rather like Stan Laurel. 'I didn't know that.'

'Nor me, but why would we?'

'Why was he going there? It's shut up, isn't it? COVID and all that.'

'He said he was checking up on the place, repairs, maintenance . . . He said the guys in the Range Rover behind him were his workmen. There was a woman in the back of the Bentley who looked half-bladdered. I think she was Gorst's wife.'

Henry frowned, thinking about Simpson Hall, the second time in two days he'd heard it mentioned, the first time being the tradesman guy the day before, asking for directions.

Jake pulled out his mobile phone. 'I took photos of the drivers of both vehicles and the registration plates. Here.' He handed the phone to Henry. 'Just swipe through until you get to the photos of my wife in the shower, then you know you've gone too far.'

Henry eyed him.

'Just kidding.'

'Damn!'

He slid his forefinger across the screen, nodding as he looked at the photos Jake had taken, recognizing Gorst in the passenger seat of the Bentley, and also the wife whom Jake had managed to snap, too. She'd been present when Henry and Blackstone had 'invited' Gorst for a chat at the cop shop. Henry didn't recognize the driver or the men in the following car.

'He was very eager to get out of our mitts yesterday,' Henry said. 'His brief told Debbie he had an important business meeting to attend today.' He screwed up his nose. 'At Simpson Hall? In shutdown premises? Can you send these to me?' He handed the phone back to Jake. 'I take it you haven't managed to track down and arrest the person who bopped me on the head?'

'Well, y'know, been a tad busy.'

'Too busy to help an old mate?'

'Y'know – dead people and all that. They are so time-consuming.'

'Fair dos.'

Jake said goodbye and got back into the Land Rover, needing to get back to the comfort of home. Henry gave him a quick wave, then called Blackstone who, it seemed, was out for a run. She frequently ran around Preston Docks to keep fit.

Before she answered, Henry heard the breathlessness and the pounding of feet. Then, 'What?'

He told her what he'd just learned, and she was intrigued.

'Is the place worth a nose around?' she asked, referring to Simpson Hall.

'Well, I'm certainly curious.'

'Go look, then. You don't need my permission, old fella.'
'I might just.'
They ended the call, and Henry weighed up whether or not to jump into his car and do just that: see what was happening at Simpson Hall.

As it transpired, what was happening at Simpson Hall came to him, and less than a minute later he was looking down the barrel of a snub-nosed revolver.

Max Janus had been shot before. Once, while he had been in Helmand Province, Afghanistan.

A Taliban sniper had put a round into his thigh. At the time, Janus thought the guy was trying to shoot his cock off, but he later learned that his aim had been put off because an SAS squad had just stepped on to the rooftop on which he'd been secreted for the past four days and interrupted his concentration. And then interrupted his life.

So he knew what it was like to take a bullet.

In the Middle East it had been brutal, painful in the extreme, and now here in north Lancashire it was just the same: somehow initially numbing as the body's endorphins reacted to quell the agony, then, very quickly, horrifically painful as that battle was lost because the body needed help, preferably in the form of morphine.

That's what he got in Afghanistan, but here, hiding in the shrubbery of a garden in the more verdant countryside of north-west England, there was no medic on hand to jab that phial of blissful relief into his body.

He stayed hidden, riding the waves of pain and nausea for about five minutes, thinking he would pass out. But didn't. He knew he had to move or there was every chance he would bleed to death, even though his wounds, with treatment, were probably not life-threatening.

He crawled slowly back through the bushes towards the house, hid behind a large rhododendron and looked up the steps of the terrace where he could see the sprawled bodies of his two men.

'What a piece of work,' Janus said, feeling some admiration for the ruthless efficiency of Sofia Bashkim, not only in the way she had taken out Gorst's protection detail but also in the pre-planning. It didn't take an idiot to work out that she and Viktor would have been frisked for weapons on arrival, so somehow she had managed to get weapons secreted in the toilets beforehand.

'Fuck her,' Janus then added, furious with himself for letting it all happen. He should have been more thorough, second-guessed everything, but he hadn't. Now he had to survive, but also check on his boss, who he assumed was as dead as the rest of the guys. And Melanie Gorst . . . *Had Sofia taken her out, too?* he wondered.

Or was she lucky enough to be in an alcoholic stupor up in her bedroom, blissfully unaware of the carnage enacted one floor below? If that was the case, she was in for a shock when she sobered up.

Nothing moved.

Every chance father and daughter had fled.

Sofia probably didn't have the time or inclination to see if he, Janus, had taken a fatal bullet. The main objective would have been to put Gorst down and make the point: the Bashkims were in charge and no one had the right to say otherwise or try to muscle them out.

Still no movement.

Janus rose higher to get a better angle and could almost see into the conference room through the shattered glass of the French windows. But not quite, so he went back to a crawl and dragged himself painfully to the foot of the steps and started to move up them one at a time until his face was level with the head of one of his men, the guy's features contorted grotesquely in a death mask. Janus could now see into the room and could also see Gorst's body lying on the floor next to the table, drenched in blood.

He looked very dead.

Janus seethed. He had been Gorst's bodyguard for three years and been well treated by him. Gorst even respected him, which was saying something. Mostly, Janus despised the people who employed him – including the Queen – but the relationship with Gorst had at least been amicable.

Janus rose unsteadily to his feet, picking up the revolver that had come out of his grasp when he'd been shot, and carefully approached the windows, ready to be ambushed and realistic enough to know if that did happen, he would be unlikely to survive.

He stepped over the other guard and went into the room where he looked at Gorst's body, immediately realizing he had been stabbed, not shot.

Janus assumed this was Viktor's doing, and unless he had used a piece of cutlery, the old man had somehow sneaked a blade in. Even then, Janus knew how – the walking stick!

'Bastards!' he hissed.

Then Gorst gasped, 'Max.'

Bennett had been dealing with a double death earlier that day, and as much as he would have preferred to be within closer proximity to whatever action was to take place, a seven-year-old girl in bits over the sudden, unexplained and concurrent demise of her two hamsters was not something even he could easily walk away from.

He had quickly built a joint casket for the two little mites, fashioned from a shoebox, obviously, but painted up professionally to look like wood and inlaid with a cushioned lining that looked like silk but was in fact cheap cotton.

The two little fellas looked ever so peaceful in those precious moments before their remains were cremated into ash.

The distraught little girl, accompanied by her mother (her of the rolling eyes who clearly did not share her daughter's grief), carried the casket in on the palms of her hands, tears streaming down her pretty little face.

Bennett's heart was almost bursting as he performed a dignified service for Cheech and Chong (as he had named them; they were actually Ant and Dec), the two little guys who had brought so much pleasure to little Lisa over the past year and died simultaneously in what looked suspiciously like a hamster suicide pact. Bennett gave his best hamster eulogy, talking about short, full lives, cheekiness and love.

All bollocks, he knew, but it paid the rent.

As the conveyor started to move to the strains of a song from *Frozen* and the purple curtains slowly closed, Lisa ran up to the casket to place one more sloppy kiss on the lid before, she was led to believe, it finally disappeared into the hidden flames of a furnace behind the screens that would consume their tiny bodies within seconds.

Money for old rope, Bennett thought as he held out his wireless card reader for Lisa's mum to insert her debit card which would instantly take £300 from her current account.

Bennett watched them drive away in a fancy car which must have cost a small fortune, and he decided that when he revisited that particular bank account under another name in a few weeks' time he would help himself to oodles of money.

Then he went back into the crematorium and picked up the shoebox casket from the back of the conveyor belt. He had decided not to waste money by lighting the burners but would simply do the cremation on a little garden waste fire he intended to light later that week. It was pointless going to the actual expense of a cremation just for two fucking hamsters, he thought.

As he strolled across to the garage and workroom with the box tucked under his arm, he got the phone call from Sofia. He flung the casket down, rushed to his van and was on his way within minutes.

Janus could hardly believe it as he knelt down next to his boss.

'Max,' Gorst hissed again.

His boss was alive.

'Stabbed me,' Gorst spluttered with a mixture of blood and saliva flecks. 'Gutted me.'

He was drenched in his own blood. Janus lay down his revolver and slowly eased up Gorst's saturated shirt to inspect the dreadful wound just below the ribcage, the lips of which oozed a continual, pulsing flow of bright red blood.

'Old man,' Gorst said. He tried to focus his eyes on Janus. 'You've been shot by the bitch,' he said.

'Yeah. I'm OK, though.'

'Others? The others?' Gorst asked weakly. 'I heard a fucking machine gun or something.'

'All our guys are dead,' Janus said bleakly.

'Jeez . . . what about Melanie? Go check, see if she's OK, will yuh?'

'I don't know about her yet, but look, Albert, you've lost a ton of blood. I need to get you to a hospital.'

As he was speaking, Gorst's eyelids fluttered and closed, and for a moment he thought he was gone, but the harsh breathing continued . . . just.

He snatched a handful of napkins from the table and pressed them gently over the wound, applying firm pressure to try to stem the flow. They were almost immediately saturated.

Janus gritted his teeth.

Gorst's eyes opened again. 'Find Melanie.'

'Only if you hold on to this.'

Gorst moved his hand on to the napkins as Janus took his away.

'Be back in a minute . . . don't go anywhere.'

He picked up his gun, then dragged himself to his feet and staggered to the door where his instinct for self-preservation kicked in. He paused, made himself stand upright and opened the door an inch at a time, expecting a volley of bullets to batter into him.

None came.

He sidestepped into the corridor and saw a mirror image of the carnage on the rear terrace. Here the bodies of his other two men were splayed out in their own blood and, he was pretty sure, dead.

'Oh no,' he said between his clenched teeth as he saw Melanie's body, too.

He stumbled across to her and knelt down, feeling for a pulse in her neck. There was nothing. She was just another body in the massacre, just a piece of collateral damage.

Rising to his feet, the agony of his own wounds still coursing through him, he went back to Gorst to find that, somehow, his boss had found the strength to sit upright with his back against the wall, still clutching the napkins to his gut.

'We got to get you to a hospital, Bert. I'm going to get the Bentley and bring it closer to the front steps, and one way or another I'm going to get you into it, OK?'

'Melanie?' Gorst asked.

Janus shook his head.

Janus found a first-aid kit in the office behind the reception desk in the foyer. He ran back to his boss, then pulled his hands away from the napkins he was holding over his wound, wincing as he saw the blood start to flow again from deep within the torso. He replaced the napkins with a wound dressing from the kit over which he tried to plaster a gauze pad.

Gorst started to shiver. 'Cold . . . this hurts,' he said.

'Bet it does . . . but this is going to hurt a damn sight more, boss. We're going to the car and you've got to move, OK?'

Gorst swallowed and nodded.

'I'll help you to your feet, and once you're up, we'll try and do it in one, OK?'

Gorst grunted.

It felt like the slowest journey Janus had ever undertaken, even though it was maybe thirty-five metres at most, but finally he managed to heave Gorst into the front passenger seat of the Bentley and strap him in. Gorst insisted that Janus put Melanie in the car, too. He would not contemplate leaving her behind.

'She's a bitch, I know,' he quipped at one point, grinning with blood-smeared teeth, 'but she's my bitch.'

'OK, OK.' Janus reached into the glove compartment and found a blister pack of paracetamol. He flipped two out, opened Gorst's mouth and tipped them in, then held a bottle of water to his lips and made him swallow.

'Better than nothing,' Janus said, glancing down at the wound dressing which was now neither use nor ornament. There was an emergency blanket in the first-aid kit which he laid around Gorst's shoulders, then, after necking two paracetamols himself, he went back to claim Melanie's bullet-riddled body.

Bennett had been – still was – furious with himself for having to stop and ask for directions from the guy outside the pub. It rankled him. A guy who had then inadvertently captured his van on the phone while taking a video of deer ambling through the village. That was why he'd felt the need to revisit him later, bop him on the head and steal the phone.

Bennett liked to travel incognito, in vehicles that didn't draw attention to themselves, such as tradesmen's vans, and while there was every chance nothing would come of the video, he wasn't willing to take the risk.

That was why, just on the off-chance his van was spotted travelling through Kendleton again, he decided to get to Simpson Hall via a more circuitous route this time, coming at it from the opposite direction, avoiding Kendleton.

Setting off from the pet cemetery, the journey took him about five minutes longer than if he'd gone through Kendleton, but it also meant that – although he would never know it – he missed bumping into a Bentley SUV driving away at speed from the hall by about three minutes.

The Bentayga surged through the gates of Simpson Hall and accelerated towards Kendleton.

It was Max Janus's intention to get his boss to the A & E unit at Royal Lancaster Infirmary which, if he pushed the super-fast vehicle, he reckoned he could get to with fifteen minutes of reckless driving.

His plan was to simply abandon the car under the ambulance canopy outside the A & E department and leave Gorst there to be discovered by staff.

For himself, he wanted to avoid any interaction with the authorities and hoped he would be able to patch himself up, because now, more than anything, he wanted revenge on Sofia and her daddy.

He glanced at Gorst, strapped in there by the seat belt, his draining blood now covering the beautiful leather upholstery. Then he looked over his shoulder at Melanie whose loose-limbed body lay along the back seat.

Gorst made a gurgling sound. He tried to look at Janus.

'Is she dead?'

'Sorry, mate. Sofia shot her, too.'

'Bitch . . . she never did any harm to anyone. Didn't deserve it.'

'No, you're right. Look, just hang in there, boss.'

'No hospital, Max . . . no hospital.'

'I don't think so. It's not like you just grazed your knee, is it?'

'He must've missed my vital organs.' Gorst looked down. His right hand was holding the dressing that Janus had put in place. He angled it slightly away from his body, then on seeing the mess, clamped it back and said, 'Or not.'

He slumped sideways against the door as pain overwhelmed him.

Janus put his foot down but then he too was engulfed in a wave of agony and nausea and his vision misted over. The sickening swerve of the car jerked him back to a kind of wakefulness and he narrowly avoided pitching the car into a drainage ditch.

It was at that moment he realized this journey might just end in disaster all around. He was getting groggy and uncoordinated as a result of his own wounds. They might be nowhere near as bad as Gorst's, but even so he could feel a worrying rising tingle in his legs and the strength seemed to be leaving them with each passing second. And then he had to shake his head to restore his vision.

No. This was not going to end well.

The car entered the main street of Kendleton.

TWELVE

Because COVID lockdowns had made the village so quiet, it was unusual to hear even the sound of a car engine, let alone the screech of tyres, so hearing both made Henry Christie pause just as he was going to get into his car and back out into the main road with the intention of, as he'd described it to Blackstone, 'doing a low fly past' of Simpson Hall.

He stopped and leaned on his car roof, frowning as he gazed towards the village.

And then the big car came into view, going far too quickly, like a tank on speed.

Henry recognized it instantly. There were very few of these cars on the road and they were immediately identifiable because of their bulk.

And, of course, he had come face-to-face with it earlier that day when it had almost barged him off the road. As Henry's cop instinct came to life (it had never really left him), he thought, 'I'm going to have words with you, pal' – and not just for this morning's little incident, but because the car was now hurtling dangerously through a lovely sedate village that Henry bloody well liked.

He slammed his car door shut and ran to the car park entrance, still with Ginny's phone in his hand, and waved the car down to stop, waggling his finger at it, already thinking about the occupants and how glad he would be to connect with Albert Gorst again and find out what he had been doing at Simpson Hall that was so important. He was already thinking that the business meeting Gorst had used as part of his excuse to get released from custody was a lie, and that there would be some good mileage in teasing Hortense Thorogood about it when they next came face-to-face.

That said, if he was honest, he expected the Bentley to zoom past him and send him spinning, not least because he didn't have any legal power to pull the vehicle over, first because he wasn't a cop and second because he wasn't a cop in uniform.

He was surprised when the car slewed towards him, braked hard and came to a suspension-rocking halt just feet away.

Henry saw two people on board.

One would probably be the driver that Jake Niven spoke to earlier that day, Henry guessed; the other, the front-seat passenger would be Albert Gorst and, possibly, if Jake had been correct in his assumption, Mrs Gorst would be slouched in the back, drunk.

He walked up to it.

The passenger side was closest to him and Albert Gorst was in the front with his head tilted forwards, as if asleep or drunk.

The driver's door opened and a man Henry did not know but assumed was the Max Janus character Jake had mentioned swung himself out on to the road. He seemed to lose his balance momentarily, right himself and come quickly around the front of the Bentley, having to put a hand on the bonnet to keep steady, a hand Henry noticed was covered in blood, leaving a smear across the paintwork.

Henry's face dropped.

And then he saw the gun which was aimed at him – a small revolver – and the man, Janus, was thumbing back the trigger.

Henry backed off, bumping into his own car.

'You! Fucker! Ditch the phone, get in behind the wheel and drive.'

Stunned by the unreality, Henry did not react.

Janus staggered towards him and jammed the gun into his face while keeping himself upright by using the roof of Henry's car for support.

'Throw the phone, get in the car and drive,' he screamed rabidly into Henry's face.

He grabbed Henry's jacket and dragged him around, jabbing the muzzle into the back of his head, frogmarched him around the front of the Bentley and hustled him into the driver's seat, which was the moment when Henry got a proper look at Gorst as Janus climbed into the back, having to rearrange Melanie Gorst's thin legs so he could fit in behind Henry and hold the gun to Henry's side.

'What the . . . Jesus!' Henry said on seeing Gorst's condition, then looking over his shoulder to see a very dead Melanie Gorst.

'Just drive,' Janus said wearily, 'or I will blow a hole in you, too, man.'

'Then I wouldn't be able to drive,' Henry said reasonably.

'And I won't be any worse off than I am now,' Janus said and rammed him again with the gun. 'But you'll be dead, so just do it: get us to a hospital.'

Henry blew out his cheeks. 'Bit late for her.' He jerked his head backwards. 'And probably for him, too.'

At which, Gorst raised his head and looked through half-closed eyes at Henry. 'Not dead yet.'

Henry wasn't sure if Gorst recognized him or not. Unlikely.

'I've never driven one of these before,' he complained. The car looked and felt huge and ungainly.

'Just press go,' Janus said.

Henry put his foot on the accelerator, the car leapt forwards and Melanie Gorst's body rolled off the back seat with a thump.

Bennett was whistling as he drove up the gravel driveway to Simpson Hall and did a quick, fancy half-doughnut with his van when he reached the turning area in front of the property, putting up a satisfying spray of stones across the Range Rover parked there.

Still whistling tunelessly, he got out and opened the sliding side door, reached in and took out a forensic suit with over-boots, a tight-fitting cap and a surgical face mask, all of which he pulled on over his clothes. Then he trotted up the steps to the front doors where he immediately stopped and took a moment to fully understand what he was seeing: a trail of blood across the terrace and down the steps, indicating that someone, badly injured and bleeding, had been dragged or assisted across.

He arched his eyebrows. 'Unexpected,' he muttered, reading the scene.

Backtracking to the top of the steps, he saw the trail of blood was visible across the gravel, but then stopped suddenly.

'A story unfolds,' he commented, imagining things in his head, working it out. 'And a story someone I know will not be happy with.'

He walked back and entered the foyer, noticing the first-aid kit open on the reception desk, its contents tipped out and depleted.

The next obvious thing to him was a whole lot of blood on the tiled floor close to the foot of the stairs, but with no body to accompany it and with trail marks in the blood indicating someone had been dragged towards the exit.

He took it in, looking at the bodies of the two men in the foyer, still working it all out, applying it to the scenario described by Sofia over the phone, then turned into the corridor leading to the toilets, noticing flecked blood on a door frame, a shoulder-height splatter, plus bullet holes ripped into the door frame and surrounding wall.

He walked past this and into the ladies' toilet where he found the bodies of two men, shot to death, the reek of cordite in the air.

He nodded: they were there as expected.

Backing out carefully, avoiding stepping in any of the blood, he walked back to the conference room, pushing open the door and stepping in just beyond the threshold where he stopped, letting his eyes rove, seeing the shattered French windows and the two bodies on the rear terrace.

Again, expected.

However, what was directly in front of him was not.

On the left side of the conference table was blood on the tabletop and the carpet, plus a trail of blood out into the foyer, out of the front door. But no body.

He backtracked again and followed this trail which took him out across the front terrace, down the steps and to the point where it mingled with the other blood trail he had just followed from the foot of the steps in the foyer.

'Another compelling story,' he remarked to himself.

He went back into the foyer, walked through the conference room and checked the bodies of the men on the back terrace before returning inside and once more assessing the blood patterns, reading them.

He shrugged. It was what it was.

He went back out and looked at the dead men on the rear terrace, picked up the legs of the lightest-looking one so they were tucked under his armpits and dragged him through the conference room, out across the foyer, through the front doors, down the front steps – the back of the man's head cracking on each step as it bounced down – and to his van, heaving him into the back of it. Then he went back for body number two.

As he walked through the premises, he made a phone call.

'It's the Tradesman,' he announced, putting on his broadest northern accent for fun. 'Got an update, lass.'

'Speak.' Sofia's voice was brittle.

'You told me to expect nine parcels, but I'm disappointed to report there are only six of the rascals and they seem, at first glance, to be the less important ones, if you get my drift?' By this time, he was dragging the second body in from the terrace and speaking via Bluetooth.

'I'm sure nine were delivered.'

'In that case, someone has some stolen property in their possession. Are you certain there were nine?'

Bennett sensed hesitation.

'Well, definitely eight . . . but I was certain there would be nine . . . have you checked the grounds? One may have been delivered there.'

'I'll look.'

'Get back to me.'

He dropped the dead man's legs with a thud, returned to the grounds behind the hall for a quick search but found no trace of a further body, although he did discover another trail of blood from someone who had exited the rear of the hall through a fire-exit door which was ajar.

He followed the route back through this open door, across a bar area and to the door in the corridor where the toilets were located, the one on which he had earlier seen blood and bullet holes.

He went back to continue dragging the body out to his van, making a second call as he did.

'No parcel,' he said.

A tense silence. 'So what are you saying?'

'Six parcels remain here. Three are missing. I notice that the first-aid kit has been opened. This could mean that although the parcels may have been damaged, they are still useable, if you see what I mean?'

To be honest, he hated this cryptic shit but played the game because the money was good: for preparing the ground by leaving the guns in the toilets – and something else – and for this clean-up, he had been paid thirty thousand euros into a Spanish bank account.

'I do see what you mean. Any vehicles?'

'One.'

More silence.

'So?' Bennett said. He was breathing a bit heavily now from his body-dragging exertions.

'Complete your task there, as per instructions.'

'Will do.'

'Then make arrangements to track and dispose of the missing parcels, please.'

'OK. Should I invoice you and, if so, for how much?'

'Same again, plus a ten-per-cent bonus on completion.'

'Agreed.'

He ended the call and went to retrieve the remaining bodies.

He collected the weapons that had been used to create the carnage at the hall; they had been left, as per instructions, in the cloakroom by the front entrance. That was useful for Bennett's purposes because he had set off that day armed only with a Glock pistol loaded with nine rounds. The Skorpion and Makarov would come in handy for his next task because still in the hidden recess in the van floor were two extra magazines for each weapon.

And he was going to need them, he thought, because as cryptic as his orders had been, they were simple, really: hunt down and execute those who were still alive.

Having had a further cryptic conversation with Sofia with regard to the wounds these people might have sustained, one thing he knew for sure was they would need urgent medical treatment. The A & E department at Royal Lancaster Infirmary would be a very good place for him to begin his hunt, and if luck would have it, end it there, too.

But before that he had a few more things to do at Simpson Hall.

Besides hiding the guns in the toilet on his first visit to the hall while 'bleeding the radiators', as he told Goatee (who, he was pleased to see, was among the dead), he had secreted a dozen small, wirelessly activated incendiary devices in various locations around the building, including the kitchen, behind the ovens. First, though, he made his way up to the first floor where he'd hidden four of these mini-bombs in four separate bedrooms. With him on this journey, he carried two cans of petrol which he splashed around the rooms and along the corridors. Back in the kitchen he dismantled and broke two burners on the cooker hob so that when he turned on the gas, which he did next, it flowed without automatically igniting.

Then he sloshed more petrol around, including all through the conference room (in which he had also hidden two incendiary devices) and the ladies' toilets where Sofia had begun her killing spree.

When all this was done, he returned to his van and placed the Skorpion and Makarov in the passenger footwell after reloading them, then covered them with a travel blanket. Still dressed in his forensic suit, now smeared with the blood of the six bodies in the back of the van, he drove to the front gates and stopped to close them. When he got back in the van, he paused a second or two for a quick mental recap.

Bodies collected, tick.

Incendiary devices, tick.

Gas hissing away, tick.

Accelerant deployed, tick.

Very, very big explosion followed by a raging inferno, tick.

Simpson Hall gutted and destroyed, tick.

He reached across to the glovebox and rooted out the wireless remote control which was no bigger than a key fob. As he drove away, he pressed the button, secure in the knowledge that very soon indeed Simpson Hall would be engulfed in a fireball.

He had no need to stay and witness his handiwork.

THIRTEEN

Henry adjusted the rear-view mirror and angled it so he could look at Janus.

'You know he'll be dead way before we get to Lancaster,' he said.

'Just drive and let me worry about that.'

Henry's eyes flicked to Gorst, who had slumped forwards again, chin on chest.

'Might even be dead now,' he commented.

'Still here,' Gorst mumbled. Obviously, his hearing was fine.

'Who stabbed you?' Henry asked.

'Look, shut it, just get us to A and E, eh?' Janus growled, jabbing Henry with the gun again.

Henry threw the big car around the next curve and in a parallel chain of thought was impressed by the vehicle which reminded him of a Thwaites Brewery horse with the undercarriage of a Grand National winner.

'Bastard! Old man did me.' Gorst spluttered blood down his front.

Henry guessed he was starting to lose it now, in those awful moments before death overwhelmed him.

He checked the mirror.

Janus had removed his jacket and was trying to inspect his own wounds.

'And who shot you?' Henry inquired, recognizing gunshot wounds when he saw them.

Janus raised his bloodshot eyes, which locked with Henry's in the reflection. He was clearly in agony but fighting it, and while Henry may have been under threat here, his cop instinct had kicked in again and he was curious to get to the bottom of this situation into which he'd suddenly been thrust. He also wanted to save lives if possible, including his own, which at that moment seemed to hang in the balance. Mrs Gorst, though, was obviously a lost cause.

'What were you doing at Simpson Hall? I assume that was the location of your urgent meeting?' he asked, aiming the question at Gorst.

The look in Janus's eyes changed to one of confusion. 'How the hell did you know that?'

Henry shrugged. 'We almost met this morning.'

'You're the guy in the Audi, the one who almost forced us off the road!' Janus blurted, now understanding.

'That's a matter of perspective.'

'You reported us. That cop pulled us because of you.'

'Correct.' Henry threw the big car around another tight bend. 'Where are your four mates in the Range Rover?'

'Dead!' Gorst exclaimed. 'Bitch killed 'em. And the old bastard, Bashkim . . . he shivved me.' He coughed up more blood.

'Keep quiet, boss,' Janus warned him. 'This guy doesn't need to know anything. All he has to do is get us to hospital, and if he's good, I won't blow his brains out.' He leaned forwards and tapped

Henry on the side of his head with the gun, just to reinforce his point.

'Who's Bashkim?' Henry asked in all innocence. The name, though slightly familiar, really meant nothing to him.

Janus tapped his head with the gun again. 'Hospital. Drive.'

Gorst coughed up yet more blood, spraying the dashboard.

Janus had been mulling over what Henry had said a few moments earlier, suddenly realizing the significance of one of the remarks. 'How did you know it was an urgent meeting?'

Henry could feel and smell the guy's breath close to his ear. 'We met the other day, me and Mr Gorst.'

'What do you mean?' Then it dawned on him. 'You're a cop. A detective.'

Henry didn't bother taking the time to put him absolutely right on that one, but it was close enough, even though he was neither cop nor detective.

Janus tipped back and said, 'Jeez,' with a shake of his head.

'Small world,' Henry said.

'Perhaps I should shoot you anyway?' Janus suggested and seemed to be about to say more, but in the mirror Henry saw him crease up in agony and the expression on his face betrayed that.

'You need A and E just as much as your boss.'

'Just drive. Get us there, OK? I'll be fine.'

Another sharp bend came up, negotiated at speed as Henry got the feel of the car, the most expensive one he had ever driven, though he guessed that after this episode it might be going for a bargain price unless the bloodstains could be removed.

'What's that?' Janus said suddenly, jerking forwards as a sign on the road whizzed by.

'What's what?'

'What did that sign say?'

'Don't know.'

'Stop . . . back up . . . let me see.'

Henry anchored on, flicked the car into reverse, swerving slightly as he did and also remembering what the sign actually said, having driven past it many times himself over the years.

Gorst groaned at the effect the sudden change of direction had on him and opened his eyes, but then they fluttered closed.

Henry stopped the car by the road sign which read *Kendleton Community Hospital 1 mile.*

'Thought I'd read it right,' Janus said. 'That's where we're going, mate.'

'It's a community hospital,' Henry pointed out. 'They don't do emergency admissions or stuff like that. It's a place where old people go for post-operative care.'

'It's a hospital, isn't it? It'll have doctors and nurses and such, won't it?'

'I guess, but they won't admit you or him. They don't have the facilities.'

'I think they will.' Janus brandished the gun so Henry could see it in the mirror. 'I'll make 'em have facilities.'

Kendleton Community Hospital, built ten years earlier, was a fifteen-bed inpatient facility, which meant it remained operational twenty-four seven. It was managed by district nurses; during the day, medical care was provided by locally based general practitioners, while out-of-hours cover was provided by Royal Lancaster Infirmary when necessary.

Henry was almost correct in that post-operative care was provided, but there was also rehabilitation and palliative care, plus day-clinic rooms for such services as podiatry and physiotherapy.

It rarely seemed to be buzzing with activity, and there were persistent rumours that the KCH would be closed down, although it seemed to stagger on.

Henry drove into the car park which was almost deserted apart from maybe half a dozen cars.

'Up to the front door,' Janus ordered him.

He did as instructed and pulled up within feet of the door.

Janus eased himself painfully out of the car and opened the driver's door, keeping the gun pointed at Henry. He leaned in and said, 'You help him out and get him to the front door, OK? Anything daft and I'll shoot you, cop.'

'OK.' Henry's voice was thick.

Initially, he hadn't had the time to be afraid, just got sucked into the vortex of the situation, but it was getting that way now. He knew he would have to go along with it as it developed for the time being.

He'd assessed Janus, could see he was a strong, fit-looking guy who, under normal circumstances, would probably have been capable of beating Henry to a pulp, but with the weakened shoulder that was obviously slowing him down – and possibly another wound in his back that Henry had spotted – Henry half wondered, if the chance arose, whether he should give overpowering him a shot. He imagined himself repeatedly punching the wound with his fists – but then thought not, not least because that probably wasn't in his armoury. He also believed Janus when he threatened he would use the gun, and Henry had no desire to get shot again.

Janus jerked the weapon in a 'get out' gesture. Henry stepped out and walked around the front to the passenger side, covered by Janus and the gun. He opened the door and looked at Gorst; had it not been for the almost inaudible rasp of his breathing, he would have sworn he was a dead man.

'Albert,' Henry said, 'I'm going to help you to get to the front door of this hospital, OK?'

Gorst grunted, 'We're at a hospital? I said no hospital.'

'Tough,' Janus said over Henry's shoulder. Then to Henry: 'Move him.'

Henry crouched down slightly and flipped Gorst's left arm across his shoulder and slid his own right arm behind Gorst and into his armpit and slowly lifted and manoeuvred him out of the car, easing him on to his feet, at which point Gorst's legs gave way and Henry had to grip him more tightly than he would have liked to keep him upright. The only thing going for Henry was that Gorst was of a fairly slim build, and Henry was a good head taller and broader and hadn't been stabbed.

Finally he had him balanced.

Janus watched, gun ready.

Henry looked at him. 'I think you might have to buzz the door to get in. It's not like the infirmary here; you can't just walk in.'

'Get moving,' Janus said coldly.

Henry took Gorst's weight and began to make towards the door which was about ten metres away across an area of paving. Already, Henry was covered with Gorst's blood as it was impossible to manhandle him without this happening. Henry half supported, half lifted him across the gap, as if assisting a drunk. As the blood-soaked trio reached the door, it opened and a man stepped out and looked at them in shock.

Henry immediately spotted the guy's ID photo badge on a lanyard around his neck, saw the NHS logo in one corner of it and hoped he was a doctor.

The man swooped across to them.

'He's badly hurt,' Henry said, stating the obvious. 'He's been stabbed and needs emergency treatment. The other guy's been shot.' He indicated Janus. 'I'm OK. Are you a doctor?'

'Yes, but you can't bring him in here, there are no facilities . . . he needs to go to A and E at Lancaster.'

Henry held back from giving Janus an 'I told you so' look.

Janus stepped up to the doctor and held the gun in his face. 'You're a doctor, that's good enough for me . . . Now fuckin' take him in and treat him and fix him up or I'll put a bullet in you.'

The doctor backed away, hands up. 'Hey, I can't. No facilities.'

'Why? What sort of bloody doctor are you?'

'I'm a vascular surgeon . . . I'm here visiting one of my patients, post-op.'

'Just the guy we need,' Janus said. 'Now turn around, go back in and sort this now, pal.'

Henry watched Janus's face as he spoke, all twitching muscles and flaring nostrils and tight lips on bloody teeth, signs of desperation and a battle against debilitating injuries that were taking a terrible toll on him physically and mentally.

Henry saw he was a tough cookie but close to breaking point, and it was probably better for all concerned to comply with his wishes.

'Do what he says,' Henry said to the doctor.

The doctor saw no option, nodded and turned back with Henry, Gorst and Janus close behind him. He swiped his ID badge and the door slid open and all four entered the hospital foyer. To the right was an unstaffed reception desk and the whole place seemed eerily deserted.

'Where is everyone?' Henry asked.

'All the day clinics were done this morning and the only people here now are in the upstairs ward; no one down here on the ground floor,' the doctor explained. Then: 'In here.'

He directed them to a consulting room off the corridor just beyond the reception area. They left a trail of dripping blood behind them.

Inside the room was a desk, a couple of chairs and an examination couch.

He said to Henry, 'Turn him around and let's get him on the couch.'

Henry did a slow pirouette and gently sat Gorst on the edge of the couch, propping him there, and then, with the doctor's help and guidance, slowly turned him around, lifted his legs and laid him down.

Gorst groaned in agony as he lay back.

Henry stood aside as the doctor rummaged in a cupboard, pulled on a pair of latex gloves, fitted a new face mask, then took a pair of scissors and got to work cutting open Gorst's shirt like a seamstress, exposing the open knife wound just below the ribcage which was still pumping blood.

'He's lost a lot of blood. How long ago did this happen?' the doctor asked as he reached up to a shelf above the couch and took down a box containing individually packaged sterile swabs. He tore one open and began to clean and wipe away the excess blood around the cut. 'How long?' he asked again.

'Forty minutes . . . dunno,' Janus answered vaguely as he plonked down on one of the chairs.

'It's a wonder he's still alive,' the doctor said, peering at the wound, opening it with his finger and thumb. 'What happened?'

The doctor glared at Henry. 'I wasn't there. I'm here because of bad luck . . . y'know, innocent passer-by kind of thing?'

'Look,' Janus interrupted, 'you don't have to know what happened. He got knifed, I got shot, so just treat him, save his life and then treat me. Isn't that what you're paid to do?'

'I'll tell you now, he's going to need a blood transfusion, and if he doesn't get it, he will die before I or any other doctor can get inside him to see what damage has been done.'

'You must have some blood here,' Janus said.

'We have plasma and saline drips, both of which he will need, too . . . but blood, no, we don't have blood.'

'What blood type is he?' Janus asked, pointing at Gorst.

'I can't tell just by looking,' the doctor said sardonically, making Henry's mouth twitch with a suppressed grin.

Janus looked chillingly at the doctor. 'Can you test it?'

'Why? What are you thinking?'

'Test it, then find someone with the same blood type here – then take their blood and feed it into him.'

The doctor snorted contemptuously. 'Even if that were possible, to take someone's blood – which under these circumstances would be classed as a serious assault . . .'

'Look at me,' Janus snapped. 'Look at him. I think we've moved past caring if we assault somebody or not, don't you think?'

The doctor sighed irritably, making Henry like him even more; clearly, the guy didn't suffer fools or stupid ideas gladly.

'You can't just take blood out of one person, even if it's the right group, and just shove it into another . . . it has to be processed and tested. And not only that, even under normal circumstances a transfusion takes at least two hours.' He had stood away from Gorst as he spoke. 'This man,' he said, pointing at Gorst, 'does not have two hours. He needs to be stabilized, he needs to be in a fucking operating theatre surrounded by a trauma team who will give him the best care possible – and even then I wouldn't lay odds on his survival. But I cannot give him a transfusion.'

'Not good enough.'

It seemed apparent to Henry that Janus was beginning to lose all sense of reason as he raised his gun and pointed it squarely at the doctor's chest and curled his finger around the trigger. Henry went rigid as he saw that the hammer was still cocked; only a tiny amount of pressure on the trigger would fire it.

Quickly Henry said, 'Can you get a drip into him?'

The doctor, who was staring at the gun, said yes.

'Do it, then.' Henry turned to Janus. 'Look, we're wasting valuable time here.' He looked at Gorst, then at Janus. 'Let the doctor get a saline drip into him – quick! Then let's get moving. Let's phone ahead and get a trauma team on standby at RLI to receive him, yeah?' He turned to the doctor. 'You can arrange that, can't you?'

The doctor nodded.

'Then do it.' Looking back at Janus, he said, 'We get him in the back of that Bentley with the doctor treating him and then we go like shit off a shovel to the hospital. In that beast, with a good tailwind, I'll do it in less than ten minutes.' He paused, then said, 'It's his only chance.'

Janus seemed unable to decide what to do for the best. Henry could not even begin to imagine what was swirling through his head. Clarity fogged by craziness, he guessed, all intermingled with pain.

Finally, after what appeared to be some soul searching, Janus lowered the gun and nodded.

Bennett couldn't be completely sure how far behind his newly contracted targets he was, but he guessed at least half an hour, which gave them an advantage in some ways, obviously, but not in others. His main claim to having the upper hand was that he was a skilled hunter in any environment (in his time, he had hunted down and executed insurgents in jungles and terrorists in city centres) and he was supremely confident of catching up with the survivors of the Simpson Hall carnage and dispatching them with his usual ruthless efficiency.

What he really didn't plan for was just how easy it would be. Even so, he didn't even feel the need to put his foot down in the van to make up for lost time.

He already knew his first port of call would be A & E at Royal Lancaster Infirmary. It didn't cross his mind to think that if they had been admitted and were already undergoing treatment, it would prevent him from completing his task, or that cops might be swarming around. Cops rarely bothered him.

This time he journeyed back through the valley from Thornwell towards Kendleton rather than going via the more circuitous route to avoid the latter village. This was the obvious route to RLI; as a hunter, it was always wise to choose the obvious route your prey would take before adopting tactics to ambush them.

He drove into and through Kendleton, emerging on the road that went past The Tawny Owl where he'd asked directions from the bloke out front and later separated him from his mobile phone, since destroyed.

He didn't slow down or stop, just kept up the 'normal' pace of any 'normal' vehicle tootling through a picturesque Lancashire village.

Normal with the exception of having six dead bodies in the back of the van, plus various items of weaponry.

However, he did rubberneck something happening in The Tawny

Owl car park, where three men and a woman were standing clustered around a convertible Audi. The woman was holding a mobile phone in her hand, gesticulating in a concerned way at the three men, one of whom was a cop in uniform next to a police Land Rover.

As Bennett drove past, the cop turned away from the group and said something into his radio, raising his eyes to Bennett's van as he drove past.

Bennett wasn't too concerned. The cop's eyes may have been looking in his direction, but his attention was actually on whatever message he was sending or receiving, rather than on Bennett's unprepossessing, normal van.

But in the glimpse Bennett got of the little scenario, he wondered if there was some connection with his own manhunt.

He drove on, unhurried, unworried.

After having briefed Henry Christie about the Bentley that had almost forced him off the road first thing that day, Jake Niven had returned home to his police house in Kendleton pretty much exhausted by his day of assisting traffic with the fatal accident. It had taken a lot out of him and after passing what information he had to Henry about the Bentley, he scuttled off to the nice warmth of his home.

His wife, Anna, was there; she had been a police officer before marrying Jake but had quit the force when the kids came along and afterwards went back to work doing admin for various businesses. Now in Kendleton, she worked for a number of small firms and was able to do most of this from home during the lockdowns.

Jake's two kids were in their rooms, but he didn't intrude into their online worlds.

All he wanted was a long hot shower, then feet up in front of the TV, so after kissing Anna and getting slightly hot under the collar as a result, he went for that shower.

When Anna tapped on the shower door, Jake was facing the rear of the cubicle, soaping up nicely and when he looked, sexily he thought, over his shoulder to see Anna there, he hoped this might be a continuation of the welcome-home kiss.

That she was fully clothed, holding his mobile phone, told him a different tale.

The lifestyle of a rural cop, he thought. Plans were frequently disrupted.

He opened the shower door a touch. 'Can I help you?'

'You need to take this. It's Ginny.'

'Henry's Ginny?'

'Yep.'

A few moments later, with a bath sheet wrapped around his midriff, he took the phone from Anna. Minutes after that, he was dry, back in uniform and on his way to meet Ginny outside Th'Owl.

'I saw him arrive home and talk to you, yeah?' Ginny was saying to Jake. 'I watched through the bar window . . . then you left and I went back into the kitchens and sort of expected him to be in a few minutes later. When he didn't come, I came back out to check and there was no sign of him . . .'

Henry's 'adopted' stepdaughter – the *actual* stepdaughter of his late fiancée, Alison – was not a person who ever seemed to panic or worry too much. She'd had far too much of that in her very short life, particularly a few years earlier when Alison had died under tragic circumstances and when (even though Henry and Alison were not married) she had asked Henry if she could call him her dad. Since then, she'd felt happy and secure with Henry, even more so when he gave her fifty per cent of the business that was The Tawny Owl which Alison had left Henry in her will.

'Just his phone on the ground – the one I'd given him – and what looks like blood on the roof of his car.' Her voice was dithery.

Jake took in the scene and what Ginny was telling him, trying to get his mind around it and come up with a reasonable explanation – which he couldn't – when a car drew into the car park, stopped and two men got out.

The doctor administered two phials of morphine – one into Janus's thigh through his jeans – and another into Gorst, even though he believed the latter would be of no use whatsoever. Gorst was drifting in and out of consciousness; he had little idea of what was going on around him now and was probably beyond pain, in that twilight, pre-death world.

Working quickly, the doctor inserted a cannula into the vein in Gorst's inner elbow and attached a bag containing saline solution to it, which he gave to Henry and told him to hold it high.

Again, he wasn't sure if it would be of any use.

Then he disinfected the stab wound and redressed it.

'That's all I can do here,' he said to Janus. 'Take him to the hospital now.'

'You're coming, too,' Janus said. The effects of the morphine shot had had an almost instant effect on him. He was back on his feet, buzzing and pain-free for the moment, though still bleeding. 'Let's get him to the car.'

Bennett drove on, now picking up a bit of speed on the rising road away from the village.

Just a few minutes later, he passed the sign for Kendleton Community Hospital, barely registered it and would have gone on if he hadn't happened to glance to his left as he passed the opening to the car park and spot the Bentley.

He slammed on the brakes, swerving to a halt, hearing the multiple thuds in the back as the mass of bodies rolled towards the bulkhead.

'Sorry guys,' he said. He selected reverse and slewed backwards past the entrance, braked hard, hearing the bodies all shift again. 'Oops, sorry again,' he chuckled, then turned into the car park and accelerated across the tarmac, stopping sharply again, just to make the bodies roll about once more, next to the Bentley.

As he stepped out of the van, he pulled the peak of his baseball cap down and refitted his face mask. He peeked into the car and saw the body of a woman wedged between the front and back seats, obviously dead.

'One down, two to go,' he said to himself. 'Thank you, Lord.'

He slung the Skorpion across his chest and, with the Makarov dangling in his hand at his side, he walked swiftly to the door of the hospital, noticing again a trail of blood from the Bentley. As he got to the door, it opened.

The doctor had grabbed a wheelchair from the corridor outside the consultation room and reversed it in, manoeuvring it alongside the examination couch.

Henry watched, standing on Gorst's left side while holding the saline bag aloft. One-handed, he assisted the doctor to sit the patient upright and gently heave him into the wheelchair, where he immediately slumped forward; the doctor had to grab him to sit him upright.

Holding him in place, he nodded for Janus to open the door, through which he pushed the wheelchair into the corridor towards the exit.

The make-up of the line was saline-bag holder Henry on the left, the doctor alongside him pushing Gorst, then Janus on the right.

The door was movement activated from the inside and opened automatically as they approached it.

Bennett's mind worked quickly, making an assessment, making a decision.

First, he took in the whole scenario: wheelchair containing a man being pushed by another man who was clearly a doctor, hence the NHS ID card on his lanyard; then a guy holding up a drip bag to one side, that guy being the one from the pub who, it seemed, had somehow become unwillingly embroiled in this shit-show; then the guy on the other side carrying a revolver.

He easily worked out the one in the wheelchair and the one with the gun were his targets; he didn't know their names, didn't want to, didn't need to. So right now he knew everything he needed – that they were in front of him and he had tracked them down very easily indeed.

So – doctor guy, pub guy – your lucky day.

Another quick assessment in among the tumble of others: who among this crew presented the greatest threat to him?

The one with the gun, which was already coming up in his direction.

All these thoughts intermingled in a flash of dendrites across Bennett's brain.

The Makarov came up and he shot Janus – a double tap into the chest, then an extra one in the head. Fast, precise, deadly shooting.

Before Janus hit the floor, already dead, Bennett shot Gorst as he sat there in the wheelchair, the three bullets in a triangle in his heart.

As Janus fell and Gorst choked his very last breath, Bennett arced the Makarov menacingly between the doctor and Henry (who had dropped the saline bag), both of whom cowered, expecting to be mown down.

Then he turned and sprinted for his van.

*   *   *

Jake recognized the two men who had arrived, but before he could greet them, his PR came to life as the comms operator called his number.

Jake gave the two new arrivals a quick nod and turned away from Ginny to acknowledge the call and listen to what was being said.

'PC Niven – just had a report from a gamekeeper saying that smoke and flames are billowing from Simpson Hall in Thornwell. Are you aware of that location?'

'Yes.'

'In that case, can you attend? Fire service en route.'

'Roger that.'

As he listened to the transmission and spoke himself, he watched a van drive past from the direction of the village, and although he saw it, he wasn't really thinking about it or attaching any importance to it. His attention returned to Ginny, who was talking to the new arrivals, and he thought no more about the vehicle and stepped back into the conversation.

'Guys – good to see you . . . Er, Ginny,' Jake said, 'I think I need to go and check this out – a big fire at Simpson Hall.' He tapped his PR.

'Yeah, yeah, OK.'

'I'll be back as soon as possible . . . but if you don't hear anything from Henry within half an hour, get on to me.'

'I will.'

One of the men cut in, 'Did you say Simpson Hall, Jake?'

'Yep, why? Does that mean something to you?'

'It sure does,' he responded in an American accent. 'That's the reason we're here.'

The other man said, 'Can I jump in with you?'

'Yeah, of course.' Moments later, they were on their way.

Even before they reached the hall, they saw smoke billowing and flames reaching high above the trees. As Jake drew up at the front gates, the whole building was beset by a huge explosion, the force of which rocked the Land Rover on its springs. At the same time, an urgent call came over the radio: '*Patrols . . . report of shots being fired at Kendleton Community Hospital and possibly two fatalities . . . patrols to attend . . . again, shots fired at Kendleton Community Hospital . . . possible fatalities . . . patrols to attend . . .*'

FOURTEEN

Following a very comprehensive swabbing of his skin by a CSI, and having handed over all his clothing for forensic analysis, Henry had a long shower, then stepped out of the owner's accommodation at The Tawny Owl into the main bar area.

He unlocked the bar, raised the shutters and helped himself to a double Jack Daniel's from the optics – doing so because he knew if he poured himself one from his own stock, it would be much more than a double. Then he walked to the bay window where he sat down, his body aching, placed the drink on a table and rubbed his face with still-dithering hands.

There was no doubt that over the course of his life as a cop he had experienced and witnessed many terrible things, probably more than any one person should have done. And as a very proactive murder squad detective, he had seen many brutal deaths and had almost been the victim himself on occasion.

But mostly, and to stay relatively sane (though this assertion might be contested by others), he had been able to do the 'compartmentalization of the grey matter' trick and keep a tight lid on things that included the times when he had been personally in imminent danger of death.

However, he was already wondering if today's incident would be the straw to break the camel's back.

For a start, he knew for certain he had been completely and overwhelmingly terrified when the killer, dressed in an already blood-splattered forensic-type suit, had confronted him, the doctor, Gorst and Janus at the front door of the community hospital.

Somehow it was a different kind of fear to the one he'd experienced when Janus had hijacked him from the car park just before. He could have been misguided, but he'd seen that as a situation he might have been able to talk himself out of, and even though Janus was threatening him with a gun, Henry felt as if he had some degree of control of the outcome – not much, but some. There had been dialogue, and where there was talk, there was hope, as he had found on many occasions in hostage negotiations.

Plus Janus and Gorst needed his help.

They needed medical treatment and he, unwittingly and unwillingly, was their conduit to it, even though there was nothing he could have done for Mrs Gorst, already dead in the back of the Bentley.

But when facing the assassin at the door, there had been no negotiation, no dialogue, no connection. The fear he had felt was different. It was the most basic fear imaginable: the fear of imminent death.

This man, this terrifying spectre, had come solely to murder, and unlike in films where the killer usually has some sort of 'chat' with the intended victim, there was no such luxury here in real life.

The only relief had been that the man was a paid killer, getting a job done, and Henry and the doctor hadn't been on his hit list.

That said, he could easily have killed all four of them. It probably wouldn't have made any difference to him, but that wasn't what he was being paid for.

So Henry and the doctor were still alive and the terror lived on in Henry. The terror of how close he had personally been to death and that the two people he'd been trying to save had been gunned down coldly and mercilessly in front of him.

He reached for the Jack Daniel's. His hand was unsteady. He took a sip, trying to avoid the temptation to neck every drop which would have been very easy to do. Followed by another, and another.

Instead, he placed the glass back down and looked at the police activity in the front car park of the pub.

A mobile incident unit had been brought in, occupying a very large proportion of the space, and numerous police vehicles of all sizes and descriptions were parked haphazardly around it and on the road, plus countless cops who seemed to have appeared from nowhere and were like busy ants, coming and going, all carrying files and looking very important with their tasks.

Henry watched dispassionately, wondering if he should feel more like being part of this sudden thing that had happened, which was all now being pieced together by the Force Major Investigation Team, led by Detective Superintendent Rik Dean.

He sipped more of the Jack Daniel's. Tasted good, had a nice effect.

Truth was today's experience had numbed him – but he did shoot upright when he spotted a car hurtling across the bridge towards the pub. It slithered to a halt and the occupant jumped out and raced to the front door.

Henry stood up, but even before he managed to get to the door, Diane Daniels had burst through and they had thrown themselves into each other's arms.

'Henry, oh God, Henry,' she sobbed.

He closed his eyes and clung on tightly, feeling some of the tension drain out of him.

'I'm still here,' he said, stroking her hair, but then he exhaled a long, unsteady breath.

'I couldn't get here fast enough,' she said.

'I couldn't wait for you to get here.'

They had been in constant contact and she had dropped everything she had been doing and raced back just to hold him.

Finally, they drew apart and looked each other over.

'You didn't have to, though. I'm OK.'

'Yes, I did,' she said firmly.

'And I'm glad you did. I needed that hug more than anything . . .' And with that they fell into each other's embrace again until they were rudely interrupted.

'Jeez, you guys, get a room, will ya?'

Henry kept hold of a giggling Diane and looked over her shoulder at the next person to enter the pub, Debbie Blackstone; behind her was Rik Dean and, behind him, a cluster of individuals including Karl Donaldson and Steve Flynn.

'Hey, old guy,' Blackstone went on remorselessly and over the top as usual, 'do you make a habit of getting kidnapped off the street?'

'What have we got, then?'

It was almost midnight. The question had been posed by Detective Superintendent Rik Dean, Henry's brother-in-law and the man who had stepped into Henry's shoes when he had retired in less-than-glowing circumstances a few years earlier. Henry didn't blame him for either. Rik was in love with Henry's sister and he would have been a fool to turn down the job offer. That said, the latter move did leave a sour taste in Henry's mouth, even though he thought of Rik as a good mate and former colleague fully deserving of the position. In fact, it had been Henry who'd been instrumental in getting Rik on to the CID in the first place all those years ago, but Rik's subsequent promotions were all his own doing.

So Rik was a good detective and, as Henry was often at pains to point out, he'd had a bloody good mentor.

After posing the question, Rik looked expectantly at the people assembled in front of him.

Those people were Henry Christie, Diane Daniels, Debbie Blackstone, Steve Flynn and Karl Donaldson.

'Right, I'll tell you what we've got,' Rik said. 'We have three people shot to death and currently lying in the public mortuary at RLI with an armed guard, just in case the offenders get twitchy and start worrying about forensics. Post-mortems cannot be carried out until tomorrow, first one booked for ten a.m.

'We also have a huge fire and explosion at Simpson Hall, the first indications being that they were caused by incendiary devices placed in various locations throughout the building, plus accelerants, plus the gas being deliberately turned on in the kitchen.' Rik finished with: 'The bodies and the fire-slash-explosion are connected.'

He was standing in front of a flipchart easel on which he had written *Simpson Hall* across the top and also the names of the three murder victims, Albert and Melanie Gorst and Max Janus.

Looking at him, Henry was reminded of an Agatha Christie-type detective as he scribbled stuff on a board in front of a selected audience.

Henry waited patiently, watching a great detective at work. He crossed his legs and reached across to Diane to hold her hand, getting a scowl from Rik as, clearly, such behaviour was frowned upon in a work environment. Henry gave him a smile, but Diane pulled her hand free from Henry's.

Henry had offered the function room of The Tawny Owl for use as an incident room, even though the mobile unit had arrived. The first-floor room could be used for officers and staff engaged in enquiries in the area to meet up and get some shelter as much as anything, and Th'Owl would provide hot drinks and some sustenance. Henry knew a lot of people would be busy for days to come both at the community hospital and Simpson Hall, and somewhere local to crash out, share intel and chill would be welcome, though the main investigation would be run from Lancaster Police Station.

Rik had gladly taken up the offer, which made sense and cost the cops nothing, always a consideration.

This 'get together' currently taking place in the bar was really just an unofficial bout of spitballing on the hoof while Rik tried to get his head around the enormity of the task ahead and how he would tackle his first 'real' briefing of almost one hundred personnel at eight a.m. the next morning, which would include all specialists from HQ and support from surrounding divisions.

He was going to have a long, sleepless night and, for a moment, Henry was a teensy bit jealous . . . but only for a moment.

'So, Henry, what about Albert Gorst?' Rik asked.

All heads swivelled to Henry. Blackstone gave him a wink, although Henry had noticed that she was having problems keeping her eyes off Steve Flynn.

Just to keep her on track, Henry said, 'I think Debs should take that one, Rik.'

She shot him a mean look, glanced once more at Flynn, then cleared her throat. 'Well, boss, you know me and Henry have been involved in Operation Sparrow Hawk for the last few months which . . . can I?' she asked Rik, indicating the non-cop newcomers Flynn and Donaldson and asking by means of her body language if it was OK for her to carry on. Rik nodded. 'Well, we uncovered a huge, interlinked conspiracy going back many years and it seems every stone we flip, more creepy-crawlies slither out, the latest one being Albert Gorst, who was involved in children's homes way back, which were very questionable to say the least.' She took a breath and then swallowed dryly when she noticed Flynn watching her. 'Ahem, anyway, me and Henry arrested Gorst on suspicion of various – and I suppose I might admit – nebulous, possible offences relating to missing children over the years. Thing was his brief pleaded for his release from custody with one of the reasons put forward being he had a very important business meeting to attend today – which was obviously to be held at Simpson Hall, although we didn't even know he had anything to do with the place because we haven't really had the chance to dig deep into him as yet, and the place has been shut down due to COVID for the best part of a year now. Anyway, he was released.'

Rik nodded at Jake Niven.

'Early this morning, Henry asked me to stop two cars that had almost forced him off the road on his way to work, which I did. A Bentley and a Range Rover. Janus was driving the Bentley, Gorst was in the passenger seat and his missus was in the back. Four heavies were in the Range Rover and they were all on their way to Simpson Hall.'

'Did they say why?' Rik asked.

'Maintenance. The guys in the Range Rover were the workmen, according to what Gorst told me. Unfortunately, I had to leave at that point to attend a fatal RTA.'

'Oh, yeah,' Rik said. 'So, Gorst and Co. were presumably on their way to Simpson Hall, not really to repair it but to attend this meeting, the result of which was he, his missus and Janus are now dead. We don't know the fate of the guys in the Range Rover, other than what Gorst told you.' Rik was looking at Henry. 'Which was?'

'They were dead, all killed by a woman and her father, an old man who had managed to stab Gorst . . . so we can be sure that Gorst was into something we don't yet know about.' He looked meaningfully at Donaldson.

Rik said, 'We'll come to that in a moment . . . Henry, do you want to tell us what happened to you today, then?'

'As Debs said, I was kidnapped off the street. Again.' He gave Blackstone a wry look, remembering vividly that last time that happened she had saved his life. 'Anyway . . . I'd landed home from work and Jake had told me about stopping Gorst earlier. I'd just phoned Debs to pass this information on when the Bentley pulls up, Janus gets out, blood everywhere, gun pointed at me, and demands I ditch my phone, get in and drive them – I guess because he's too weak from his injuries by now. In order to save my brains being blown out, I comply and next thing we pull into the community hospital and get that poor doctor to help out, which, bless him, he tries to do. But Gorst needs to get to a trauma unit ASAP, and as we're leaving the hospital, a guy in a blood-spattered forensic suit, armed with two guns, meets us and kills Gorst and Janus but not me and the doctor.'

Henry stopped as his mouth dried up while reliving the brutal incident. He lubricated it with some more Jack Daniel's.

Everyone seemed to fall into a reverential silence until Blackstone said, 'You don't have a lot of luck with mobile phones, do you?'

Something clicked in Henry's mind with these cynical words spoken in jest, but before he could work it out, Rik said, 'And you didn't manage to get a look at the getaway vehicle?'

'No. Too busy cowering and shitting myself,' Henry said.

'But if you'd acted quickly, we could have had a number or at least a make.'

Henry gave him the evil eye and said, 'Discipline me if you like, mate.'

He recalled those moments post-shooting. The bullet-riddled body of Gorst slumped in the wheelchair; the bullet-riddled body of Janus on the tiled floor, blood gushing from his wounds initially like a power shower and then wilting as the source of that power, Janus's heart, failed completely.

Henry had been transfixed by the spectacle and reacted far too slowly to get a sighting of the getaway vehicle. For a few moments, his mind had been blank with the horror of what had happened.

He added, 'I wish I had, Rik, but two people had just been murdered right in front of me and I guess my reactions aren't what they used to be now I'm slow and old.'

'Oh, I don't know,' Blackstone said, then corrected herself. 'Hang on, no, you're right, you are old and slow!'

Her intervention broke the rising tension and Henry winked at her again.

'What about ANPR?' Diane asked. 'Any cameras in the vicinity? It's got to be worth checking the database around the appropriate times.'

Rik said he would get on with it.

Henry looked at Steve Flynn and Karl Donaldson. Up to that moment, he'd had very little time to engage with them. Donaldson was an old friend he'd met twenty-five years before when the American had been in the UK investigating mob-based criminal activity in north-west England. Their friendship had blossomed and been ongoing since; occasionally, when Henry had been a 'real' cop, they had worked together on some serious, high-level investigations. Henry and Flynn's relationship was slightly more fraught because Henry had been instrumental in drumming Flynn out of the cops over the little matter of Flynn's alleged involvement in the disappearance of over a million pounds of a drug dealer's money. Flynn had eventually been exonerated, and his and Henry's paths had crossed several times since; over the years, they'd discovered a mutual tolerance of each other, though neither would have called it a friendship. That said, Flynn had become Henry's unofficial go-to guy for backup when things had the possibility of getting hairy. Flynn was someone Henry was very glad to have behind him, or in front, and looking at him and Donaldson now, Henry recognized a very formidable combination he would not like to go up against.

'So, guys,' Rik said, interrupting Henry's thoughts, and addressing Donaldson and Flynn. Henry knew that Rik and the pair had already had a hurried discussion. 'It's over to you – time to fill in a few gaps.'

Donaldson shifted in his chair and took a sip of his fresh orange juice (Henry knew that despite his size, Donaldson was not great with alcohol; not that he was a drunk, just that it didn't take very much to *make* him drunk, so generally he avoided it).

'Long story short,' he began.

After their restaurant-based confrontation with Nico Bashkim and as a result of what he divulged, Donaldson and Flynn decided they needed to get to England as quickly as possible to chase down the specific whereabouts of Viktor; Nico had told them the old man and his daughter were scheduled to have a high-level criminal conference with a certain Albert Gorst in order to, as Nico phrased it, 'iron out' several difficulties the Bashkims and Gorst were experiencing with each other.

Nico sounded cagey about the meeting and didn't greatly expand, other than to say Gorst had been making certain demands that had been received coldly by Viktor and Sofia.

Although Nico denied knowing very much about this and claimed his information came from eavesdropping conversations because he had been effectively cut out of all decision making, he did blab he'd heard that a 'contingency plan' had been put in place in case the meeting went bad and 'certain steps' needed to be taken by Viktor and Sofia.

When pressed by Donaldson, Nico revealed one of the family's 'contractors' in the UK – known as the Tradesman – had been told to hide some firearms in the meeting venue and also rig it to go up in a ball of flame – but only if necessary, he'd stressed.

'*If necessary.*'

Two words Donaldson took with a pinch of salt.

'Next few days, dunno.' Nico had shrugged when Donaldson asked him for a specific time and date. 'All I know is that I got my old plaything back,' he'd said, referring to the superyacht *Halcyon* which, up to pulling the double-cross on Donaldson, had been Nico's floating home for almost ten years, crisscrossing the Aegean and the Mediterranean. His existence had been one of continuous debauchery at sea; it seemed he was thrilled to be back on board, resuming that fulfilling life. He went on, 'My father's away for I don't know how long – maybe he won't return – and with the help of the little blue pill, I'm fucking everything I can lay my hands on . . . so, no, I don't exactly know when the meeting will take place because I'm not part of the inner circle any more,' he had concluded acidly.

Donaldson and Flynn set about making arrangements to get to England as quickly as possible.

And like anyone else, they had to use public transport.

In times gone by, Donaldson occasionally had an FBI jet at his beck and call, but now that his influence seemed to be waning within that organization, where he was regarded as the old guard, he was forced to book a seat on the first available flight from Ibiza to the UK with Flynn, using the Wi-Fi connection and laptop on board Flynn's boat.

Flynn himself felt a little guilty sitting with his battered computer on his knee, scrolling through flights while Molly watched on.

Nico had given them the name of the place where the meeting would take place. Flynn found a couple of cheap seats to Liverpool for the next day and booked them for himself and Donaldson.

Later, he and Molly had gone for a stroll hand in hand along the marina, giving a wide berth to some sort of kerfuffle further down the quayside where a crowd had gathered around an ambulance at an incident on the water's edge. They cut across to the resort centre and found a café to sit outside at on the main street where Flynn admitted, 'I just jumped in and booked flights without thinking about you, Molls. Sorry.'

She remained impassive, did not look at him for a moment, but then turned her head slowly, her eyes on fire and said, 'I know.'

'Blokey thing,' he said contritely, feeling a little shaky for a big, tough man.

She sighed despondently, then smiled. 'It's OK. You've got more invested in this than I have – people's lives have been lost – so it's your baby, shall I say? I'll stay here, watch the boat . . . not such a bad part of the deal really.' She leaned back in her chair and closed her eyes. 'Just thinking about a well-endowed Spaniard,' she teased him.

It was time for Flynn to return the eyes-on-fire look.

The flight to Liverpool was almost empty, such were the vagaries of COVID, and both men – big, broad, tall guys – were able to stretch out and get some sleep.

They had done some online research into Simpson Hall; they were surprised and pleased to find it was located near to Kendleton, which meant they could factor in a touch-base with Henry if time and circumstances permitted.

Flynn had pre-booked a hire car, and within half an hour of landing at John Lennon Airport, they were travelling north on the M6, coming off at the Lancaster junction to pick up the road to Kendleton, which they reached as Jake Niven was talking to a very distraught-looking Ginny in the car park of The Tawny Owl.

Henry listened to Donaldson and Flynn explain how they came to be in Kendleton.

Although he knew the two guys well enough, the tale of the Bashkims was riveting because he had no clue whatsoever of the involvement of either man with the Albanian crime family; he had heard of the Bashkims when he had been in the police but hadn't had any direct dealings with them. He knew their network was strongly established across the north and that was about it.

That Donaldson was on their tail was no surprise – it was what he did. Flynn's involvement fascinated him, although he doubted if he would ever get the full story until everything here had calmed down, and maybe not even then.

'So, yeah,' Donaldson drawled without revealing any great detail,

'I've been investigating them for a few years now and we thought old man Viktor had been killed in a car bomb in Malta.'

'Turned out not to be the case,' Flynn added.

Henry decided to be a bit cheeky and asked Flynn, 'What exactly is your involvement with them, then?'

And almost for the first time ever, Henry saw a vulnerable side to Flynn with the uncomfortable body language he displayed. It flickered only for a moment before Flynn closed it down and said, 'It's personal; let's leave it at that.'

Henry was intrigued but didn't push it as there were more immediate concerns. He would do so later.

He turned to Donaldson, about to ask a further question, when Rik Dean butted in and said abruptly, 'Hold on. You had information that the head of an organized crime gang was going to meet up with someone from this neck of the woods and you didn't see fit to share this intelligence with us before you got here?'

Donaldson gave him a look that could have shrivelled him up. 'We didn't have a full picture,' he said.

Rik rounded on Blackstone. 'And DS Blackstone – Gorst. Who exactly is this man and why didn't you know more about him?'

She was taken aback by the bluntness of his question.

Henry cut in, 'Hey, Rik, don't come at us with twenty/twenty hindsight bullshit. He's just someone we uncovered with Sparrow Hawk.'

'No, no, you misunderstand me, Henry.' Rik pointed at him – too aggressively for Henry's liking. 'Not who *was* he thirty years ago . . . who the hell he is *now* to be meeting up with the head of one of the most successful organized crime gangs in Europe, probably the world? *Who is he?*'

'Whoever he is, he's dead now,' Blackstone said, miffed by the tone of Rik Dean's voice.

Rik went on as though he hadn't heard her. 'And this Janus guy – who is he?'

Henry fixed him with a stare. 'It'll all come out in the wash.'

Donaldson tried to calm down an increasing fractious dialogue. 'Likelihood is that Gorst was running supply networks for the Bashkims into the UK. We'll speak with my source,' Donaldson said, meaning Nico but not naming him, 'when I get a chance to try to get more out of him.'

'Hmm,' Rik muttered, unimpressed. Then he asked Donaldson, 'What do you think happened at Simpson Hall, then?'

'That Viktor and his daughter, Sofia, who is or will soon become the new head of the organization, went for a meeting with Gorst, who probably thought he held all the aces. They prepared for it to go wrong and, if it did, have the means to take Gorst out of the picture. I think Gorst may have wanted too much or even everything, and the Bashkims do not give anything to anyone.'

'What do you mean by "prepared"?'

'Hidden guns and enough explosives to ensure that Simpson Hall would go up like a nuclear bomb.'

'Bit extreme,' Rik said.

'That's what they're like, aren't they, Steve?' Donaldson asked Flynn.

'They are psychopaths,' Flynn confirmed.

'Sounds to me like they'd already decided what the outcome of the meeting would be,' Blackstone said.

Donaldson agreed. 'I think so, too . . . they went to kill Gorst, whatever.'

'Which all fits in with what Gorst said to me in the car,' Henry added. 'The old man stabbed him, and the woman shot Janus and the other bodyguards, whose bodies could still be in the remains of the hall.'

'But where does this other guy come into it?' Blackstone asked. 'The one in the forensic suit. That's not the old man or young woman, is it?'

'It's a good question,' Donaldson said.

There was a silence then as the brainstorming session ground to a slight halt.

Until Flynn said, 'It's got to be the Tradesman . . . the guy who set up the contingency plan for the Bashkims at the hall.' He turned to Henry. 'You said his forensic suit was blood-splattered?'

Henry nodded. 'You also said Gorst had been stabbed by the old man, that Janus and the others had been shot by the woman, so what about . . .' Flynn collected his thoughts. 'The Tradesman turns up and his job is to do a clearance of the scene after the deed is done, but he finds that Viktor and Sofia weren't quite as successful as they thought they'd been.'

Henry sat forwards, picking up on this. 'Father and daughter left the scene believing they'd killed everyone in sight, and when this guy, the Tradesman, gets there to do his cleaning up work, he realizes that not everyone's dead who should be dead . . .'

Flynn said, 'Yep.'

Henry said, 'His job was to clean up by burning Simpson Hall to the ground . . .'

'And blowing it to smithereens,' Blackstone added excitedly.

'And cleaning up the scene may mean collecting the bodies and disposing of them separately in some other location and destroying any evidence left behind. But what he discovers is that . . .'

'He's a few bodies short of a mass funeral,' Blackstone said, really warming to this.

'Three short to be precise . . . which meant the Tradesman has got more work to do, so after he's collected the bodies of the six bodyguards – and I know I'm jumping to conclusions here because they could yet be found in the remains of the hall and tomorrow we'll know for certain – he tells Viktor that not everyone is here and then Viktor contracts him to complete the task by ensuring the missing people are assassinated.'

'Gotta be,' Flynn agreed.

'OK, OK, people,' Rik said, patting the air down in a calming gesture. 'Tomorrow morning . . .' He checked his watch – six past midnight – and corrected himself. 'This morning I have a briefing to deliver and I need to get my head around what I'm going to say. I think the various threads we're going to have to follow are formulating in here.' He tapped his head.

Jake Niven, who other than when he'd been asked to contribute, had listened to all this toing and froing and speculation, raised his hand.

'Yep, Jake,' Rik said.

'Err, purely coincidental this, maybe . . .' He eyed Donaldson and Flynn. 'Remember when you guys arrived and we were talking to Ginny about Henry's sudden disappearance?' They nodded. 'Then I got the call about Simpson Hall being on fire?' More nods. 'I was trying to concentrate on what was being said over the radio, not really taking any notice of anything passing . . . except something did drive past.' He paused. 'A van. Transit type. Grey. I really wasn't looking but I did see it had some writing on the side.'

He looked around the room.

'I know this sounds really silly, but I'm one hundred per cent sure it had the words "The Tradesman" written on the side.' He almost laughed at the ridiculousness of it, but all the others were stunned to silence.

Rik said, 'Surely not.'

'Honest, boss. Now I think hard, I can see it going past and a bloke at the wheel but in shadow. It really had the words "The Tradesman" on the side. It was coming from the direction of Thornwell and went out on the Caton Road towards the community hospital. Timing-wise, it fits in with what happened there.'

Rik looked sharply at Donaldson. 'Could it be?'

'I've heard sillier stories.'

Henry took all this in, his memory knowing something but unable to unearth exactly what.

He tried to focus his mind on something he knew was important, once more visualizing the shooter at the hospital, trying to make a connection. That guy had been wearing a forensic suit from top to bottom, like a onesie with the hood pulled over his head and tightened with a drawstring around his face so he looked like a polar explorer. He also wore a face mask, thereby covering the bottom half of his face underneath his eyes.

But there was something else.

He was wearing a baseball cap underneath the hood with the peak pulled down – literally all Henry could see were the man's eyes and they were in the shade of the peak.

What was it about that baseball cap?

It was a camouflage pattern, like something the military might wear.

Henry sat upright as the realization clobbered him.

He had seen the cap before. He had seen the man before. He had seen the van before.

He looked sharply at Diane who said, 'What?'

'A man and a van.'

'Lots of men with vans,' she said.

'Not many who go around planting bombs and clearing up crime scenes for the mob for a living,' Henry said, 'which might just explain something that's been nagging me.'

Diane said, 'What?'

'Why I got robbed just for my phone.'

'So why did you get robbed just for your phone?' Blackstone asked, a bit like a knock-knock joke.

'Because I took a video of something I shouldn't have done . . . I think.'

'Even if that's the case, what has it to do with this and what is the video of?' Blackstone asked, before pointing out, 'You haven't got the phone anyway.'

Henry smirked. 'Look, it could have absolutely nothing to do with all this, but a guy in a van stopped to ask for directions the other day. He had a hoodie pulled over his face, had a face mask on, and was wearing a camouflage-patterned baseball cap, the peak of which stuck out, and all I could see were his eyes. The guy who shot Gorst and Janus was also wearing a camo baseball cap under the forensic hood.'

Blackstone pulled a face. 'Coincidence.'

Henry kept smirking. 'And you know how much I like a good coincidence.'

'Ugh,' Blackstone uttered. Yes, she did.

'But guess what?' Henry asked. 'The guy asked for directions to Simpson Hall.'

Rik said, 'You're fucking kidding . . . who, what . . . Would a killer would be so brazen and stupid?'

'Or smug and conceited?' Henry countered. 'Anyway, it might be nothing whatsoever, I admit.'

'And you videoed it on your phone? Why the hell did you do that?' Rik asked.

'I wasn't deliberately videoing the man or the van; I was video-ing a herd of deer walking down to the village.'

'A herd of deer?' Rik asked incredulously.

'What's wrong with that?'

'Nothing, I suppose, if it catches a murderer . . . but you haven't got the footage, so it's a moot point.'

'I haven't,' Henry said, then looked at Diane, 'but I know someone who has . . . haven't you, dear? If you'll excuse the pun.'

It was probably one of the worst pieces of footage of the natural world ever taken, a sin compounded by the whispering, David Attenborough-like narration by Henry as he recorded the progress of the herd of deer mooching past the front of The Tawny Owl towards the village.

Henry cringed.

Especially because he had managed to rig up a feed to a large-screen TV in the bar from Diane's phone which amplified his voice and made him sound a bit daft. It had not been intended for public consumption.

'And as you can see,' the voice said softly, 'the herd of deer, which in these unprecedented times, appears to have taken the bull by the horns and moved lock, stock and barrel into the village . . . they really are magnificent creatures, particularly Horace the majestic red stag who, with his virility unchecked, has probably inseminated every single female surrounding him . . .'

As he spoke this award-winning voiceover, the lens tracked the herd trotting off the village green, on to the road and going towards the village itself and thereby caught the grey van parked further down the road, but at such an angle that all that could be seen were the back doors and not the sides, so any writing there was impossible to make out. What was easy to read, though, was a mobile phone number painted on the rear doors and the rear registration plate.

'David Attenborough, eat your heart out,' Blackstone quipped.

The footage also captured the driver climbing into the driver's side of the van and driving away.

Jake said, 'Could well be the van I saw.'

A shimmer of invisible excitement went through everyone.

'Henry, you brilliant bastard,' Rik said in awe, his eyes stuck to the screen.

They all kept watching.

Henry re-ran it.

The man in the hoodie walking towards the van but with his back to the camera. Getting in, closing the door, starting the engine. Then his hand coming out of the window as he adjusted the door mirror and the reflection of his face as he looked into it and then . . .

'Hellfire, Henry!' Rik said.

The man pushed up the peak of his baseball cap with his thumb, then pulled down his face mask with his finger and actually revealed his full face for a very, very brief moment in the mirror as the van moved away and the short nature video ended.

Henry, who was holding Diane's phone, pressed pause, backed up the footage once again and, after a few misses, managed to stop it at the exact moment the guy's face was revealed.

Then, using his finger and thumb, he expanded the view.

As he did, the image lost some of its clarity and became grainy, but Henry knew that the Technical Support Unit had the wherewithal to enhance and sharpen it.

'You videoed him, Henry . . . he knew it, so he came back and nicked your phone,' Blackstone said. 'Cheeky git.'

'Hmm.' As a reflex, Henry massaged the back of his head, which was still very tender.

Rik was already on his phone to the control room. 'Detective Superintendent Dean here, PNC check, please . . . a Ford van, registered number . . .' He paused and waited for a response, scribbling down the name and address of the registered keeper on the flipchart, thanking the operator, then looking around triumphantly. 'Got him!'

Henry didn't want to put a damper on it, but said, 'Hmm.'

Blackstone asked, 'What?'

'Were it all so easy,' he replied.

'Let's hope, eh?'

'What about the phone number on the van, boss?' Blackstone asked Rik.

'Let's not jump the gun with that . . . I don't want anyone ringing him and alerting him until our ducks are in a row.'

'It'll be fake,' Henry said. 'The whole thing will be fake.'

Diane's phone was still connected to the TV screen, showing the enlarged, paused photo of the driver's face captured in the mirror. Henry got up and walked to the TV, peering closely at the guy, wondering if this was the one who had smashed him over the head, the one who had cold-bloodedly murdered Gorst and Janus.

He spun on his heels. To Diane, he said, 'Babe, you said you'd had to avoid a van that night when you found me out cold. Not many vans out and about on our roads at that time of night – could it have been this one?'

She shook her head. 'I really don't know. Possible.'

'I'll mention that for the ANPR trawl in the morning,' Rik said.

'And I'll get a team on CCTV camera footage, public and private, from Simpson Hall all the way to the motorway – see what we can uncover.'

'In the meantime, what do you propose to do about that guy?' Flynn asked.

'Well, we need to move quickly, that's a given . . . I'm going to arrange a firearms entry team backed up by Support Unit and other specialists to his address.' He tapped the flipchart; the address of the vehicle owner was in Blackpool, so there wasn't too far to go. 'I'll be arranging a five thirty a.m. briefing for that with a view to going in as early as possible.'

'I'd like to be there,' Henry said.

Rik nodded yes.

'I think we would, too,' Donaldson said, indicating himself and Flynn.

Rik nodded. 'Observing only.'

'We'll take that,' Donaldson said.

'You with Henry?' Rik asked Blackstone.

'Great, boss.'

Rik then looked at Diane. 'I want you to manage the Major Investigation Room, Diane.'

'Will do.'

Her phone was still connected to the TV screen and it bleeped to indicate an incoming text which appeared in full across the TV, making it impossible for anyone not to see and read.

At that moment Henry was the closest to the TV, so he could hardly miss it.

Hi, hun, how u doin? Missin u. Love u loadz. T. XXX

FIFTEEN

'**A**re you OK?' For once, Debbie Blackstone's concern seemed genuine until she added, 'Despite the public humiliation?'

Henry rubbed his very tired face with the palms of his hands. He felt like one of those dogs, the breed of which he did not know, which seemed to have too much loose skin, and that his insides had been scooped out and flushed down the toilet.

Then Blackstone chuckled. 'Got to see the funny side of it: one hell of a way to find that out, man. I mean, talk about humiliation.'

Henry's face turned very slowly towards her. 'I think that's enough.'

'Fair dos.'

It was six fifteen a.m. They were parked up in a side street in north Blackpool in the maze of terraced houses behind the Imperial Hotel on the promenade. Henry wasn't completely sure how he'd made it through the night following that gut punch of a text message.

The other people who had witnessed it had disappeared like cockroaches when the lights were switched on.

Henry had sorted out rooms for Flynn and Donaldson upstairs in the hotel and for Blackstone to bed down in the guest room in the owner's accommodation area. Rik Dean had gone home.

Leaving Henry and Diane alone in the bar.

Henry swore. He could see Diane swallow.

'I'm sorry,' her voice croaked.

'For which bit?'

'All of it.'

He switched off the TV and sat in the chair next to her and uttered a derisive laugh, probably at himself. 'Long shifts, few phone calls, nights back at your flat . . . supposedly alone.'

She opened her mouth to interrupt.

Henry held up a finger. 'Please, don't deny anything . . . all the signs were there, I suppose, and here's me, the former high-flying detective who, seemingly, couldn't detect a fart in a lift.' His voice faded, but then he said, 'I was living in cloud cuckoo land. Sending you the video, thinking you'd enjoy it . . . what a toss-bag I am!'

'I did want to see it. I wanted to want it,' she said miserably.

'And you came back and lied to me.'

She hung her head. 'I tried. I wanted to convince myself that I love you . . . and I did . . . I mean, I really, really like you . . . you saved my life and I'll always be in your debt for that.'

'And you saved mine . . . but it's not debt. You don't owe me anything for saving your life, Diane, certainly not in terms of having to pretend to be in love with me, or any other terms for that matter.'

He gave one of those helpless shrugs. 'I feel pathetic and stupid. I mean, how could it possibly have worked? Looks like I might end up with Maude Crichton after all.'

He was referring to the rich widow who lived on the other side of the village and who definitely had the hots for Henry. Age-wise they were compatible, whereas the age difference between him and Diane was a good twenty years, in her favour.

'You don't mean it!'

'It's the only way I'll get an Aston Martin,' he admitted, then sighed pathetically again. 'Anyway.' He patted his thighs. 'No fool like an old fool.' He stood up, not even daring to glance at her, let alone make eye contact, and said, 'I'm not even going to ask who "T" is. Please make sure the door's locked on your way out.'

He went through the door into the owner's accommodation, closed it, leaned on it and listened for the sound of Diane leaving.

Then he went to bed. He didn't sleep.

Less than four hours later, he was sitting at the back of a briefing room at Blackpool police station where Rik was addressing a fire-arms rapid-entry team with Support Unit backup. Later, he was in a car with Blackstone, Flynn and Donaldson, and after Blackstone's piss-taking, they settled down to wait for the raid to happen.

Rik Dean had been up all night on the phone, arranging things like crazy, and Henry thought he'd done a good job of it.

Although the name and address of the registered owner of the van didn't ring warning bells on any police databases, that did not stop Rik pulling together a full-scale hit on the guy's house. The police dealt with false identities and purposely misleading information on a daily basis, so the fact that the van owner wasn't on the cop radar was hardly a surprise, and when Rik led the dawn briefing, he couldn't overstress that the teams should exercise extreme care for two main reasons: one, the person in this house could be armed and dangerous; two, he might not be the person they were after.

'You know your jobs,' he'd told them. 'I want this swift, firm and absolutely spot-on. Obviously, you react to what you find, but keep it reasonable . . . yet do not hesitate to use your weapons if necessary . . . and only step up the response if required – safe and efficient, I can't stress this enough. I want everyone going in there to come out unscathed and that includes the target and any other occupants if at all possible.'

'Seriously, are you OK?' Blackstone asked Henry again as they sat in the car. 'I don't want you in emotional cloud cuckoo land if the shit hits the fan. You need to be focused, yeah?'

He did not reply, so she pounded his arm. 'Say yes, boss.'

'Yes, boss,' he said grudgingly.

They were listening to the radio transmissions between the members of the strike team, control room and the briefing room (where Rik was), and they also had an iPad linked to a split-screen video/audio feed from various bodycams of selected officers.

'But to be honest, knowing what I do, if this is the guy we're after, I'll show my bum in the pound shop,' Blackstone promised.

'I'll show mine, too,' Henry said.

'Crims do make mistakes, though. That's why us dim cops catch 'em usually.'

'They do . . . but I'll bet the only mistakes this one made were having to ask for directions and looking in his wing mirror, and he knows it – hence his revisit to me.'

'Alpha Three in position,' came a transmission over the secure radio channel dedicated to the operation.

Henry knew this was from the team covering the rear of the property, consisting of armed officers and Support Unit.

After a short pause, the 'Strike! Strike! Strike!' instruction was given.

Two hours later, Henry peered through the sliding hatch in a cell door at the prisoner inside, a man in his late thirties, dressed in a forensic suit with a harsh blanket wrapped around his shoulders. He was ashen-faced and traumatized by what at first had seemed to be the most realistic nightmare he'd ever had: the surge of uniforms into his bedroom, being dragged from underneath his quilt by many grappling hands, being slammed face down into his nice bedroom shag-pile carpet and being cuffed, while also being screamed at and guns and Tasers pointed at him, all inducing him to pee himself.

'T'ain't him,' Henry said, slowly closing the hatch.

By that time, though, that fact had pretty much been established beyond all reasonable doubt.

As it happened, he *was* a tradesman – a joiner with a grey Transit van which was parked up overnight in the yard of his small business premises on a nearby industrial estate. The van had been seized and was currently being minutely examined by a forensic team and the stolen vehicle squad, but early indications were that it was legit; it did have writing on it, which was this man's name and phone number, again genuine, and the number did not match the one in the video Henry had taken. That number had been checked by the telephone unit and found never to have been issued, just a random string of numbers that went nowhere.

'Awks,' Blackstone said, as she, Henry, Donaldson and Flynn walked into the Major Incident Room on the top floor of Lancaster Police Station and spotted Diane Daniels sitting at the office manager's desk, head down in paperwork.

'Only if you're fifteen years old,' Henry said.

The MIR was very busy.

Having been at the arrest early that morning, Henry and Blackstone had missed the eight a.m. briefing that Rik Dean had rightly decided to go ahead with. Even if the arrest had been a good one, there would still have been much to do, not least of which was tracking down Viktor and Sofia Bashkim, the strategy for which was going to be decided after discussion with Karl Donaldson, with Steve Flynn listening in.

It was almost midday when Henry, Blackstone, Flynn and Donaldson entered the buzzing room.

Diane glanced up, but her eyes quickly returned to the paperwork stacking up in front of her.

A bank of HOLMES computers had been set up – HOLMES being the acronym for the Home Office Large and Major Enquiry System – and vast amounts of data were already being uploaded. Tasks had been and were still being allocated to detectives, uniforms and specialists. Henry breathed it all in, feeling again that slight pang of jealousy as he recalled the numerous murder investigations he had either run or been involved in.

Rik Dean was at the front of the room on a small, raised stage, looking at more flipcharts that had been sticky-tacked to the wall and were more professional versions of the ones he'd been scribbling on in the early hours of that morning. There was a DCI at his shoulder, his number two, and both looked super stressed – the one thing Henry definitely did not envy.

He walked past Diane who did not look up, and he saw Blackstone scowling very obviously at her, although the scowl gave way to an innocent smile when she realized Henry had clocked her antics.

'Stop it,' he hissed.

'Well.' She shrugged. 'What a bi—!'

'Shut it,' he snapped before she could complete the insulting word.

She ran her thumb and forefinger across her lips, indicating they were now sealed as if by a zip.

Rik said something to the DCI at his shoulder, who nodded and peeled away. Rik turned to the four of them.

'Hi, guys – and gal,' he added quickly, not wishing to offend Blackstone because no one wished to offend her.

Before he could say anything further, Diane rose from her seat and came towards them, holding a sheaf of photographs. 'Boss, these have just arrived from TSU,' she said, shouldering past Blackstone who looked ready to punch her lights out. She handed them to Rik. 'Blow-up from the video,' she said.

He took them, and Diane turned, making chilly eyeball contact with Blackstone complete with a 'Just you watch it' expression, then caught a fleeting glance at Henry whose features were tightly drawn. It was obvious to her he was hurting and trying to keep all the emotional stuff in check. In fact, the break-up was killing him inside and being in such close proximity to Diane was agony.

Rik looked at the photos. 'Very good.' He smiled with satisfaction, took the top one to go on the wall and gave the remainder of the pile to Henry who handed one to each of his compatriots.

As ever, the Technical Support Unit had done a great job in a short turnaround.

They had homed in on the van driver's reflection in the door mirror and enlarged it, but kept it sharp so that the image of his face was very identifiable.

Rik said, 'My office, folks.'

It was tight and cosy in Rik's temporary office off the MIR, but he managed to squeeze four chairs into a snug semi-circle around the desk, seating himself behind it.

Henry guessed it was for his benefit that Rik went laboriously point by point through everything he'd pulled together to get the ball rolling on the investigation and what everyone was doing. Although Henry was interested, he was finding it hard to concentrate.

The stress of the previous day was definitely getting to him.

Finally, thankfully, Rik's speech was drawing to a close.

'. . . And I've got a DI down at the mortuary covering the post-mortems with Scenes of Crime and Forensics . . . I'm going down there shortly.' He arched his eyebrows at Donaldson and Flynn. 'So, guys, I've nothing on the task pads as regards the Bashkims yet, even though they are the catalyst to all this. I'd be grateful if you could let me know what the plan is to bring these people to justice.'

All eyes swivelled to Donaldson, although Blackstone's did linger on Flynn for a moment too long and Henry also noticed she'd sneakily managed to get on a chair alongside him, so they were sitting thigh to thigh.

Donaldson drew in a breath. 'No problem, but I need to speak to my boss to ensure we establish a formal link between us, the FBI and yourselves. We need to get the NCA and Interpol on board, too . . . My gut feeling is that the Bashkims, if they are not already there by now, will run fast to Albania; if that's the case, we're in for big problems. As much as that country has opened up, its police, judiciary and politicians are still in the grip of organized crime. At best, it will be a waiting game; at worst, a game without end.'

'Pretty bleak summary,' Henry observed.

Donaldson shrugged. 'Saying it as it is. I would be astounded if they hadn't planned their getaway to the nth degree, and I'll bet they were either in the air or at sea within hours of the killings.'

'In our conversation last night, you mentioned this superyacht – *Halcyon*, is it? Moored in Ibiza. Do you think they will return to that?' Rik asked.

Donaldson pondered this for a moment, then said, 'No. If the meeting with Gorst had ended amicably, then maybe – but then, of course, we wouldn't be having this discussion – but now I think they'll head for the hills where they're almost untouchable. Once they're bedded in, it'll be like extracting a splinter from your fingertip.'

'Bugger,' said Rik.

'Tell you what, though – let me get back down to my office in London, make some connections and get the ball rolling with law enforcement across Europe.'

'I don't want to waste time,' Rik said. 'This is a hot investigation.'

'Understood. I'll leave now and get back to you before the end of the day,' Donaldson promised.

Rik accepted that. He looked at Henry. 'Meanwhile, we've still got this Tradesman guy to nail. Can you get your witness statement written?'

'Yep – I'll go home and do it, if that's OK?'

'Sure. Debbie . . . Gorst and Janus – everything you can unearth on them. *Everything*,' he stressed.

'On it, boss.'

The meeting was over.

Henry and Donaldson managed a quick 'elbow' on the ground-floor car park of the police station. They almost hugged but stopped just in time.

'Catch up soon, pal,' Donaldson promised.

'Out of work and once this COVID thing is over,' Henry said.

To Flynn, he said, 'Good to see you. We'll catch up soon, too – yeah?'

'Yup,' Flynn agreed. He and Donaldson then got into their rental car which they'd arranged to drop off at a depot in London and drove off with a quick wave to Henry and Blackstone. Henry noticed Blackstone's tongue-on-the-floor look at Flynn as he disappeared down the one-way street.

'If you were a bloke, I'd say you were like a dog with two dicks,' Henry said. 'You clearly have – how shall I say? – a longing for him.'

'What, me?' she blustered, and Henry was actually surprised to see this side of her. Obviously she had something for Flynn, as Henry had so brilliantly worked out. Her face was in turmoil. 'I want to mother him,' she admitted.

'Mother him? Jeepers!'

'And then, after that . . . something more basic.'

'OK, sorry I broached the subject,' Henry said, rooting for his car keys. 'I'm back off home. I'll write my statement in peace and quiet.' He held up some statement forms, plus the mugshot of the Tradesman.

'I'll get on with Gorst and Janus.'

'You do that.'

Just as Blackstone was about to get into her Mini Cooper, she said to Henry, 'Hey, regarding Flynn.'

'What about him?'

'Do you know what Viktor actually did to his Spanish cop girlfriend?'

Henry shook his head.

'He decapitated her.'

With that, she got into the Mini with Henry watching, mouth agog, fired it up, revved the beautifully tuned engine which she herself had rebuilt from scratch, then screamed out of the car park, making the tyres squeal.

Within five minutes, Flynn and Donaldson were speeding south down the motorway, Flynn flooring the accelerator.

Both men were consumed by their own thoughts.

Flynn was thinking – and hoping – that his involvement with Viktor was now over. He wasn't a cop anymore and had no right or authority to be on any official investigation; he didn't want to plead that case anyway. What he wanted to do now was head back to Ibiza, team up with Molly and reveal his true feelings for her: that he was madly in love and wanted a life together. He'd suggest they head back to Gran Canaria on the boat, taking their time and, once there, see how things stood. He knew he had issues to resolve in Puerto Rico, not least that he was executor and sole beneficiary of the estate of Adam Castle, his friend who had been drawn into the world of the Bashkims and died as a result.

Flynn had inherited Adam's businesses which included bars, clubs, safari tours and fishing boats and property throughout the Canaries. They were in a bureaucratic tangle, not least because of Spanish law, but were not far off being sorted out.

Flynn's plan was to sell everything with the exception of a fishing boat in Lanzarote, which he wanted to run as a business alongside *Faye*. Other than that, he did not want the money. He was going to give half to Adam's family and a quarter to the widow of Jose, his crew member who had also been a victim of the Bashkims; he would retain what was left for himself, a little nest egg to give him time and space to plan a future with Molly.

But his first need was to get back to her and not screw up the relationship, which, historically, he was very good at doing.

Donaldson was thinking along the same lines.

He had been far too consumed by the Bashkims over the last four years and perhaps it was now time to let go. His boss was at breaking point with him and maybe the best course of action would be to cruise into a nice retirement with his wife, travel the world when it reopened, look forward to grandkids and grow tomatoes.

That, he thought, was the right thing to do.

He glanced at Flynn, who had suffered more than most at the hands of the Bashkims; he wouldn't blame him if he wanted to continue the fight to the death.

However, if Viktor was arrested, he would probably see out his life in a cell before he even reached trial, which wouldn't be a satisfactory conclusion for either him or Flynn.

'What're you thinking, Steve?'

'Me? About going fishing, I guess. You?'

'Me? Grandkids. None on the way yet, but someday they will be.'

'Nice.'

'Good thoughts.'

Two things happened in fairly quick succession that put all those dreamy thoughts on hold.

Henry enjoyed the ride home. He slowed down as he passed the entrance to the Kendleton Community Hospital, which was still sealed off as a major crime scene, but didn't stop. Not long after, he was at The Tawny Owl, where he had a long chat with Ginny about the business and their plans for reopening when it was permitted. Both wanted to hit the ground running.

After that, he brewed himself a cafetiere of rich Kenyan coffee, took it through to the lounge of the accommodation and settled at his desk overlooking the rear garden. He flattened out the witness statement forms, poured a mug of the steaming brew, gathered his thoughts and picked up a pen.

About half an hour into this process, a message landed on his phone. He opened it and looked at the photograph attached to it, frowning.

Then the phone actually rang: Rik Dean.

'You received that photo?' Rik asked without preamble.

'I have. Explain.'

'It's from the techies sifting through what remains of Simpson Hall,' Rik explained, referring to the scientists covering that crime scene. 'They've been going through what's left of the CCTV system and some of it is undamaged, including the computer that recorded from the security cameras around the hall. What I've sent you is a still lifted from footage which shows Gorst and Janus together with an old man and a younger woman on the front steps of the hall. It looks like the arrival of Viktor and Sofia Bashkim . . . so it puts them there undeniably – if that is, in fact, Viktor and Sofia. At the moment we don't have any more mugshots of them; that's one thing we're waiting for from Donaldson.'

'That's excellent.' Henry had already forwarded the image to his laptop, downloaded and opened it to look at full size. Gorst and Janus were instantly identifiable. It was great evidence against the Bashkims.

'I'm circulating a cropped version to all ports and airports,' Rik said. 'Trying to see if we can pinpoint if they have been seen leaving the country by air or sea. No doubt they'll be on false documentation, but someone might be able to ID them.'

'If these two are anything like Karl describes, they'll be well gone now,' Henry mused. 'But, yeah, it's something that needs to be done. Have you sent this to Karl and Flynn and Debs?'

Rik confirmed he had. 'Thought you'd like a copy, too.'

'Thanks. I'm just doing my statement. I'll scan it and send it to the MIR when I've finished it.'

The call ended, but almost immediately the landline of the pub began to ring. Henry ignored it, expecting Ginny to pick it up somewhere else, but when she didn't, he did.

'Hello, The Tawny Owl, Henry Christie speaking . . .'

Before he had managed to fully introduce himself, an enraged lady said loudly, 'I have never, ever been to your bloody pub and I certainly won't be going now. In fact, I'm going to report you to the police for accessing my bank account and ripping me off!'

Henry held the phone a foot away from his ear until she finished the rant, then said, 'Uh, exactly what do you mean, Mrs . . . Miss . . . Ms?'

'My name is Mrs Ellen Tong and, as I say, I have never been anywhere near your establishment – what's it called?'

'The Tawny Owl.'

'Yes, The Tawny Owl, and I have certainly never spent, let me look, six pounds and forty pence three days ago.'

'OK – can you just explain what you mean and I'll try to help you, Mrs Tong,' Henry said equably but with a furrowed brow because no one had been to his pub recently, other than the morning breakfast and coffee crowd . . . a thought that made his stomach do a quick somersault and also jarred his brain into action.

Mrs Tong took an impatient breath before relaunch. 'I'm online, looking at my current account, and the pending transactions show that I bought something from The Tawny Owl three days ago.'

'Right,' Henry said, trying to recall what details appeared in the 'pending transactions' on his online bank account. 'What exactly does it say, please?'

'The Tawny Owl, Kendleton. Six pounds, forty pence.'

'Does it give a time?'

'A time? No, it doesn't.'

'OK . . . the thing is, as you'll probably know, like other businesses in the hospitality sector, this business is closed other than for some takeaway food we do in the morning . . . so you definitely haven't been here?'

'I don't even know where The Tawny Owl is. I got your number from the Internet.'

'And you haven't let anyone borrow your bank card?'

'Nope!'

'Where do you live, Mrs Tong?'

'Preston.'

'Hmm, looks like you might have had your card stolen, or cloned, or something. Have you reported it to the police?'

'Nope.'

'And is there any other suspicious activity on your account?'

'Hold on, I logged out . . . don't think so . . . oh.'

'What is it?'

'There's another appeared. McDonald's on Riversway, Preston.

Oh God, and three hundred pounds taken from an ATM at Morrison's on the docks . . . oh my . . . now five hundred pounds from Morrison's itself.'

'And that's not you?'

'I do not eat unhealthy food. I haven't been to a cash machine for six months because of this pandemic and all my food is now delivered by Waitrose.'

'Have you checked your purse or wallet or wherever you keep your card?'

'Hold on.'

Henry heard rustling, then she came back on the line. 'It's still here.'

'Then somehow, someone has got your card details, maybe someone you bought from online, possibly,' Henry suggested. 'Either way, you need to tell your bank, get the card cancelled' – here he heard Mrs Tong emit a deep, very pissed-off sigh – 'and get a new one.' But as he said that, he had a juddering thought. 'Sorry, Mrs Tong – you said three days ago?'

'I did.'

'Look, give me your number and the last four digits of your card and I'll call you back shortly . . . I just need to check something.'

He took the numbers, hung up and went to see Ginny who was working in her tiny office just off the pub kitchen. Her desk was overflowing with paperwork, but when Henry asked her where the card receipts were from three days ago, she immediately found them and handed the slips to him, all pinned together with a bulldog clip.

'What are you after?'

'Not sure yet. Are these in chronological order?'

Ginny nodded. 'Who are you after?' she asked.

'Why? Do you know which receipt belongs to which individual?'

'Mostly, with it being a regular crowd. Here.' She waggled her fingers and Henry gave her the slips back.

'Can you tell which one was a stranger's?'

She started to flip through them. 'Yes, I know all the regulars like the gamekeepers. Just do.' She shrugged. 'There were only a couple of people I didn't know.' She pulled one slip out of the stack, then another, and handed them to Henry. 'These.'

He looked at them and gave her one back, kept the other, then exhaled. He didn't even know he'd been holding his breath. The one he kept was dated three days ago, timed at just after seven a.m., and bore the four digits Mrs Tong had given to him.

His mouth dried up and, as it often did when he got a tad over-excited, his arse twitched tightly.

This was the time he had been waiting outside for Debbie to arrive to pick him up to then go and see Albert Gorst.

The time when a tradesman had turned up and asked for directions, bought a breakfast sandwich and a coffee – with a stolen or cloned bank card – for £6.40.

Ginny was watching him, her mouth slightly open. 'What is it?' She knew the story of the Tradesman.

Henry wafted the slip at her. 'Is this the payment from him?' She looked at it again and nodded.

Henry thanked her, rushed back to his desk and picked up the landline, but before calling Mrs Tong he phoned Debbie Blackstone.

Donaldson's phone beeped, announcing the arrival of a text. He clicked on the message which was from Rik Dean and contained the photograph culled from the security camera footage at Simpson Hall. He gave a snort of a laugh and angled his phone so Flynn could see it.

'Our guy and girl arriving for their meeting,' Donaldson said, noting Flynn's face become tight with distaste. 'She's even got a bunch of flowers.'

'No argument they were there, then?' Flynn said.

'None whatsoever . . . and suddenly I'm not thinking about grand-kids anymore. Are you thinking of fishing?'

'No,' Flynn said, once more fired up because of the photo and the thought that just maybe revenge would be a good thing where Viktor Bashkim was concerned.

'Debs, it's Henry. Where are you?'

'As usual, naked in a bath of warm ass's milk surrounded by eunuchs from headquarters rubbing me down with loofahs.'

'Still at work, then?' Henry laughed.

'What do you want, old guy?'

He could hear the sound of an engine and assumed she was on the move.

'Any chance you could head towards McDonald's on Preston Docks?'

'Why, oh great detective? Do you need a quarter-pounder?'

'I need you to check something for me.'

'Hang on, I thought I was boss. I give the orders around here.'

'You are, my lovely, you are and you do. Just do my bidding one time and I'll meet you there as soon as possible.'

'Sounds intriguing,' she purred.

Henry explained.

Flynn's phone, which he'd put in the cup holder by the gear lever, rang. He asked Donaldson to answer it for him.

The American picked it up and checked the screen. 'It's Molly. Want me to answer it?'

'Yep.'

'Hi, Molly, it's Karl Donaldson. Steve's driving right now.'

He put it on speakerphone.

'Where are you guys?' she asked.

'M6 southbound, on our way to London.'

'Oh, OK.'

'What d'you want, darling?' Flynn asked her.

'I need to talk to you both . . . any chance you can pull on to a service area maybe?'

They had just passed the 300-metre mark for the exit to Stafford services. Flynn swerved across from the outside lane and just made it on to the slip road without causing too much mayhem.

SIXTEEN

Molly knew Flynn had his demons and they stemmed from several sources: a very sour divorce way back; not being able to see his son, Craig, anywhere near enough; being harried out of the cops by Henry Christie after being accused of doing something he hadn't done; and, most recently, getting involved with the Bashkims, something that would have sent most decent people spinning into an early grave. Molly knew if she'd been in his position, she would now be being cared for in some kind of institution.

But she saw good in him.

True, he was as tough as nails on the outside, but underneath, once the brittle exterior had been chipped away, he was a slush puppy, and it was that she was relying on to see them through to the other side of the journey they were on.

Which is why she said to him, 'Go, go,' when the information came through about the possible whereabouts of Viktor Bashkim. She knew she had to let Flynn have his head of steam on this one and maybe, once it was over, their lives could blossom.

Deep down, she knew it would all come good.

So sending him off and her staying aboard *Faye* wasn't such a terrible option. Some time to herself was welcome and she intended to get as much out of it as possible.

Following the long sea journeys recently undertaken to Cyprus and back, the boat was in need of a serious clean, even though Flynn had already given her the once over, so Molly got going with that almost as soon as Flynn and Donaldson had gone.

After this, she showered and had a slow meander around Santa Eulalia, which was still spookily quiet, but it was a pleasant stroll. She returned to *Faye* with a takeaway pizza and a bottle of rosé, which she demolished without guilt, and went to bed. Next day was just plain lazy, stretched out on the rear deck, reading and listening to music in the sun.

It was only later in the day that something interesting happened.

She had walked along the marina again, checking that *Halcyon* was still berthed there and the four supercars were still in a line, seemingly not having moved. She carried on walking up on to the promenade and around to the curved beach where she was standing, taking in the view and air, wondering if she could find time for a nice coffee somewhere, when she noticed some activity on the beach itself.

Two uniformed cops were talking animatedly to a woman who was obviously drunk, despite the time of day.

The trio were about one hundred metres away from where Molly was standing but even so she could hear raised voices and it seemed the cops and the woman were having some sort of skirmish. Fingers were being pointed. And when the woman gesticulated wildly, she staggered back a few feet, trying to keep her balance.

The officers seemed simply to want her to move on for whatever reason.

Finally, after more shouting, the woman stuck her middle finger up at the cops, turned, almost lost her balance and staggered away in the sand, coming in Molly's direction.

It took a few moments but Molly realized who this woman was – Nico Bashkim's escort, Lulu. At least, that was her professional name.

Molly watched her unsteady progress across the beach, then up the steps, gripping the handrail to stay upright, until she finally reached the level of the promenade where she sank down on to her hands and knees and began to bawl her eyes out.

Molly rushed across to her.

'Lulu? Are you OK? What's the matter, love?' She went down on to her haunches so she was more or less at Lulu's eye level. 'Lulu?' she cooed.

Lulu looked up, face streaming with tears, her make-up smeared across her cheeks. She looked a mess. Her eyes were blurred and she seemed to have problems focusing on Molly's face until, finally, she did recognize her.

'Lulu, what is it?' Molly wasn't necessarily expecting an intelligent response: the woman reeked of alcohol and, as she had rightly surmised from a distance, being close up confirmed she was very drunk.

'Nico,' she blabbed, 'Nico.' Her face was distorted with misery.

'What about him?'

'Heart attack. He's had a heart attack and they've thrown me off the boat. Bastards!'

Those were the last lucid words that Lulu said as Molly helped her to her feet and supported her all the way back to *Faye* where she helped her clamber on board and steered her into the master stateroom where she let her flop face down on to the bed, removed her high-heeled shoes, then covered her with a blanket. She fell asleep immediately.

Like having a drunk in a cell, Molly kept a regular eye on her to make sure she didn't choke on her own vomit – or indeed vomit at all on the bed – and apart from one waking moment when she needed to pee and then drink copious amounts of water and fall asleep again, Lulu did not really wake for another twelve hours, which was the next morning.

Molly bedded down on the single bed and toyed with the idea of letting Flynn know, but decided against it until she really had something interesting to tell him.

Finally, as Molly fried some bacon and toasted some bread and the wonderful aroma filtered through to Lulu, she appeared in an awful state and said, with her knees grazed, micro-skirt up around her waist and her thong at such an angle that all was revealed, 'Need a shower,' pathetically, her bottom lip quivering.

Molly found a towel and ushered her into the en-suite shower room and closed the door behind her, saying there was a T-shirt and shorts she could borrow after if she liked (although she was aware that the pencil-thin Lulu might need a belt to keep the shorts up).

She reappeared twenty minutes later, scrubbed, minus make-up and everything else, and Molly saw just how beautiful she was under it all.

'Bacon sandwich and a coffee sound good?'

Lulu looked on the verge of crying again, but nodded and responded with a pitiful and grateful, 'Yes, thank you.'

Molly was eagerly looking forward to listening to her tale, which she expected to be full of woe.

It was.

Seeing Nico clutch his chest and pitch into the cold water of the marina and not knowing what to do other than scream had been the start of it.

This was followed by looking on as two waiters from a quayside restaurant dived in and dragged Nico's apparently lifeless body out, laying him out like a dead fish at the water's edge and then performing CPR on him with no regard for their own personal safety, getting up close, one of them compressing his chest, the other using rescue breaths, with a real chance of catching COVID if Nico had been infected.

Lulu watched on, stunned, as a crowd gathered to gawp at the event. Finally an ambulance arrived and the paramedics took over. An oxygen mask went on Nico's face and a defibrillator was deployed to shock Nico's system, making his whole body spasm obscenely until he was finally hefted on to a stretcher into the back of the ambulance, with Lulu climbing aboard, too. Then she had the unreal experience of the blue-and-red-lighted and siren-accompanied journey to the hospital in Ibiza Town while the paramedics worked relentlessly to try to save him.

'Fucking horrific,' Lulu concluded as she shovelled the bacon sandwich into her mouth and swallowed it down with mouthfuls of coffee. 'And when we arrived at the hospital, seeing him rushed into the trauma unit and then having the doors slammed in my face, because I'm sure they knew I was just his fucking hooker,' she said bitterly.

'It must have been awful,' Molly agreed empathetically, refilling Lulu's mug and plying her with more toast because she looked as if she needed the sustenance. She scoffed it.

'I thought I'd never see him alive again. I was sure he was dead.' She drank more coffee. 'Except he wasn't . . . they saved him.'

'I stayed at the hospital all the while, and I rang the captain of the boat and told him what had happened, and next thing there were people from the boat there and they just told me to fuck off back to the boat and get my things, and that I had to leave because there wasn't any reason for me to be on board if Nico wasn't there. The bastards.'

'Oh, so what did you do?' Molly asked.

Lulu shrugged. 'Slept on the beach. I have nowhere to go. I have no money. I depend on Nico to look after me, and now he isn't there, they won't put up with me. I'm just property to throw away.'

Lulu looked sick.

Molly's heart went out to her. Another used, abused and abandoned female in the grand scheme of the unpleasant world of men. It would have been easy to ask her what she had expected, but things were never that cut and dried.

'Where are you from?' she asked her.

'Kiev, Ukraine.'

'Family?'

'Sort of.'

'Could you get back there? *Would* you go back there?'

'I don't know, I just don't know.'

'Would there be any use in getting to see Nico? He could speak
for you, couldn't he? I presume he's still in hospital and it's a public
place, so no one could stop you visiting him and maybe asking for
money from him – or am I being naive, Lulu?'

Lulu looked at her steadily and said, 'Yes, you are. And anyway,
he's not in a public hospital anymore. Once he was stabilized, they
moved him out to a private clinic in Santa Eulalia where he's under
guard. I don't have a hope in hell of getting to see him, so I'm
screwed, but not in a nice way this time.'

Molly left Lulu on board *Faye* while she made the phone call to
Flynn and Donaldson to update them on her breaking news. She
found an empty bench on the Paseo del Port to sit on while she
spoke to them.

When she returned to the boat, Lulu had gone but left a scribbled
note on a pad saying: *Thank you, L.*

The two men were silent for a long time after the phone call ended,
sitting in their rental car on the motorway service area, churning
over what Molly had just told them.

Donaldson was on his own phone, connected to the Internet,
tabbing and flicking through various pages until he found what he
was looking for, saying, 'Hmm,' and taking in a deep breath.

Eventually, they looked at each other and Flynn said, 'Are you
thinking what I'm thinking?'

Donaldson said, 'Yes.'

'Got him,' Blackstone said triumphantly. She pressed pause and the
image on screen stopped moving, focused on the windscreen of a
car at the drive-through ordering point at the McDonald's on
Riversway in Preston. The vehicle was a white Peugeot Partner and
the driver's face was caught clearly on the CCTV footage as he
stuck out his face and called his order across to the speaker – a Big
Mac Meal, white coffee, extra fries – although the sound of his
voice could not be heard. 'I've tied it in to the card details you gave
me, and this is definitely him. Our boy.'

They were in the manager's office at the restaurant, Henry

standing behind Blackstone; the manager had left them to skim through the footage.

In his hand, Henry held the enhanced photograph that TSU had managed to extract from his natural history film. He looked at it – the man in the van, pulling down his face mask – and compared it to the face on the screen in front of him.

He swallowed dryly, because the man in the car at McDonald's was definitely the same one, using the same cloned card belonging to Mrs Tong to buy his meal.

'What about PNC?' Henry said, knowing that, sometimes, getting information out of Blackstone was like being on a drip feed.

Henry could see that the registered number of the van had been picked up by another security camera on the drive-through route.

'Comes back to a bloke in Runcorn . . . so probably this is like the other van, stolen with false plates, but just real-looking enough to fool cameras and cops,' Blackstone said.

'Still, we need someone to visit the Runcorn address,' Henry said.

'I've got the ball rolling with that, via Ricky Boy,' she said, using her pet name for Rik Dean. 'Cheshire police will be knocking on a door soon.'

'Good girl.'

'I am, aren't I?' She looked demurely over her shoulder at Henry with her trademark crooked grin and batted her very long false eyelashes.

'Can we seize the disk?' Henry said.

'No, but I've run a copy off on to another disk and the manager's happy for me to have that. We'll need a warrant for the original.'

'OK . . . thoughts?' Henry checked his watch: time was getting on.

'Would it be worth visiting Mrs Tong? Try to establish if she's had any interaction with this guy? She might recognize him, unless it was an online scam, which will make it much harder to track him down.'

'Let's do it.'

Mrs Tong lived on a housing estate north of Preston, close to the M55 motorway. When Henry knocked on the front door, he heard

a cacophony of barking behind it, which made his heart sink somewhat. He turned to Blackstone and said, 'Little dogs.'

'Pekingese is my bet – about ten of 'em,' Blackstone guessed.

'Little shits,' Henry countered.

'Shih Tzu, you mean?'

'I know what I mean,' he said glumly.

The door opened on a security chain to reveal Mrs Tong's eye
peering out, and the snouts of several tiny dogs vying for position
at ankle level, barking, snarling, yapping and generally misbehaving.
Henry could not work out how many there were.

'Yes?'

'Mrs Tong? Henry Christie . . . I phoned, told you I was on the
way with my colleague, DS Blackstone. Regarding The Tawny Owl.'

Henry leaned slightly aside so she could see Blackstone behind
him and at the same time he showed her his identity card, while
Blackstone flashed her warrant card.

Mrs Tong then appeared to sweep all the dogs backwards with
her foot, pushed the door to and slid the chain off.

'Come in.'

There were six dogs in all and Henry didn't really know the breed
of any of them, but two of them were sitting on his lap, one on
each thigh, looking up at him, two were sitting on Blackstone's
lap in the same position and the other two were on Mrs Tong's lap,
looking jealously at their family members on someone else's laps.

Henry had tried stroking one of the dogs on his lap – he thought
it might have been called Poochy-poo – but it had snapped at
him and now he dared not put a finger near either canine, both
of whom seemed to have the eyes of the devil and continually
bared their teeth at him, clearly sensing his dislike of them and
playing on it. The two dogs on Blackstone's lap seemed to love
her stroking them and she gave Henry a smug look that said, 'This
is how you do it.'

The living room was dedicated to Mrs Tong's pets and the mantel-
piece was simply a display shelf for photographs of her animals,
Henry assumed, dead and alive, past and present.

'I think Poochy likes you,' Mrs Tong said.

'I don't think he does,' Henry said.

'She.'

'She, then.'

'Don't be fooled by the aggression. It's just a front for affection.'

Out of the corner of his eye, he saw Blackstone smirk.

'Anyway,' Henry said. 'Your bank card . . .'

'Ah, yes . . . I'm quite amazed the police have reacted so quickly.'

'It's what we do,' Blackstone said.

As Henry glanced around the living room, he saw a photograph of a dog on the front windowsill accompanied by a selection of sympathy cards and a small urn next to the photo. It looked like any of the other dogs, but maybe an older version, and it had obviously passed away fairly recently.

He said, 'I'm sorry to see you've recently lost one of your pets, Mrs Tong.'

Her gaze moved to the photograph. 'Yes . . . Tommy Too-too . . . two months ago . . . He was run over outside . . . very flat. He was a good dog and I still have his ashes. I'll be keeping them with the ashes of my other dogs in the back garden.'

Henry didn't bother to ask how many that might be in case he started to get a creeped-out feeling.

'Anyway, your card,' Blackstone said, getting the conversation back on track. She and Henry had decided to work through this systematically rather than show Mrs Tong the photo of the van driver straight away. 'Have you any idea who might have got hold of your details?'

'Not really. Lockdown, you know . . . I've used it more than ever but mostly always with the same companies online, such as Waitrose and Pets at Home – people like that.'

'I know it's a very personal thing, but is there any chance of us just having a quick peek through your bank statement to see if anything strikes us?' Blackstone suggested.

'I don't see why not. I've nothing to hide. And I printed a copy off because I thought you might ask.'

'That was very thoughtful,' Henry said. Poochy-poo snarled at him for talking. Henry fought the urge to flick her nose with his finger.

Mrs Tong reached the telephone table next to her chair and picked up a few sheets of paper – her bank statements – and handed them across to Blackstone, who skim-read them. She saw that most transactions were regular, as Mrs Tong had said, and it seemed unlikely that these would be the source of any fraud.

The only one that appeared just once was a payment of £450 to Broughton Pet Cemetery Ltd.

Blackstone handed the sheet to Henry who had to hold it out of reach of the snapping fangs of Poochy-poo.

'Broughton Pet Cemetery,' Blackstone said. 'That seems to be the only one that's a bit different – just a one-off payment by debit card.'

'Oh yes . . . that's where Tommy Too-too was cremated. It won't be him. He was such a nice man, such a nice man, gave a wonderful service, so sympathetic . . . it won't be him. I trusted him with my pet, I'd trust him with my savings if I had to.'

'You paid directly to him with your card?' Henry asked.

Mrs Tong nodded.

'Do you remember how that went, just out of interest?' he asked.

'I gave him my card, he inserted it into one of those wireless card-reader things, I put my PIN in, as you do, paid, he gave me my card back. It won't be him.'

Henry and Blackstone gave each other the nod, and Blackstone extracted a photograph from the folder she had brought in with her. She handed it over to Mrs Tong and asked, 'Do you recognize this man?'

Mrs Tong took it, reached for her glasses, fitted them and looked at the TSU still. Henry and Blackstone watched her as she suddenly become rigid and sat upright.

'The fucking bastard,' she said.

SEVENTEEN

Henry and Blackstone stood reverently aside, giving the family respectful looks and reassuring nods and sympathetic smiles as the mother, father and daughter filed out of the small chapel. The mother and daughter were hugging each other, tears flowing, while the father tried to maintain some kind of macho dignity, but even he was deeply affected following the wonderful service for their West Highland terrier, who, according to the notice board by the door on which the services for the day were listed, was called McDougal, or Mackie for short. He had been twelve years old.

The next service was due in just over an hour and that was for a pet named Aloysius, although the species was not specified. Henry and Blackstone had speculated and hoped that Aloysius might be a bird of prey or something equally unusual. It was a Golden Retriever rather than a Golden Eagle, although they would never know this. It was a service that would never take place, and in some ways Henry felt bad about that, but needs must and thieves, fraudsters and murderers had to be arrested.

They had managed to earwig some of Mackie's slick eulogy and were almost moved by it themselves and probably would have been if someone else had been delivering it.

After watching the grieving family depart, Blackstone said, 'Are you ready, old guy?'

'As I'll ever be.'

Underneath his zip-up jacket, Henry was wearing a bulletproof vest, much lighter and more flexible than any of the hefty, old-fashioned ones he'd worn during his actual police career. He was wearing jeans and a T-shirt, and his lanyard was dangling around his neck; Blackstone was dressed similarly, but her warrant card was displayed on her belt. In her back pocket she had her extendable baton and her rigid handcuffs were in a pouch at the small of her back.

Henry, being merely a civilian investigator, wasn't allowed such trappings, but he wasn't too concerned because he had total confidence in Blackstone's ability to deploy them to great advantage. Plus she also had a canister of CS spray in her jacket pocket that Henry knew she was itching to use.

And if all else failed, Henry had already decided he would cower behind her while she used her kung fu skills. He felt reasonably well protected.

It also helped his peace of mind that four armed officers were getting out of their vehicle and jogging towards them and around the small chapel, covering the two other doors – one on the side, one at the rear – armed cops had already deployed silently, backed up by Support Unit officers, all dressed in protective gear as though they were going to a Star Wars convention as storm troopers.

Henry and Blackstone were wearing earbuds connected to their personal radios and had listened to the transmissions between the various units deployed on this operation as they got into position. They were now all in place, and Rik Dean, who was controlling the operation from police headquarters, said to Blackstone, 'Delta Two, are you sure you want it to go this way?'

Blackstone checked Henry with a look and he nodded.

Yes, this was how they wanted things to progress. There were obviously dangers in it, but both had a feeling that if the troops went in, Tasers and guns at the ready, there would be another bloodbath and Henry had had enough of that. He wanted to make a peaceful, boring arrest if at all possible, although he wasn't completely certain this would be the outcome.

Since leaving Mrs Tong's house after her foul-mouthed outburst – which took Henry and Blackstone by surprise and made Poochy-poo lunge at Henry – and getting her word she would not contact the pet cemetery to complain about her bank card, they had been excessively busy throughout the night. With Rik Dean, they pulled together a fast-entry team to go in the following day.

There had been a lot of discussion about how best to do this. Rik was pushing for something hard and violent if necessary, but Henry wanted to ease back a little and have hard and violent in reserve, not least because the police would be going in blind in some respects: so far, there was nothing on any police or government databases they had access to that matched the man they were after. He seemed to be a ghost, a person without a history, nothing online as such – other than a name at a pet cemetery, which Henry guessed was as false as the vehicles he used.

As Henry had perused the website of Broughton Pet Cemetery, he saw that several pet cremations were listed for the next day, the first one at ten a.m., next one at noon; with that in mind, he and Blackstone plumped for a ten forty-five a.m. visit. That way, he hoped they would be able to catch the owner of the business, who was listed on the website as one Martin Bennett. There was no photograph, but they might find Mr Bennett alone once the first cremation had finished and the guests had just left, although that could not be guaranteed.

'Affirmative,' Blackstone said. 'Me and Henry will go in first.'

'Roger that,' Rik acknowledged. 'Take care.'

Blackstone raised her eyebrows at her older partner and asked, 'Is your bodycam on?' He checked to see if the tiny green light was glowing on the device clipped to his vest and gave her a thumbs up.

They were ready to go.

Bennett looked up and saw the woman followed by a man step into the chapel.

Using a soft broom, he had been sweeping the floor around the conveyor belt to the furnace which was strewn with delicate white rose petals in remembrance of the Westie. He wanted the place to be immaculate for the next family due at twelve, and although he didn't like people scattering stuff like this, for £500 it was worth the hassle.

'I'm afraid we're closed,' he called out pleasantly. 'Any time tomorrow would be good, if you don't mind.'

His professional smile faded quickly, though, as the man closed the door and turned to face him, standing just behind the woman, and gave him a little wave; both then tugged open their jackets just wide enough to reveal the *POLICE* logo stamped across their ballistic vests; this status was then confirmed when both flipped on their chequered baseball caps, so that Bennett would realize there would be no misunderstandings. These were cops he was dealing with.

Bennett leaned on the broom handle and sighed.

The pair walked slowly towards him.

'So, you're a cop,' he said, directing the remark to Henry. 'I knew I should've killed you. Fucking loose ends.' He chuckled and shook his head. They were about halfway across the chapel now, walking past the two rows of chairs. Bennett said, 'I wouldn't come any closer,' in a very matter of fact but cautionary way.

They stopped.

'How many mistakes did I make?' he asked. 'I'm intrigued to know.'

'Too many to list,' Blackstone said. 'We'll cover them in due course when we question you . . . but the main one was getting lost.'

'Ah, yeah . . . that old chestnut. Happens to the best of us.'

'So, Mr Bennett, or whatever your real name might be,' Blackstone said, 'my name is DS Blackstone from the Force Major Investigation Team at Lancashire Police headquarters, my colleague is civilian investigator Henry Christie, and I am arresting you for the murders of Albert Gorst and Max Janus – to start with. You do not have to say anything, but it may harm your defence if you do not mention when questioned something which you later rely on in court. Anything you do say may be given in evidence.'

Bennett looked at her askance. 'Did you say he was a civilian investigator? I'm being arrested by a fucking woman and a fucking civvie?'

Ignoring him, Blackstone said, 'Put the broom down, put your hands on your head and go down on to your knees, please. And do not make this hard work.'

She and Henry took a step towards him.

Bennett was already thinking of how he could escape and how quickly he could access the ten-square-foot secure storage unit he rented in a warehouse on the outskirts of Preston in which he kept an old ammunition box containing cash in mixed currencies to the value of £100,000, several false passports which he constantly updated and replaced, bank cards which gave him access to a number of accounts throughout Europe, and several handguns plus ammunition. He had another two such units in other parts of the country, similarly stocked.

He allowed the brush to fall over with a clatter.

'Please don't think we've come alone,' Blackstone said. 'That would be a big mistake.'

Bennett nodded sagely and raised his arms, interlocked his fingers on the top of his head and slowly lowered himself to his knees.

'Turn a blind eye, look away for sixty seconds, say I wasn't here, and you'll both have half a million euros in your bank accounts in twenty-four hours,' he said.

'Nah, what do you say, Henry?' Blackstone asked, keeping her eyes firmly on Bennett.

'We're not even in the EU now,' Henry said. 'What good are euros these days? But thanks anyway.'

The two officers resumed their walk towards him and both could see him weighing them up, knowing exactly what he was thinking.

Just so he knew for certain, Blackstone tapped her body cam and said, 'There's a live feed being monitored from here, there are armed officers at every door wanting to come in with bated breath. If you do anything that tempts them, they'll be in, Mr Bennett, and they will deal with you appropriately – do you understand?'

He licked his lips, then nodded.

'We want to do this without any fuss, OK?' she said. 'But that's down to you. Now, raise your hands high, please, and then very slowly bend forwards on to all fours, go face down on your belly and then spread your arms. Do you understand?'

He began that process, following the instructions.

Henry and Blackstone took some more steps towards him, both wary.

His face was cheek down on the floor and by tilting his head he could see them approaching and saw that the woman cop had her cuffs in her right hand now.

'Put your left arm behind your back, please,' she instructed him.

He didn't respond.

'Won't ask again,' Blackstone said.

Slowly, his arm moved and he angled it around his back, palm up, but then his right arm began to move too, fast, mirroring the left, and Henry realized why as he saw the slight lump in the waistband of his jeans under his shirt.

'Gun!' Henry shouted.

The distance between Blackstone and Bennett was about ten feet now; suddenly, Blackstone moved in a blur of speed across the gap as Bennett's right hand yanked a small handgun out from under his belt at the small of his back and started to roll his body in order to bring it round to fire.

The side door of the chapel burst open as two armed cops smashed their way in, weapons drawn, screaming something that was unintelligible to Henry's ears as Blackstone, much to his dismay, threw herself the last few feet across the gap like a goalkeeper.

But Bennett had moved quickly, twisting his body, and the muzzle rose just as Blackstone flew through the air, her hands outstretched going for the weapon. Henry watched, even as he too kept moving forwards, as Blackstone corkscrewed like a leopard and at the same time lashed out with a chopping motion of her right hand, which was holding the handcuffs. In that nanosecond before the firing pin hit the bullet and the gun fired, she managed to strike the short barrel with the handcuff bar, knocking the aim askew. The gun fired and the bullet went harmlessly upwards into the ceiling, but that did not stop Blackstone. In another flurry of speed, skill and strength that astounded Henry, she grabbed Bennett's wrist with her free hand and ended up flattened across him, pinning his wrist down and slamming the back of his hand down repeatedly on the floor, even as he fought back, until his fingers opened and the gun skittered away across the floor like a spinning top – at which moment Henry dropped on to the guy's legs and the two armed cops stood over Bennett with their guns pointed directly at his head, screaming orders at him.

He stopped struggling, went limp and began to laugh.

EIGHTEEN

The view from the first-floor balcony of the suite at the exclusive private clinic was stunning, looking north across the bay of Santa Eulalia with the marina in the distance and beyond to the rocky promontory that formed the backdrop behind the Hotel Ses Estaques, which was called the Punta de s'Esglesia Vella.

But at that moment, the magnificence of the vista was completely lost on the huddled, miserable figure of Nico Bashkim who sat in a wheelchair on the balcony with an intravenous drip, supported by a mobile stand, feeding into the cannula inserted into the back of his left hand, one blanket over his shoulders and another tucked under his knees.

He was grateful he was still alive. The Spanish paramedics had been on the scene within minutes of him being dragged out of the water, and their actions, combined with those of the two waiters who had selflessly dived into the sea in the first place, had kept him going. Ultimately, he had survived a very serious heart attack. He had made a generous donation to a charity for retired paramedics and had ensured that a substantial wad of euros had been pressed into the hands of both waiters.

But he could not even remember it happening.

In fact, the last thing he recalled was blabbing information to the American FBI agent and that bastard Steve Flynn who had a gun screwed into the back of his neck. After that, nothing, until he came to many hours later to learn that in order to save his life he'd undergone triple heart bypass surgery and was now living on borrowed time unless he made some huge sacrifices in terms of his lifestyle – sacrifices that had to start now. Such as cut out the cocaine, cut out the booze and fatty food. He had meekly inquired about Viagra but had been assured that its use, even in his circumstances, was fine, but that he probably wouldn't be thinking about sex for quite a few months.

He'd been quickly transferred to this private clinic on the outskirts of Santa Eulalia, where he'd continued to receive the best care available on the island and in a location that was also easier to guard; he knew two armed heavies were now stationed outside his door.

So yes, he was alive, but he was particularly unhappy as he looked across the bay, because having watched the smoke rise into the air from the exhaust of the engines of the *Halcyon* a couple of hours earlier, the beautiful boat was now nudging its way out of the port.

Without him aboard.

He knew this was being taken away from him, and in spite of the calming drugs coursing through his newly repaired blood vessels, he was growing angrier by the second, and his heart was beating faster than was healthy at each metre the boat moved away from him, out of his grasp . . . just like his life.

He heard voices he recognized out in the corridor and stiffened up in the wheelchair to brace himself; he knew that what was about to come was a destiny-changing meeting. For the life of him, he could not get the hateful expression off his face at the prospect of seeing his father and his sister who, he knew, were making a secret visit to him before they vanished into Albania for the foreseeable future.

But one thing he knew: he did not want to return to that godforsaken country to live among the hills and peasants who would murder you as soon as look at you. That was a life that was long gone and he had no desire to ever revisit. Cyprus had been bad enough, but at least it had been civilized.

There was a knock on the door, which opened, and his sister poked her head around and cooed, 'Nico,' softly. 'It's me and your father.'

Their journey had been much easier than anticipated and they stuck to their previously planned route, knowing there was another they could take if necessary.

Following the getaway from Simpson Hall, Sofia and Viktor had been whisked across the north of England to Leeds–Bradford Airport. On the drive, both changed clothing in the vehicle – Sofia helping her father to get out of his blood-splattered suit into a tracksuit. The clothing from the crime scene was bagged up and handed to the guy in the front seat of their transport who had been tasked with disposing of it permanently. At the airport they were met by a courier who gave them their onward flight tickets and new passports which would take them to Limoges in France.

During the journey across country, Sofia had dealt with the almost casual phone calls from the Tradesman who had been contracted to move in and clean up the crime scene. She had expected to be told that there were nine bodies at the hall and it had been a shock to learn there were only six. From what the Tradesman described, it seemed that Gorst, his wife and Janus were possibly still alive and had somehow managed to drag themselves away.

She immediately told the Tradesman to follow that up and, if they were indeed alive, to kill all three of them. He said he would, and after the phone call ended, Sofia transferred thirty thousand euros to his bank account in Spain and photographs of Gorst and Janus to his mobile phone.

She was furious. She knew what had happened. She hadn't made certain Janus was dead and the knife into Gorst's guts hadn't done the business with him, either. She was sure Mrs Gorst was dead, though.

She tried not to worry as they waited for their flight.

The Tradesman was good, dependable, and once they were back and settled in Albania, they would summon him and brief him about Steve Flynn and Karl Donaldson: Viktor literally wanted their heads on a silver platter in front of him, a job the Tradesman would relish. He had done similar jobs for them over the last couple of years.

As they waited for the flight to be called, Sofia decided against telling Viktor the job at Simpson Hall was incomplete; it was stress he didn't need, but was the sort of thing that she, as prospective head of the family, was expected to deal with. Which she had. Until the Tradesman reported back to her, she would not concern herself with it.

However, there was something else her father did have to know.

As they waited in one of the pre-booked lounges, sipping tea, Sofia turned to Viktor and said, 'I have something to tell you about Nico . . . and it's not good news.'

She made her position clear that it was not necessary, nor was it a good idea, to visit Nico, who had been transferred from the public hospital in Ibiza Town to a private clinic near Santa Eulalia following his life-saving surgery. What they should do, she argued, was keep to their scheduled route and get back to Albania as agreed, but Viktor would not have any of that: he wanted to see his son; he demanded it.

Sofia understood and knew she was fighting a losing battle, so she capitulated. When they landed in Limoges, she began to make arrangements for the change in travel plans and the visit to Nico.

She was under no illusion that until they were back home in Albania, they would not be safe from the clutches of law enforcement, so the next leg of the journey through France, down into Spain and across to Ibiza had to be done with extreme caution and speed.

She hired a car at Limoges and drove south, making a series of phone calls along the way, calling in favours from people she knew in Marseilles so that she and Viktor were able to stay overnight at a farmhouse near Narbonne, which was used as a staging post for a drug route up from Marseilles to Paris. It was not the most salubrious of locations, but the men there, knowing they were hosting celebrities of the crime world, made them welcome, fed and watered them, gave them a bed for the night and provided security.

Although Viktor was exhausted by the journey, which seemed to exacerbate his prostate problems, he insisted on keeping moving. The next morning, they crossed the Spanish border in a new car with new passports and made their way to Barcelona, where they

booked into an airport hotel for another night and caught a flight
to Ibiza the following morning.

During the journey through France, Sofia heard nothing from the
Tradesman, but that did not concern her because she had read a
newsfeed on the Internet concerning a double murder at a rural
hospital in the Lancaster area. Details were sparse and the police
had launched a major enquiry, but no arrests were mentioned, so
she was sure that the Tradesman had gone to ground. She guessed
he would be in contact soon.

The other issue she had to deal with was that the new owner of
Halcyon, the head of the Lyubery crime syndicate, contacted her
and said he wanted his boat back, after having allowed Nico full
use of it for a few weeks. Sofia knew she had to agree to this, but
that it would not go down well with her brother – something else
she would have to deal with firmly when she came face-to-face with
him. But that was only a minor thing. What was important was to
visit Nico so that Viktor could see him and, if he was fit to travel,
arrange transport to Albania. If not, he would have to come home
later.

The almost empty flight was uneventful, and as they made their
way slowly through immigration at Ibiza Airport, they were not
challenged or even given a second glance by anyone in uniform.

They were on the road in yet another hire car an hour after
landing, heading north along the coast to the private clinic to which
Nico had been transferred.

As they drew up in the car park and Sofia helped Viktor out of
the car and through the entrance doors, they failed to notice the
Renault Captur parked in shadow under trees at the far edge of
the car park, containing two men who had been waiting patiently
for their arrival.

It was not going well.

'We had to,' Sofia was insisting. 'It is no longer our boat – not
yours, not ours. That was the agreement we made in exchange for
security.' She was very quickly losing her cool with Nico. 'So it
had to go back. It is not your toy any longer. Get used to it.'

'Some fucking security that turned out to be!' Nico snarled.
'Basically guarded by a bunch of amateurs.'

'Anyway, the deal is done,' she stated.

Leaning on the balcony rail, Sofia could see *Halcyon* slowly disappearing in the distance. She wasn't going to miss it. While Viktor had used it as his floating fortress over the years, she had spent little time on it and had little affection for it.

'And if you think I'm traipsing back to Albania for the rest of my life, you can go screw,' Nico snarled, returning to a half-finished argument they were already having. He was becoming more and more furious.

He scowled at Viktor, who was sitting with a sad old face on a chair on the balcony, resting his hands on his walking stick, which Nico knew was just a sheath for a stiletto.

Nico said to him, 'You two can go. I might have a weak heart, but I've got a life to lead and it's not in that shithole of a country.'

Sofia spun and looked at her brother, feeling rage and dislike ignite within her. 'Which proves exactly why you do not have the necessary qualities to lead this family into the future it deserves. I am the one who will bring new blood into it and steer it through and' – here she looked at Viktor with affection – 'make Father proud, something that has eluded you all your life with your debauchery and pleasure-seeking.'

As she said these words, she pushed herself away from the balcony rail and began to walk over to Nico in an intimidatory way, having had enough of her whining sibling.

Nico watched her approach.

His eyes, though, were glued on the chunky gold necklace she wore, the one with the blood of over sixty years on it.

She leaned over him with her face only inches from him and her eyes wild.

'I am ashamed of you, Nico.' She almost spat into his face.

'Sofia!' Viktor said, trying to rein her in. He rose from the chair, using his walking stick as a lever to do so.

'No, Father,' she said without turning, but gesticulating with a backward flick of her hand for him to stay where he was, not to get involved. Somewhere deep inside told her this was the moment of truth with Nico, the final nail in his coffin that once and for all would see her move to take complete control of the family business.

Nico remained static in his wheelchair, hardly breathing.

He could smell her. The perfume, the sweat of travel and the anger that was bubbling over.

'I am in charge now. What I say goes,' she said through grinding teeth. 'If you do not come home with us, you will be cut off. No more money, no more whores, no more cocaine up those fat nostrils of yours. You will die a pauper . . . with nothing . . . you will be nothing – a pathetic, big fat pig of a failure!'

Flynn and Donaldson slid down the seats of the Renault and watched Sofia and Viktor walk into the clinic.

'Knew they wouldn't be able to resist it,' Flynn said. 'They had to visit him. Good shout,' he said, harking back to Molly's call to tell them about Nico's near-death experience. It had dawned on both men at exactly the same moment that there was every chance Viktor and Sofia, driven by the so-called 'family values' of the Bashkims, would walk into a trap of their own making.

They had caught a flight that night to Ibiza from East Midlands Airport and set up their stall to await the family reunion. Both men had a history of waiting and watching, Flynn with the Special Boat Service and Donaldson with years of FBI surveillance operations under his belt. They would have remained as long as necessary; as it happened, the wait was much shorter than expected.

'We give them five minutes, then we go in,' the American said.

'Yep.' Flynn reached down between his legs for the Ruger automatic and ensured it was cocked, the safety on. He slid it under his jacket.

Likewise, Donaldson picked up his automatic pistol and checked it.

'Last chance, pal – are you OK with this? We are going to kill those two, you know? No half measures,' Donaldson warned Flynn.

Who nodded.

Spot on five minutes, they moved, walking swiftly to the revolving door which was the clinic entrance, crossing the foyer diagonally, ignoring the receptionist and taking the flight of stairs to the first floor, then along the corridor towards the luxury suite at the far end, where Nico had been ensconced for his care and convalescence; by the time they reached it, their weapons were out, held discreetly down by their sides.

From their reconnaissance, they already knew there would be two guards posted outside the door and that, more than likely, they would be leaning out of the window at the far end of the corridor, smoking and chatting.

Not that they assumed this, but as they approached, the two men were indeed leaning together side by side at the open window, chewing the fat and blowing smoke into the atmosphere.

On the word 'failure', Nico snapped.

Sofia's gurning face, now twisted so ugly with hatred for him, was just inches from his. The gold chain was dangling loose from her neck, taunting him with its significance.

His hands shot up and grabbed her by the throat, followed by the rest of his body as he rose from the wheelchair, dragging the drip over with a clatter as he went for her in an uncontrollable fit of rage, feeling her neck beneath his fingers as, with his bulk and the help of the sudden attack, he forced her over.

She struggled and writhed, trying to get a grip of his larger hands and peel them off her windpipe, but as he smashed the back of her head down on to the tiled floor, the blow stunned her and allowed Nico to tighten his deadly grip, rearrange his weight so he was properly above her, squeezing. Her eyes began to bulge as she gagged for air.

Viktor screamed, 'Get off her! Stop this!' and jumped out of his chair and began raining blows on to Nico's back with his walking stick. 'Stop it, stop it!'

Nico felt nothing. Everything he had was now focused on the two hands around Sofia's neck, getting tighter and tighter, denying her air for her lungs as he crushed her larynx and blood for her brain as he compressed her carotid arteries, throttling her to death.

She fought wildly, but only for moments, until finally she died underneath him.

Viktor continued to beat Nico, but that faded out in its intensity as he saw his daughter relax in death and he slumped down, gasping and clutching his chest.

Nico stood up, panting, feeling weak but also triumphant.

He turned to Viktor and said, 'I am now the head of this family.'

He reached down and tore the gold necklace from Sofia's neck and, straddling her, held it up aloft to the gods.

But then something happened within him. He emitted a gasp and dropped the chain as he recognized the symptoms of a renewed heart attack: the fierce heat and pain shooting up from his chest, across his left shoulder and down to his fingertips; the sudden blur of vision, the helplessness as he sank to his knees and pitched forward across Sofia's still body as his own death engulfed him.

Viktor watched, still clutching his own chest, knowing something very bad inside him was happening. He knew what it was – the dangerously thin and weakened wall of his aorta had burst from the exertion, and blood was gushing uncontrollably into his abdominal cavity.

He fought for breath, but it did not come. Suddenly, he was very weak, sweating profusely; his skin became clammy and his heart-beat went wild as he tugged at his collar and then pitched head first out of his chair across Niko's legs. His cane rolled away and he was dead.

The pair of guards did not even see them coming, so engrossed were they in an argument about a recent football match.

One moment they were in deep discussion about the brilliance of Lionel Messi and the next, as Flynn and Donaldson tipped them out of the open window, they were spiralling towards the landscaped garden below.

Even before they hit the ground, Flynn and Donaldson were positioned either side of the door to Nico's room, readying their weapons, hearts pounding and nodding as they did their silent countdown, knowing their moves exactly. When they reached 'one', Flynn turned the door handle and threw the door open.